1 MONTH OF
FREE
READING

at
www.forgottenbooks.com

By purchasing this book you are eligible for one month membership to ForgottenBooks.com, giving you unlimited access to our entire collection of over 1,000,000 titles via our web site and mobile apps.

To claim your free month visit: www.forgottenbooks.com/free215853

ISBN 978-0-484-36559-8
PIBN 10215853

This book is a reproduction of an important historical work. Forgotten Books uses state-of-the-art technology to digitally reconstruct the work, preserving the original format whilst repairing imperfections present in the aged copy. In rare cases, an imperfection in the original, such as a blemish or missing page, may be replicated in our edition. We do, however, repair the vast majority of imperfections successfully; any imperfections that remain are intentionally left to preserve the state of such historical works.

MAGGIE MILLER

OR

OLD HAGAR'S SECRET.

BY

MRS. MARY J. HOLMES

AUTHOR OF "TEMPEST AND SUNSHINE," "LENA RIVERS,"
"ENGLISH ORPHANS," "DORA DEANE," ETC.

CHICAGO
M. A. DONOHUE & COMPANY

MAGGIE MILLER.

CHAPTER I.

THE OLD HOUSE BY THE MILL.

'MID the New England hills, and beneath the
shadow of their dim old woods, is a running brook
whose deep waters were not always as merry and
frolicsome as now; for years before our story opens,
pent up and impeded in their course, they dashed
angrily against their prison walls, and turned the
creaking wheel of an old sawmill with a sullen,
rebellious roar. The mill has gone to decay, and the
sturdy men who fed it with the giant oaks of the forest are sleeping quietly in the village graveyard. The
waters of the mill-pond, too, relieved from their confinement, leap gaily over the ruined dam, tossing for
a moment in wanton glee their locks of snow-white
foam, and then flowing on, half fearfully as it were,
through the deep gorge overhung with the hemlock
and the pine, where the shadows of twilight ever lie,
and where the rocks frown gloomily down upon the
stream below, which, emerging from the darkness,
loses itself at last in the waters of the gracefully winding Chicopee, and leaves far behind the moss-covered
walls of what is familiarly known as the "Old House
by the Mill."

'Tis a huge, old-fashioned building, distant nearly

a mile from the public highway, and surrounded so
thickly by forest trees that the bright sunlight, dancing merrily midst the rustling leaves above, falls but
seldom on the time-stained walls of dark gray stone,
where the damp and dews of more than a century have
fallen, and where now the green moss clings with a
loving grasp, as if 'twere its rightful resting-place.
When the thunders of the Revolution shook the hills
of the Bay State, and the royal banner floated in the
evening breeze, the house was owned by an old Englishman who, loyal to his king and country, denounced
as rebels the followers of Washington. Against these,
however, he would not raise his hand, for among them
were many long-tried friends who had gathered with
him around the festal board; so he chose the only remaining alternative, and went back to his native country, cherishing the hope that he should one day return to the home he loved so well, and listen again to
the musical flow of the brook, which could be distinctly heard from the door of the mansion. But his
wish was vain, for when at last America was free and
the British troops recalled, he slept beneath the sod of
England, and the old house was for many years deserted. The Englishman had been greatly beloved,
and his property was unmolested, while the weeds and
grass grew tall and rank in the garden beds, and the
birds of heaven built their nests beneath the projecting roof or held a holiday in the gloomy, silent rooms.

As time passed on, however, and no one appeared to
dispute their right, different families occupied the
house at intervals, until at last, when nearly fifty years
had elapsed, news was one day received that Madam
Conway, a granddaughter of the old Englishman, hav-

ing met with reverses at home, had determined to
emigrate to the New World, and remembering the
" House by the Mill," of which she had heard so
much, she wished to know if peaceable possession of it
would be allowed her, in case she decided upon removing thither and making it her future home. To this
plan no objection was made, for the aged people of
Hillsdale still cherished the memory of the hospitable
old man whose locks were gray while they were yet but
children, and the younger portion of the community
hoped for a renewal of the gayeties which they had
heard were once so common at the old stone house.

But in this they were disappointed, for Madam Conway was a proud, unsociable woman, desiring no acquaintance whatever with her neighbors, who, after
many ineffectual attempts at something like friendly
intercourse, concluded to leave her entirely alone, and
contented themselves with watching the progress of
matters at " Mill Farm," as she designated the place,
which soon began to show visible marks of improve-
ment. The Englishman was a man of taste, and
Madam Conway's first work was an attempt to restore
the grounds to something of their former beauty. The
yard and garden were cleared of weeds, the walks and
flower-beds laid out with care, and then the neighbors
looked to see her cut away a few of the multitude of
trees which had sprung up around her home. But
this she had no intention of doing. " They shut me
out," she said, " from the prying eyes of the vulgar,
and I would rather it should be so." So the trees remained, throwing their long shadows upon the high.
narrow windows, and into the large square rooms,
where the morning light and the noonday heat seldom

found entrance, and which seemed like so many cold, silent caverns, with their old-fashioned massive furniture, their dark, heavy curtains, and the noiseless footfall of the stately lady, who moved ever with the same measured tread, speaking always softly and low to the household servants, who, having been trained in her service, had followed her across the sea.

From these the neighbors learned that Madam Conway had in London a married daughter, Mrs. Miller; that old Hagar Warren, the strange-looking woman who more than anyone else shared her mistress' confidence, had grown up in the family, receiving a very good education, and had nursed their young mistress, Miss Margaret, which of course entitled her to more respect than was usually bestowed upon menials like her; that Madam Conway was very aristocratic, very proud of her high English blood; that though she lived alone she attended strictly to all the formalities of high life, dressing each day with the utmost precision for her solitary dinner — dining off a service of solid silver, and presiding with great dignity in her straight, high-backed chair. She was fond, too, of the ruby wine, and her cellar was stored with the choicest liquors, some of which she had brought with her from home, while others, it was said, had belonged to her grandfather, and for half a century had remained unseen and unmolested, while the cobwebs of time had woven around them a misty covering, making them still more valuable to the lady, who knew full well how age improved such things.

Regularly each day she rode in her ponderous carriage, sometimes alone and sometimes accompanied by Hester, the daughter of old Hagar, a handsome, intelligent-looking girl, who, after two or three years of comparative idleness at Mill Farm, went to Meriden, Conn., as seamstress in a family which had advertised for such a person. With her departed the only life of the house, and during the following year there ensued a monotonous quiet, which was broken at last for Hagar by the startling announcement that her daughter's young mistress had died four months before, and the husband, a gray-haired, elderly man, had proved conclusively that he was in his dotage by talking of marriage to Hester, who, ere the letter reached her mother, would probably be the third bride of one whose reputed wealth was the only possible inducement to a girl like Hester Warren.

With an immense degree of satisfaction Hagar read the letter through, exulting that fortune had favored her at last. Possessed of many sterling qualities, Hagar Warren had one glaring fault, which had imbittered her whole life. Why others were rich while she was poor she could not understand, and her heart rebelled at the fate which had made her what she was.

But Hester would be wealthy—nay, would perhaps one day rival the haughty Mrs. Miller across the water, who had been her playmate; there was comfort in that, and she wrote to her daughter expressing her entire approbation, and hinting vaguely of the possibility that she herself might some time cease to be a servant, and help do the honors of Mr. Hamilton's house! To this there came no reply, and Hagar was thinking seriously of making a visit to Meriden, when one rainy autumnal night, nearly a year after Hester's marriage, there came another letter sealed with black. With a sad foreboding Hagar opened it, and read that Mr. Hamilton had failed; that his house and farm were sold, and that he, overwhelmed with mortification both at his failure and the opposition of his friends to his last marriage, had died suddenly, leaving Hester with no home in the wide world unless Madam Conway received her again into her family.

"Just my luck!" was Hagar's mental comment, as she finished reading the letter and carried it to her mistress, who had always liked Hester, and who readily consented to give her a home, provided she put on no airs from having been for a time the wife of a reputed wealthy man. "Mustn't put on airs!" muttered Hagar, as she left the room. "Just as if airs wasn't for anybody but high bloods!" And with the cankerworm of envy at her heart she wrote to Hester, who came immediately; and Hagar—when she heard her tell the story of her wrongs, how her husband's sister, indignant at his marriage with a sewing-girl, had removed from him the children, one a stepchild and one his own, and how of all his vast fortune there was not left for her a penny—experienced again the old bitterness of feeling, and murmured that fate should thus deal with her and hers.

With the next day's mail there came to Madam Conway a letter bearing a foreign postmark, and bringing the sad news that her son-in-law had been lost in a storm while crossing the English Channel, and that her daughter Margaret, utterly crushed and heartbroken, would sail immediately for America, where she wished only to lay her weary head upon her mother's bosom and die.

"So there is one person that has no respect for

blood, and that is Death," said old Hagar to her mistress, when she heard the news. "He has served us both alike, he has taken my son-in-law first and yours next."

Frowning haughtily, Madam Conway bade her be silent, telling her at the same time to see that the rooms in the north part of the building were put in perfect order for Mrs. Miller, who would probably come in the next vessel. In sullen silence Hagar withdrew, and for several days worked half reluctantly in the "north rooms," as Madam Conway termed a comparatively pleasant, airy suite of apartments, with a balcony above, which looked out upon the old mill-dam and the brook pouring over it.

"There'll be big doings when my lady comes," said Hagar one day to her daughter. "It 'll be Hagar here, and Hagar there, and Hagar everywhere, but I shan't hurry myself. I'm getting too old to wait on a chit like her."

"Don't talk so, mother," said Hester. "Margaret was always kind to me. She is not to blame for being rich, while I am poor."

"But somebody's to blame," interrupted old Hagar. "You was always accounted the handsomest and cleverest of the two, and yet for all you'll be nothing but a drudge to wait on her and the little girl."

Hester only sighed in reply, while her thoughts went forward to the future and what it would probably bring her. Hester Warren and Margaret Conway had been children together, and in spite of the difference of their stations they had loved each other dearly; and when at last the weary traveler came, with her pale sad face and mourning garb, none gave her so heartfelt a welcome as Hester; and during the week when, from exhaustion and excitement, she was confined to her bed, it was Hester who nursed her with the utmost care, soothing her to sleep, and then amusing the little Theo, a child of two years. Hagar, too, softened by her young mistress' sorrow, repented of her harsh words, and watched each night with the invalid, who once, when her mind seemed wandering far back in the past, whispered softly, " Tell me the Lord's prayer, dear Hagar, just as you told it to me years ago when I was a little child."

It was a long time since Hagar had breathed that prayer, but at Mrs. Miller's request she commenced it, repeating it correctly until she came to the words, " Give us this day our daily bread " ; then she hesitated, and bending forward said, " What comes next, Miss Margaret? Is it 'Lead us not into temptation?'"

" Yes, yes," whispered the half-unconscious lady. " 'Lead us not into temptation,' that's it." Then, as if there were around her a dim foreboding of the great wrong Hagar was to do, she took her old nurse's hand between her own, and continued, " Say it often, Hagar, 'Lead us not into temptation '; you have much need for that prayer."

A moment more, and Margaret Miller slept, while beside her sat Hagar Warren, half shuddering, she knew not why, as she thought of her mistress' words, which seemed to her so much like the spirit of prophecy.

" Why do I need that prayer more than anyone else?" she said at last. " I have never been tempted more than I could bear—never shall be tempted—and if I am, old Hagar Warren, bad as she is, can resist temptation without that prayer."

Still, reason as she would, Hagar could not shake off the strange feeling, and as she sat half dozing in her chair, with the dim lamplight flickering over her dark face, she fancied that the October wind, sighing so mournfully through the locust trees beneath the window, and then dying away in the distance, bore upon its wing, "'Lead us not into temptation.' Hagar, you have much need to say that prayer."

Aye, Hagar Warren—much need, much need!

CHAPTER II.

THE wintry winds were blowing cold and chill around the old stone house, and the deep untrodden snow lay highly piled upon the ground. For many days the gray, leaden clouds had frowned gloomily down upon the earth below, covering it with a thick veil of white. But the storm was over now; with the setting sun it had gone to rest, and the pale moonlight stole softly into the silent chamber, where Madam Conway bent anxiously down to see if but the faintest breath came from the parted lips of her only daughter. There had been born to her that night another grandchild—a little, helpless girl, which now in an adjoining room was Hagar's special care; and Hagar, sitting there with the wee creature upon her lap, and the dread fear at her heart that her young mistress might die, forgot for once to repine at her lot, and did cheerfully whatever was required of her to do.

There was silence in the rooms below—silence in the chambers above,—silence everywhere,—for the sick woman seemed fast nearing the deep, dark river whose waters move onward, but never return.

Almost a week went by, and then, in a room far more humble than where Margaret Miller lay, another immortal being was given to the world; and, with a softened light in her keen black eyes, old Hagar told to her stately mistress, when she met her on the stair, that she too was a grandmother.

" You must not on that account neglect Margaret's child," was Madam Conway's answer, as with a wave of her hand she passed on; and this was all she said— not a word of sympathy or congratulation for the peculiar old woman whose heart, so long benumbed, had been roused to a better state of feeling, and who in the first joy of her newborn happiness had hurried to her mistress, fancying for the moment that she was almost her equal.

" Don't neglect Margaret's child for that! " How the words rang in her ears as she fled up the narrow stairs and through the dark hall, till the low room was reached where lay the babe for whom Margaret's child was not to be neglected. All the old bitterness had returned, and as hour after hour went by, and Madam Conway came not near, while the physician and the servants looked in for a moment only and then hurried away to the other sickroom, where all their services were kept in requisition, she muttered: " Little would they care if Hester died upon my hands. And she will die too," she continued, as by the fading daylight she saw the pallor deepen on her daughter's face.

And Hagar was right, for Hester's sands were nearer run than those of Mrs. Miller. The utmost care might not, perhaps, have saved her; but the matter was not tested; and when the long clock at the head of the stairs struck the hour of midnight she murmured: " It is getting dark here, mother—so dark —and I am growing cold. Can it be death? "

" Yes, Hester, 'tis death," answered Hagar, and her voice was unnaturally calm as she laid her hand on the clammy brow of her daughter.

An hour later, and Madam Conway, who sat dozing

in the parlor below, ready for any summons which might come from Margaret's room, was roused by the touch of a cold, hard hand, and Hagar Warren stood before her.

"Come," she said, "come with me;" and, thinking only of Margaret, Madam Conway arose to follow her. "Not there—but this way," said Hagar, as her mistress turned towards Mrs. Miller's door, and grasping firmly the lady's arm she led to the room where Hester lay dead, with her young baby clasped lovingly to her bosom. "Look at her—and pity me now, if you never did before. She was all I had in the world to love," said Hagar passionately.

Madam Conway was not naturally a hard-hearted woman, and she answered gently: "I do pity you, Hagar, and I did not think Hester was so ill. Why haven't you let me know?" To this Hagar made no direct reply, and after a few more inquiries Madam Conway left the room, saying she would send up the servants to do whatever was necessary. When it was known throughout the house that Hester was dead much surprise was expressed and a good deal of sympathy manifested for old Hagar, who, with a gloomy brow, hugged to her heart the demon of jealousy, which kept whispering to her of the difference there would be were Margaret to die. It was deemed advisable to keep Hester's death a secret from Mrs. Miller; so, with as little ceremony as possible, the body was buried at the close of the day, in an inclosure which had been set apart as a family burying-ground; and when again the night shadows fell Hagar Warren sat in her silent room, brooding over her grief, and looking oft at the plain pine cradle where lay the little motherless child, her granddaughter. Occasionally, too, her eye wandered towards the mahogany crib, where another infant slept. Perfect quiet seemed necessary for Mrs. Miller, and Madam Conway had ordered her baby to be removed from the antechamber where first it had been kept, so that Hagar had the two children in her own room.

In the pine cradle there was a rustling sound; the baby was awaking, and taking it upon her lap Hagar soothed it again to sleep, gazing earnestly upon it to see if it were like its mother. It was a bright, healthy-looking infant, and though five days younger than that of Mrs. Miller was quite as large and looked as old.

" And you will be a drudge, while she will be a lady," muttered Hagar, as her tears fell on the face of the sleeping child. " Why need this difference be ? "

Old Hagar had forgotten the words " Lead us not into temptation "; and when the Tempter answered, " It need not be," she only started suddenly as if smitten by a heavy blow; but she did not drive him from her, and she sat there reasoning with herself that " it need not be." Neither the physician nor Madam Conway had paid any attention to Margaret's child; it had been her special care, while no one had noticed hers, and newly born babies were so much alike that deception was an easy matter. But could she do it ? Could she bear that secret on her soul ? Madam Conway, though proud, had been kind to her, and could she thus deceive her! Would her daughter, sleeping in her early grave, approve the deed. " No, no," she answered aloud, " she would not ! " and the great drops of perspiration stood thick upon her dark, haggard face as she arose and laid back in her cradle the child whom she had thought to make an heiress.

For a time the Tempter left her, but returned ere long, and creeping into her heart sung to her beautiful songs of the future which might be were Hester's baby a lady. And Hagar, listening to that song, fell asleep, dreaming that the deed was done by other agency than hers—that the little face resting on the downy pillow, and shaded by the costly lace, was lowly born; while the child wrapped in the coarser blanket came of nobler blood, even that of the Conways, who boasted more than one lordly title. With a nervous start she awoke at last, and creeping to the cradle of mahogany looked to see if her dream were true; but it was not. She knew it by the pinched, blue look about the nose, and the thin covering of hair. This was all the difference which even her eye could see, and probably no other person had noticed that, for the child had never been seen save in a darkened room.

The sin was growing gradually less heinous, and she could now calmly calculate the chances for detection. Still, the conflict was long and severe, and it was not until morning that the Tempter gained a point by compromising the matter, and suggesting that while dressing the infants she should change their clothes for once, just to see how fine cambrics and soft flannels would look upon a grandchild of Hagar Warren! " I can easily change them again—it is only an experiment," she said, as with trembling hands she proceeded to divest the children of their wrappings. But her fingers seemed all thumbs, and more than one sharp pin pierced the tender flesh of her little grand-

child as she fastened together the embroidered slip,
teaching her thus early, had she been able to learn the
lesson, that the pathway of the rich is not free from
thorns.

Their toilet was completed at last—their cradle beds
exchanged; and then, with a strange, undefined feeling, old Hagar stood back and looked to see how the
little usurper became her new position. She became
it well, and to Hagar's partial eyes it seemed more
meet that she should lie there beneath the silken covering than the other one, whose nose looked still more
pinched and blue in the plain white dress and cradle
of pine. Still, there was a gnawing pain at Hagar's
heart, and she would perhaps have undone the wrong
had not Madam Conway appeared with inquiries for
the baby's health. Hagar could not face her mistress,
so she turned away and pretended to busy herself with
the arrangement of the room, while the lady, bending
over the cradle, said, " I think she is improving,
Hagar; I never saw her look so well " ; and she
pushed back the window curtain to obtain a better
view.

With a wild, startled look in her eye, Hagar held
her breath to hear what might come next, but her fears
were groundless; for, in her anxiety for her daughter,
Madam Conway had heretofore scarcely seen her
grandchild, and had no suspicion now that the sleeper
before her was of plebeian birth, nor yet that the other
little one, at whom she did not deign to look, was bone
of her bone and flesh of her flesh. She started to
leave the room, but, impelled by some sudden impulse,
turned back and stooped to kiss the child. Involuntarily old Hagar sprang forward to stay the act, and

grasped the lady's arm, but she was too late; the aristocratic lips had touched the cheek of Hagar Warren's grandchild, and the secret, if now confessed, would never be forgiven.

"It can't be helped," muttered Hagar, and then, when Mrs. Conway asked an explanation of her conduct, she answered, "I was afraid you'd wake her up, and mercy knows I've had worry enough with both the brats."

Not till then had Madam Conway observed how haggard and worn was Hagar's face, and instead of reproving her for her boldness she said gently: "You have indeed been sorely tried! Shall I send up Bertha to relieve you!"

"No, no," answered Hagar hurriedly, "I am better alone."

The next moment Madam Conway was moving silently down the narrow hall, while Hagar on her knees was weeping passionately. One word of kindness had effected more than a thousand reproaches would have done; and wringing her hands she cried, "I will not do it; I cannot."

Approaching the cradle, she was about to lift the child, when again Madam Conway was at the door. She had come, she said, to take the babe to Margaret, who seemed better this morning, and had asked to see it.

"Not now, not now. Wait till I put on her a handsomer dress, and I'll bring her myself," pleaded Hagar.

But Madam Conway saw no fault in the fine cambric wrapper, and taking the infant in her arms she walked away, while Hagar followed stealthily. Very lovingly the mother folded to her bosom the babe, calling it her fatherless one, and wetting its face with her tears, while through the half-closed door peered Hagar's wild dark eyes—one moment lighting up with exultation as she muttered, " It's my flesh, my blood, proud lady ! " and the next growing dim with tears, as she thought of the evil she had done.

" I did not know she had so much hair," said Mrs. Miller, parting the silken locks. " I think it will be like mine," and she gave the child to her mother, while Hagar glided swiftly back to her room.

That afternoon the clergyman whose church Mrs. Conway usually attended, called to see Mrs. Miller, who suggested that both the children should receive the rite of baptism. Hagar was accordingly bidden to prepare them for the ceremony, and resolving to make one more effort to undo what she had done she dressed the child whom she had thought to wrong in its own clothes, and then anxiously awaited her mistress' coming.

" Hagar Warren ! What does this mean ? Are you crazy ! " sternly demanded Madam Conway, when the old nurse held up before her the child with the blue nose.

" No, not crazy yet ; but I shall be, if you don't take this one first," answered Hagar.

More than once that day Madam Conway had heard the servants hint that Hagar's grief had driven her insane; and now when she observed the unnatural brightness in her eyes, and saw what she had done, she too thought it possible that her mind was partially unsettled; so she said gently, but firmly: " This is no time for foolishness, Hagar. They are waiting for us in the sickroom; so make haste and change the baby's dress."

There was something authoritative in her manner, and Hagar obeyed, whispering incoherently to herself, and thus further confirming her mistress' suspicions that she was partially insane. During the ceremony she stood tall and erect like some dark, grim statue, her hands firmly locked together, and her eyes fixed upon the face of the little one who was baptized Margaret Miller. As the clergyman pronounced that name she uttered a low, gasping moan, but her face betrayed no emotion, and very calmly she stepped forward with the other child upon her arm.

" What name?" asked the minister; and she answered, " Her mother's; call her for her mother! "

" Hester," said Madam Conway, turning to the clergyman, who understood nothing from Hagar's reply.

So Hester was the name given to the child in whose veins the blood of English noblemen was flowing; and when the ceremony was ended Hagar bore back to her room Hester Hamilton, the child defrauded of her birthright, and Maggie Miller, the heroine of our story.

CHAPTER III.

"It is over now," old Hagar thought, as she laid the children upon their pillows. "The deed is done, and by their own hands too. There is nothing left for me now but a confession, and that I cannot make;" so with a heavy weight upon her soul she sat down, resolving to keep her own counsel and abide the consequence, whatever it might be.

But it wore upon her terribly,—that secret,—and though it helped in a measure to divert her mind from dwelling too much upon her daughter's death it haunted her continually, making her a strange, cecentric woman whom the servants persisted in calling crazy, while even Madam Conway failed to comprehend her. Her face, always dark, seemed to have acquired a darker, harder look, while her eyes wore a wild, startled expression, as if she were constantly followed by some tormenting fear. At first Mrs. Miller objected to trusting her with the babe; but when Madam Conway suggested that the woman who had charge of little Theo should also take care of Maggie she fell upon her knees and begged most piteously that the child might not be taken from her. "Everything I have ever loved has left me," said she, "and I cannot give her up."

"But they say you are crazy," answered Madam Conway, somewhat surprised that Hagar should manifest so much affection for a child not at all connected to her. "They say you are crazy, and no one trusts a crazy woman."

"Crazy!" repeated Hagar half-scornfully; "crazy —'tis not craziness—'tis the trouble—the trouble— that's killing me! But I'll hide it closer than it's hidden now," she continued, "if you'll let her stay; and 'fore Heaven I swear that sooner than harm one hair of Maggie's head I'd part with my own life;" and taking the sleeping child in her arms she stood like a wild beast at bay.

Madam Conway did not herself really believe in Hagar's insanity. She had heretofore been perfectly faithful to whatever was committed to her care, so she bade her be quiet, saying they would trust her for a time.

"It's the talking to myself," said Hagar, when left alone. "It's the talking to myself which makes them call me crazy; and though I might talk to many a worse woman than old Hagar Warren, I'll stop it; I'll be still as the grave, and when next they gossip about me it shall be of something besides craziness."

So Hagar became suddenly silent and uncommunicative, mingling but little with the servants, but staying all day long in her room, where she watched the children with untiring care. Especially was she kind to Hester, who as time passed on proved to be a puny, sickly thing, never noticing anyone, but moaning frequently as if in pain. Very tenderly old Hagar nursed her, carrying her often in her arms until they ached from very weariness, while Madam Conway, who watched her with a vigilant eye, complained that she neglected little Maggie.

"And what if I do?" returned Hagar somewhat

bitterly. "Aint there a vast difference between the two? S'pose Hester was your own flesh and blood, would you think I could do too much for the poor thing?" And she glanced compassionately at the poor wasted form which lay upon her lap, gasping for breath, and presenting a striking contrast to little Maggie, who in her cradle was crowing and laughing in childish glee at the bright firelight which blazed upon the hearth.

Maggie was indeed a beautiful child. From her mother she had inherited the boon of perfect health, and she throve well in spite of the bumped heads and pinched fingers which frequently fell to her lot, when Hagar was too busy with the feeble child to notice her. The plaything of the whole house, she was greatly petted by the servants, who vied with each other in tracing points of resemblance between her and the Conways; while the grandmother prided herself particularly on the arched eyebrows and finely cut upper lip, which she said were sure marks of high blood, and never found in the lower ranks! With a scornful expression on her face, old Hagar would listen to these remarks, and then, when sure that no one heard her, she would mutter: "Marks of blood! What nonsense! I'm almost glad I've solved the riddle, and know 'taint blood that makes the difference. Just tell her the truth once, and she'd quickly change her mind. Hester's blue, pinched nose, which makes one think of fits, would be the very essence of aristocracy, while Maggie's lip would come of the little Paddy blood there is running in her veins!'"

And still Madam Conway herself was not one-half so proud of the bright, playful Maggie as was old

Hagar, who, when they were alone, would hug her to her bosom, and gaze fondly on her fair, round face and locks of silken hair, so like those now resting in the grave. In the meantime Mrs. Miller, who since her daughter's birth, had never left her room, was growing daily weaker, and when Maggie was nearly nine months old she died, with the little one folded to her bosom, just as Hester Hamilton had held it when she too passed from earth.

"Doubly blessed," whispered old Hagar, who was present, and then when she remembered that to poor little Hester a mother's blessing would never be given she felt that her load of guilt was greater than she could bear. "She will perhaps forgive me if I confess it to her over Miss Margaret's coffin," she thought; and once when they stood together by the sleeping dead, and Madam Conway, with Maggie in her arms, was bidding the child kiss the clay-cold lips of its mother, old Hagar attempted to tell her. "Could you bear Miss Margaret's death as well," she said, "if Maggie, instead of being bright and playful as she is, were weak and sick like Hester?" and her eyes fastened themselves upon Madam Conway with an agonizing intensity which that lady could not fathom. "Say, would you bear it as well—could you love her as much—would you change with me, take Hester for your own, and give me little Maggie?" she persisted, and Madam Conway, surprised at her excited manner, which she attributed in a measure to envy, answered coldly: "Of course not. Still, if God had seen fit to give me a child like Hester, I should try to be reconciled, but I am thankful he has not thus dealt with me."

" 'Tis enough. I am satisfied," thought Hagar. " She would not thank me for telling her. The secret shall be kept; " and half exultingly she anticipated the pride she should feel in seeing her granddaughter grown up a lady and an heiress.

Anon, however, there came stealing over her a feeling of remorse, as she reflected that the child defrauded of its birthright would, if it lived, be compelled to serve in the capacity of a servant; and many a night, when all else was silent in the old stone house, she paced up and down the room, her long hair, now fast turning gray, falling over her shoulders, and her large eyes dimmed with tears, as she thought what the future would bring to the infant she carried in her arms.

But the evil she so much dreaded never came, for when the winter snows were again falling they made a little grave beneath the same pine tree where Hester Hamilton lay sleeping, and, while they dug that grave, old Hagar sat, with folded arms and tearless eyes, gazing fixedly upon the still white face and thin blue lips which would never again be distorted with pain. Her habit of talking to herself had returned, and as she sat there she would at intervals whisper: " Poor little babe! I would willingly have cared for you all my life, but I am glad you are gone to Miss Margaret, who, it may be, will wonder what little thin-faced angel is calling her mother! But somebody 'll introduce you, somebody 'll tell her who you are, and when she knows how proud her mother is of Maggie she'll forgive old Hagar Warren! "

" Gone stark mad! " was the report carried by the servants to their mistress, who believed the story when

Hagar herself came to her with the request that Hester might be buried in some of Maggie's clothes.

Touched with pity by her worn, haggard face, Madam Conway answered, " Yes, take some of her common ones," and, choosing the cambric robe which Hester had worn on the morning when the exchange was made, Hagar dressed the body for the grave. When at last everything was ready, and the tiny coffin stood upon the table, Madam Conway drew near and looked for a moment on the emaciated form which rested quietly from all its pain. Hovering at her side was Hagar, and feeling it her duty to say a word of comfort the stately lady remarked that it was best the babe should die; that were it her grandchild she should feel relieved; for had it lived, it would undoubtedly have been physically and intellectually feeble.

" Thank you! I am considerably comforted," was the cool reply of Hagar, who felt how cruel were the words, and who for a moment was strongly tempted to claim the beautiful Maggie as her own, and give back to the cold, proud woman the senseless clay on which she looked so calmly.

But love for her grandchild conquered. There was nothing in the way of her advancement now, and when at the grave she knelt her down to weep, as the bystanders thought, over her dead, she was breathing there a vow that never so long as she lived should the secret of Maggie's birth be given to the world unless some circumstance then unforeseen should make it absolutely and unavoidably necessary. To see Maggie grow up into a beautiful, refined, and cultivated woman was now the great object of Hagar's life; and, fearing lest by some inadvertent word or action the

secret should be disclosed, she wished to live by herself, where naught but the winds of heaven could
listen to the incoherent whisperings which made her
fellow-servants accuse her of insanity.

Down in the deepest shadow of the woods, and distant from the old stone house nearly a mile, was a half-
ruined cottage which, years before, had been occupied
by miners, who had dug in the hillside for particles of
yellow ore which they fancied to be gold. Long and
frequent were the night revels said to have been held
in the old hut, which had at last fallen into bad repute
and been for years deserted. To one like Hagar, however, there was nothing intimidating in its creaking
old floors, its rattling windows and noisome chimney,
where the bats and the swallows built their nests; and
when one day Madam Conway proposed giving little
Maggie into the charge of a younger and less nervous
person than herself she made no objection, but surprised her mistress by asking permission to live by
herself in the " cottage by the mine," as it was called.

" It is better for me to be alone," said she, " for I
may do something terrible if I stay here, something I would sooner die than do," and her eyes fell
upon Maggie sleeping in her cradle.

This satisfied Madam Conway that the half-crazed
woman meditated harm to her favorite grandchild, and
she consented readily to her removal to the cottage,
which by her orders was made comparatively comfortable. For several weeks, when she came, as she
did each day, to the house, Madam Conway kept
Maggie carefully from her sight, until at last she
begged so hard to see her that her wish was gratified;
and as she manifested no disposition whatever to

molest the child, Madam Conway's fears gradually subsided, and Hagar was permitted to fondle and caress her as often as she chose.

Here now, for a time, we leave them; Hagar in her cottage by the mine; Madam Conway in her gloomy home; Maggie in her nurse's arms; and Theo, of whom as yet but little has been said, playing on the nursery floor; while with our readers we pass silently over a period of time which shall bring us to Maggie's girlhood.

CHAPTER IV.

GIRLHOOD.

FIFTEEN years have passed away, and around the old stone house there is outwardly no change. The moss still clings to the damp, dark wall, just as it clung there long ago, while the swaying branches of the forest trees still cast their shadows across the floor, or scream to the autumn blast, just as they did in years gone by, when Hagar Warren breathed that prayer, " Lead us not into temptation." Madam Conway, stiff and straight and cold as ever, moves with the same measured tread through her gloomy rooms, which are not as noiseless now as they were wont to be, for girl-hood—joyous, merry girlhood—has a home in those dark rooms, and their silence is broken by the sound of other feet, not moving stealthily and slow, as if following in a funeral train, but dancing down the stairs, tripping through the halls, skipping across the floor, and bounding over the grass, they go, never tiring, never ceasing, till the birds and the sun have gone to rest.

And do what she may, the good lady cannot check the gleeful mirth, or hush the clear ringing laughter of one at least of the fair maidens, who, since last we looked upon them, have grown up to womanhood. Wondrously beautiful is Maggie Miller now, with her bright sunny face, her soft dark eyes and raven hair, so glossy and smooth that her sister, the pale-faced, blue-eyed Theo, likens it to a piece of shining satin.

Now, as ever, the pet and darling of the household, she moves among them like a ray of sunshine; and the servants, when they hear her bird-like voice waking the echoes of the weird old place, pause in their work to listen, blessing Miss Margaret for the jo˙ ˙nd gladness her presence has brought them.

Old Hagar, in her cottage by the mine, has kept her secret well, whispering it only to the rushing wind and the running brook, which have told no tales to the gay, light-hearted girl, save to murmur in her ear that a life untrammeled by etiquette and form would be a blissful life indeed. And Maggie, listening to the voices which speak to her so oft in the autumn wind, the running brook, the opening flower, and the falling leaf, has learned a lesson different far from those taught her daily by the prim, stiff governess, who, imported from England six years ago, has drilled both Theo and Maggie in all the prescribed rules of high life as practiced in the Old World. She has taught them how to sit and how to stand, how to eat and how to drink, as becomes young ladies of Conway blood and birth. And Madam Conway, through her golden spectacles, looks each day to see some good from all this teaching come to the bold, dashing, untamable Maggie, who, spurning birth and blood alike, laughs at form and etiquette as taught by Mrs. Jeffrey, and, winding her arms around her grandmother's neck, crumples her rich lace ruffle with a most unladylike hug, and then bounds away to the stables, pretending not to hear the distressed Mrs. Jeffrey calling after her not to run, " it is so Yankeefied and vulgar "; or if she did hear, answering back, " I am a Yankee, native born, and shall run for all Johnny Bull!"

Greatly horrified at this evidence of total depravity, Mrs. Jeffrey brushes down her black silk apron and goes back to Theo, her more tractable pupil; while Maggie, emerging ere long from the stable, clears the fence with one leap of her high-mettled pony, which John, the coachman, had bought at an enormous price, of a traveling circus, on purpose for his young mistress, who complained that grandma's horses were all too lazy and aristocratic m their movements for her.

In perfect amazement Madam Conway looked out when first Gritty, as the pony was called, was led up to the door, prancing, pawing, chafing at the bit, and impatient to be off. "Margaret shall never mount that animal," she said; but Margaret had ruled for sixteen years, and now, at a sign from John, she sprang gayly upon the back of the fiery steed, who, feeling instinctively that the rider he carried was a stranger to fear, became under her training perfectly gentle, obeying her slightest command, and following her ere long like a sagacious dog. Not thus easily could Madam Conway manage Maggie, and with a groan she saw her each day fly over the garden gate and out into the woods, which she scoured in all directions.

"She'll break her neck, I know," the disturbed old lady would say, as Maggie's flowing skirt and waving plumes disappeared in the shadow of the trees. "She'll break her neck some day;" and thinking someone must be in fault, her eyes would turn reprovingly upon Mrs. Jeffrey for having failed in subduing Maggie, whom the old governess pronounced the "veriest madcap" in the world. "There is nothing like her in all England," she said; "and her low-bred ways must be the result of her having been born on American soil."

If Maggie was to be censured, Madam Conway chose to do it herself; and on such occasions she would answer: "'Low-bred,' Mrs. Jeffrey, is not a proper term to apply to Margaret. She's a little wild, I admit, but no one with my blood in their veins can be low-bred;" and, in her indignation at the governess, Madam would usually forget to reprove her granddaughter when she came back from her ride, her cheeks flushed and her eyes shining like stars with the healthful exercise. Throwing herself upon a stool at her grandmother's feet, Maggie would lay her head upon the lap of the proud lady, who very lovingly would smooth the soft, shining hair, "so much like her own," she said.

"Before you had to color it, you mean, don't you, grandma?" the mischievous Maggie would rejoin, looking up archly to her grandmother, who would call her a saucy child, and stroke still more fondly the silken locks.

Wholly unlike Maggie was Theo, a pale-faced, fairhaired girl, who was called pretty, when not overshadowed by the queenly presence of her more gifted sister. And Theo was very proud of this sister, too; proud of the beautiful Maggie, to whom, though two years her junior, she looked for counsel, willing always to abide by her judgment; for what Maggie did must of course be right, and grandma would not scold. So if at any time Theo was led into error, Maggie stood ready to bear the blame, which was never very severe, for Mrs. Jeffrey had learned not to censure her too much, lest by so doing she should incur the displeasure of her employer, who in turn loved Maggie, if it were possible, better than the daughter whose name she bore, and whom Maggie called her mother. Well kept and beautiful was the spot where that mother lay, and the grave was marked by a costly marble which gleamed clear and white through the surrounding evergreens. This was Maggie's favorite resort, and here she often sat in the moonlight, musing of one who slept there, and who, they said, had held her on her bosom when she died.

At no great distance from this spot was another grave, where the grass grew tall and green, and where the headstone, half sunken in the earth, betokened that she who rested there was of humble origin. Here Maggie seldom tarried long. The place had no attraction for her, for rarely now was the name of Hester Hamilton heard at the old stone house, and all save one seemed to have forgotten that such as she had ever lived. This was Hagar Warren, who in her cottage by the mine has grown older and more crazy-like since last we saw her. Her hair, once so much like that which Madam Conway likens to her own, has bleached as white as snow, and her tall form is shriveled now, and bent. The secret is wearing her life away, and yet she does not regret what she has done. She cannot, when she looks upon the beautiful girl who comes each day to her lonely hut, and whom she worships with a species of wild idolatry. Maggie knows not why it is, and yet to her there is a peculiar fascination about that strange old woman, with her snow-white hair, her wrinkled face, her bony hand, and wild, dark eyes, which, when they rest on her, have in them a look of unutterable tenderness.

Regularly each day, w.:n the sun nears the western horizon, Maggie steals away to the cottage, and the lonely woman, waiting for her on the rude bench by the door, can tell her bounding footstep from all others which pass that way. She does not say much now herself; but the sound of Maggie's voice, talking to her in the gathering twilight, is the sweetest she has ever heard; and so she sits and listens, while her hands work nervously together, and her whole body trembles with a longing, intense desire to clasp the young girl to her bosom and claim her as her own. But this she dare not do, for Madam Conway's training has had its effect, and in Maggie's bearing there is ever a degree of pride which forbids anything like undue familiarity. And it was· this very pride which Hagar liked to see, whispering often to herself, " Warren blood and Conway airs—the two go well together."

Sometimes a word or a look would make her start, they reminded her so forcibly of the dead; and once she said involuntarily: " You are like your mother, Maggie. Exactly what she was at your age."

" My mother!" answered Maggie. " You never talked to me of her; tell me of her now. I did not suppose I was like her in anything."

" Yes, in everything," said old Hagar; " the same dark eyes and hair, the same bright red cheeks, the same——"

" Why, Hagar, what can you mean?" interrupted Maggie. " My mother had light blue eyes and fair brown hair, like Theo. Grandma says I am not like her at all, while old Hannah, the cook, when she feels ill-natured and wishes to tease me, says I am the very image of Hester Hamilton."

"And what if you are? What if you are?" eagerly rejoined old Hagar. "Would you feel badly to know you looked like Hester?" and the old woman bent anxiously forward to hear the answer: "Not for myself, perhaps, provided Hester was handsome, for I think a good deal of beauty, that's a fact; but it would annoy grandma terribly to have me look like a servant. She might fancy I was Hester's daughter, for she wonders every day where I get my low-bred ways, as she calls my liking to sing and laugh and be natural."

"And s'posin' Hester was your mother, would you care?" persisted Hagar.

"Of course I should," answered Maggie, her large eyes opening wide at the strange question. "I wouldn't for the whole world be anybody but Maggie Miller, just who I am. To be sure, I get awfully out of patience with grandma and Mrs. Jeffrey for talking so much about birth and blood and family, and all that sort of nonsense, but after all I wouldn't for anything be poor and work as poor folks do."

"I'll never tell her, never," muttered Hagar; and Maggie continued: "What a queer habit you have of talking to yourself. Did you always do so?"

"Not always. It came upon me with the secret," Hagar answered inadvertently; and eagerly catching at the last word, which to her implied a world of romance and mystery, Maggie exclaimed: "The secret, Hagar, the secret! If there's anything I delight in it's a secret!" and, sliding down from the rude bench to the grass-plat at Hagar's feet, she continued: "Tell it to me, Hagar, that's a dear old woman. I'll never tell anybody as long as I live. I won't, upon my word," she continued, as she saw the look of horror resting on Hagar's face; "I'll help you keep it, and we'll have such grand times talking it over. Did it concern yourself?" and Maggie folded her arms upon the lap of the old woman, who answered in a voice so hoarse and unnatural that Maggie involuntarily shuddered, "Old Hagar would die inch by inch sooner than tell you, Maggie Miller, her secret."

"Was it, then, so dreadful?" asked Maggie half fearfully, and casting a stealthy glance at the dim woods, where the night shadows were falling, and whose winding path she must traverse alone on her homeward route. "Was it, then, so dreadful?"

"Yes, dreadful, dreadful; and yet, Maggie, I have sometimes wished you knew it. You would forgive me, perhaps. If you knew how I was tempted," said Hagar, and her voice was full of yearning tenderness, while her bony fingers parted lovingly the shining hair from off the white brow of the young girl, who pleaded again, "Tell it to me, Hagar."

There was a fierce struggle in Hagar's bosom, but the night wind, moving through the hemlock boughs, seemed to say, "Not yet—not yet"; and, remembering her vow, she answered: "Leave me, Maggie Miller, I cannot tell you the secret. You of all others. You would hate me for it, and that I could not bear. Leave me alone, or the sight of you, so beautiful, pleading for my secret, will kill me dead."

There was command in the tones of her voice, and rising to her feet Maggie walked away, with a dread feeling at her heart, a feeling which whispered vaguely to her of a deed of blood—for what save this could thus affect old Hagar? Her road home led near the little burying-ground, and impelled by something she could not resist she paused at her mother's grave. The moonlight was falling softly upon it; and, seating herself within the shadow of the monument, she sat a long time thinking, not of the dead, but of Hagar and the strange words she had uttered. Suddenly, from the opposite side of the graveyard, there came a sound as of someone walking; and, looking up, Maggie saw approaching her the bent figure of the old woman, who seemed unusually excited. Her first impulse was to fly, but knowing how improbable it was that Hagar should seek to do her harm, and thinking she might discover some clew to the mystery if she remained, she sat still, while, kneeling on Hester's grave, old Hagar wept bitterly, talking the while, but so incoherently that Maggie could distinguish nothing save the words, " You, Hester, have forgiven me."

" Can it be that she has killed her own child! " thought Maggie, and starting to her feet she stood face to face with Hagar, who screamed: " You here, Maggie Miller!—here with the others who know my secret! But you shan't wring it from me. You shall never know it, unless the dead rise up to tell you."

" Hagar Warren," said Margaret sternly, " is murder your secret? Did Hester Hamilton die at her mother's hands? "

With a short gasping moan, Hagar staggered backward a pace or two, and then, standing far more erect than Margaret had ever seen her before, she answered: " No, Maggie Miller, no; murder is not my secret. These hands," and she tossed in the air her shriveled arms, " these hands are as free from blood as yours. And now go. Leave me alone with my dead, and see

that you tell no tales. You like secrets, you say. Let
what you have heard to-night be *your* secret. Go."

Maggie obeyed, and walked slowly homeward, feeling greatly relieved that her suspicion was, false, and
experiencing a degree of satisfaction in thinking that
she too had a secret, which she would guard most
carefully from her grandmother and Theo. " She
would never tell them what she had seen and heard—
never!"

Seated upon the piazza were Madam Conway and
Theo, the former of whom chided her for staying so
late at the cottage, while Theo asked what queer
things the old witch-woman had said to-night.

With a very expressive look, which seemed to say,
" I know, but I shan't tell," Maggie seated herself at
her grandmother's feet, and asked how long Hagar
had been crazy. " Did it come upon her when her
daughter died?" she inquired; and Madam Conway
answered: " Yes, about that time, or more particularly
when the baby died. Then she began to act so
strangely that I removed you from her care, for, from
something she said, I fancied she meditated harm to
you."

For a moment Maggie sat wrapped in thought—
then clapping her hands together she exclaimed: " I
have it; I know now what ails her! She felt so badly
to see you happy with me that she tried to poison me.
She said she was sorely tempted—and that's the secret
which is killing her."

" Secret! What secret?" cried Theo; and, woman-
like, forgetting her resolution not to tell, Maggie told
what she had seen and heard, adding it as her firm belief that Hagar had made an attempt upon her life.

" I would advise you for the future to keep away
from her, then," said Madam Conway, to whom the
suggestion seemed a very probable one.

But Maggie knew full well that whatever Hagar
might once have thought to do, there was no danger
to be apprehended from her now, and the next day
found her as usual on her way to the cottage. Bounding into the room where the old woman sat at her
knitting, she exclaimed: " I know what it is! I know
your secret! "

There was a gathering mist before Hagar's eyes,
and her face was deathly white, as she gasped: " You
know the secret! How? Where? Have the dead
come back to tell? Did anybody see me do it? "

" Why, no," answered Maggie, beginning to grow
a little mystified. " The dead have nothing to do with
it. You tried to poison me when I was a baby, and
that's what makes you crazy. Isn't it so? Grandma
thought it was, when I told her how you talked last
night."

There was a heavy load lifted from Hagar's heart,
and she answered calmly, but somewhat indignantly,
" So you told—I thought I could trust you, Maggie."

Instantly the tears came to Maggie's eyes, and,
coloring crimson, she said: " I didn't mean to tell—indeed I didn't, but I forgot all about your charge. Forgive me, Hagar, do," and, sinking on the floor, she
looked up in Hagar's face so pleadingly that the old
woman was softened, and answered gently: " You are
like the rest of your sex, Margaret. No woman but
Hagar Warren ever kept a secret; and it's killing her,
you see! "

" Don't keep it, then," said Maggie. " Tell it to me.

Confess that you tried to poison me because you en-
vied grandma," and the soft eyes looked with an anxious, expectant expression into the dark, wild orbs of
Hagar, who replied: " Envy was at the bottom of it
all, but I never tried to harm you, Margaret, in any
way. I only thought to do you good. You have not
guessed it. You cannot, and you must not try."

" Tell it to me, then. I want to know it so badly,"
persisted Maggie, her curiosity each moment increasing.

" Maggie Miller," said old Hagar, and the knitting
dropped from her fingers, which moved slowly on
till they reached and touched the little snowflake of a
hand resting on her knee—" Maggie Miller, if you
knew that the telling of that secret would make you
perfectly wretched, would you wish to hear it? "

For a moment Maggie was silent, and then, half
laughingly, she replied: " I'd risk it, Hagar, for I
never wanted to know anything half so bad in all my
life. Tell it to me, won't you? "

Very beautiful looked Maggie Miller then—her
straw flat set jauntily on one side of her head, her
glossy hair combed smoothly back, her soft lustrous
eyes shining with eager curiosity, and her cheeks
flushed with excitement. Very, very beautiful she
seemed to the old woman, who, in her intense longing
to take the bright creature to her bosom, was, for an
instant, sorely tempted.

" Margaret! " she began, and at the sound of her
voice the young girl shuddered involuntarily. " Margaret! " she said again; but ere another word was
uttered the autumn wind, which for the last half-hour
had been rising rapidly, came roaring down the wide-

mouthed chimney, and the heavy fireboard fell upon the floor with a tremendous crash, nearly crushing old Hagar's foot, and driving for a time all thoughts of the secret from Maggie's mind. " Served me right," muttered Hagar, as Maggie left the room for water with which to bathe the swollen foot. " Served me right; and if ever I'm tempted to tell her again may every bone in my body be smashed! "

The foot was carefully cared for, Maggie's own hands tenderly bandaging it up; and then with redoubled zeal she returned to the attack, pressing old Hagar so hard that the large drops of perspiration gathered thickly about her forehead and lips, which were white as ashes. Wearied at last, Maggie gave it up for the time being, but her curiosity was thoroughly aroused, and for many days she persisted in her importunity, until at last, in self-defense, old Hagar, when she saw her coming, would steal away to the low-roofed chamber, and, hiding behind a pile of rubbish, would listen breathlessly while Margaret hunted for her in vain. Then when she was gone she would crawl out from her hiding-place, covered with cobwebs and dust, and mutter to herself: " I never expected this, and it's more than I can bear. Why will she torment me so, when a knowledge of the secret would drive her mad! "

This, however, Maggie Miller did not know. Blessed with an uncommon degree of curiosity, which increased each time she saw old Hagar, she resolved to solve the mystery, which she felt sure was connected with herself, though in what manner she could not guess. " But I *will* know," she would say to herself when returning from a fruitless quizzing of old Hagar, whose hiding-place she had at last discovered; " I *will* know what 'tis about me. I shall never be quite happy till I do."

Ah, Maggie, Maggie, be happy while you can, and leave the secret alone! It will come **to you** soon enough—aye, soon enough!

CHAPTER V.

TRIFLES.

VERY rapidly the winter passed away, and one morning early in March Maggie went down to the cottage with the news that Madam Conway was intending to start immediately for England, where she had business which would probably detain her until fall.

"Oh, won't I have fun in her absence!" she cried. "I'll visit every family in the neighborhood. Here she's kept Theo and me caged up like two wild animals, and now I am going to see a little of the world. I don't mean to study a bit, and instead of visiting you once a day I shall come at least three times."

"Lord help me!" ejaculated old Hagar, who, much as she loved Maggie, was beginning to dread her daily visits.

"Why do you want help?" asked Maggie laughingly. "Are you tired of me, Hagar? Don't you like me any more?"

"Like you, Maggie Miller!—like you!" repeated old Hagar, and in the tones of her voice there was a world of tenderness and love. "There is nothing on earth I love as I do you. But you worry me to death sometimes."

"Oh, yes, I know," answered Maggie; "but I'm not going to tease you for a while. I shall have so much else to do when grandma is gone that I shall

forget it. I wish she wasn't so proud," she continued, after a moment. "I wish she'd let Theo and me
see a little more of the world than she does. I wonder
how she ever expects us to get married, or be anybody,
if she keeps us here in the woods like young savages.
Why, as true as you live, Hagar, I have never been
anywhere in my life, except to church Sundays, once
to Douglas' store in Worcester, once to Patty Thomp-
son's funeral, and once to a Methodist camp-meeting;
and I never spoke to more than a dozen men besides
the minister and the school boys! It's too bad!" and
Maggie pouted quite becomingly at the injustice done
her by her grandmother in keeping her thus secluded.
"Theo don't care," she said. "She is prouder than I
am, and does not wish to know the Yankees, as
grandma calls the folks in this country; but I'm glad
I am a Yankee. I wouldn't live in England for anything."

"Why don't your grandmother take you with her?"
asked Hagar, who in a measure sympathized with
Maggie for being thus isolated.

"She says we are too young to go into society," answered Maggie. "It will be time enough two years
hence, when I am eighteen and Theo twenty. Then
I believe she intends taking us to London, where we
can show off our accomplishments, and practice that
wonderful courtesy which Mrs. Jeffrey has taught us.
I dare say the queen will be astonished at our qualifi-
cations;" and with a merry laugh, as she thought of
the appearance she should make at the Court of St.
James, Maggie leaped on Gritty's back and bounded
away, while Hagar looked wistfully after her, saying
as she wiped the tears from her eyes: "Heaven bless

the girl! She might sit on the throne of England any day, and Victoria wouldn't disgrace herself at all by doing her reverence, even if she be a child of Hagar Warren."

As Maggie had said, Madam Conway was going to England. At first she thought of taking the young ladies with her, but, thinking they were hardly old enough yet to be emancipated from the schoolroom, she decided to leave them under the supervision of Mrs. Jeffrey, whose niece she promised to bring with her on her return to America. Upon her departure she bade Theo and Maggie a most affectionate adieu, adding:

" Be good girls while I am away, keep in the house, mind Mrs. Jeffrey, and don't fall in love."

This last injunction came involuntarily from the old lady, to whom the idea of their falling in love was quite as preposterous as to themselves.

" Fall in love!" repeated Maggie, when her tears were dried, and she with Theo was driving slowly home. " What could grandma mean! I wonder who there is for us to love, unless it be John the coachman, or Bill the gardener. I almost wish we could get in love though, just to see how 'twould seem, don't you?" she continued.

" Not with anybody here," answered Theo, her nose slightly elevated at the thought of people whom she had been educated to despise.

" Why not here as well as elsewhere?" asked Maggie. " I don't see any difference. But grandma needn't be troubled, for such things as men's boots never come near our house. It's a shame, though," she continued, " that we don't know anybody, either male or female. Let's go down to Worcester some day, and get acquainted. Don't you remember the two handsome young men whom we saw five years ago in Douglas' store, and how they winked at each other when grandma ran down their goods and said there were not any darning needles fit to use this side of the water?"

On most subjects Theo's memory was treacherous, but she remembered perfectly well the two young men, particularly the taller one, who had given her a remnant of blue ribbon which he said was just the color of her eyes. Still, the idea of going to Worcester did not strike her favorably. " She wished Worcester would come to them," she said, " but she should not dare to go there. They would surely get lost. Grandma would not like it, and Mrs. Jeffrey would not let them go, even if they wished."

" A fig for Mrs. Jeffrey," said Maggie. " I shan't mind her much. I'm going to have a real good time, doing as I please, and if you are wise you'll have one too."

" I suppose I shall do what you tell me to—I always do," answered Theo submissively, and there the conversation ceased.

Arrived at home they found dinner awaiting them, and Maggie, when seated, suggested to Mrs. Jeffrey that she should give them a vacation of a few weeks, just long enough for them to get rested and visit the neighbors. But this Mrs. Jeffrey refused to do.

She had her orders to keep them at their books, she said, and " study was healthful "; at the same time she bade them be in the schoolroom on the morrow. There was a wicked look in Maggie's eyes, but her tongue told no tales, and when next morning she went with Theo demurely to the schoolroom she seemed surprised at hearing from Mrs. Jeffrey that every book had disappeared from the desk where they were usually kept; and though the greatly disturbed and astonished lady had sought for them nearly an hour, they were not to be found.

" Maggie has hidden them, I know," said Theo, as she saw the mischievous look on her sister's face.

" Margaret wouldn't do such a thing, I'm sure," answered Mrs. Jeffrey, her voice and manner indicating a little doubt, however, as to the truth of her assertion.

But Maggie had hidden them, and no amount of coaxing could persuade her to bring them back. " You refused me a vacation when I asked for it," she said, " so I'm going to have it perforce; " and, playfully catching up the little dumpy figure of her governess, she carried her out upon the piazza, and, seating her in a large easy-chair, bade her take snuff, and comfort too, as long as she liked.

Mrs. Jeffrey knew perfectly well that Maggie in reality was mistress of the house, that whatever she did Madam Conway would ultimately sanction; and as a rest was by no means disagreeable, she yielded with a good grace, dividing her time between sleeping, snuffing, and dressing, while Theo lounged upon the sofa and devoured some musty old novels which Maggie, in her rummaging, had discovered.

Meanwhile Maggie kept her promise of visiting the neighbors, and almost every family had something to say in praise of the merry, light-hearted girl of whom they had heretofore known but little. Her favorite recreation, however, was riding on horseback, and almost every day she galloped through the woods and over the fields, usually terminating her ride with a call upon old Hagar, whom she still continued to tease unmercifully for the secret, and who was glad when at last an incident occurred which for a time drove all thoughts of the secret from Maggie's mind.

CHAPTER VI.

ONE afternoon towards the middle of April, when Maggie as usual was flying through the woods, she paused for a moment beneath the shadow of a sycamore while Gritty drank from a small running brook. The pony having quenched his thirst, she gathered up her reins for a fresh gallop, when her ear caught the sound of another horse's hoofs; and, looking back, she saw approaching her at a rapid rate a gentleman whom she knew to be a stranger. Not caring to be overtaken, she chirruped to the spirited Gritty, who, bounding over the velvety turf, left the unknown rider far in the rear.

"Who can she be?" thought the young man, admiring the utter fearlessness with which she rode; then, feeling a little piqued, as he saw how the distance between them was increasing, he exclaimed, "Be she woman, or be she witch, I'll overtake her"; and, whistling to his own fleet animal, he too dashed on at a furious rate.

"Trying to catch me, are you?" thought Maggie. "I'd laugh to see you do it." And entering at once into the spirit of the race, she rode on for a time with headlong speed—then, by way of tantalizing her pursuer, she paused for a moment until he had almost reached her, when at a peculiar whistle Gritty sprang forward, while Maggie's mocking laugh was borne back to the discomfited young man, whose interest in the daring girl increased each moment. It was a long, long chase she led him, over hills, across plains, and through the grassy valley, until she stopped at last within a hundred yards of the deep, narrow gorge through which the mill-stream ran.

" I have you now," thought the stranger, who knew by the dull, roaring sound of the water that a chasm lay between him and the opposite bank.

But Maggie had not yet half displayed her daring feats of horsemanship, and when he came so near that his waving brown locks and handsome dark eyes were plainly discernible, she said to herself: " He rides tolerably well. I'll see how good he is at a leap," and, setting herself more firmly in the saddle, she patted Gritty upon the neck. The well-trained animal understood the signal, and, rearing high in the air, was fast nearing the bank, when the young man, suspecting her design, shrieked out: " Stop, lady, stop! It's madness to attempt it."

" Follow me if you can," was Maggie's defiant answer, and the next moment she hung in mid-air over the dark abyss.

Involuntarily the young man closed his eyes, while his ear listened anxiously for the cry which would come next. But Maggie knew full well what she was doing. She had leaped that narrow gorge often, and now when the stranger's eyes unclosed she stood upon the opposite bank, caressing the noble animal which had borne her safely there.

" It shall never be said that Henry Warner was beaten by a schoolgirl," muttered the stranger. " If she can clear that, I can, bad rider as I am!" and

burying his spurs deep in the sides of his horse, he
pressed on while Maggie held her breath in fear, for
she knew that without practice no one could do what
she had done.

There was a partially downward plunge—a fierce
struggle on the shelving bank, where the animal had
struck a few feet from the top—then the steed stood
panting on terra firma, while a piercing shriek broke
the deep silence of the wood, and Maggie's cheeks
blanched to a marble hue. The rider, either from
dizziness or fear, had fallen at the moment the horse
first struck the bank, and from the ravine below there
came no sound to tell if yet he lived.

"He's dead; he's dead!" cried Maggie. "'Twas
my own foolishness which killed him," and springing
from Gritty's back she gathered up her long riding
skirt and glided swiftly down the bank, until she came
to a wide, projecting rock, where the stranger lay,
motionless and still, his white face upturned to the
sunlight, which came stealing down through the
overhanging boughs. In an instant she was at his
side, and his head was resting on her lap, while her
trembling fingers parted back from his pale brow the
damp mass of curling hair.

"The fall alone would not kill him," she said, as
her eye measured the distance, and then she looked
anxiously round for water with which to bathe his
face.

But water there was none, save in the stream below,
whose murmuring flow fell mockingly on her ears, for
it seemed to say she could not reach it. But Maggie
Miller was equal to any emergency, and venturing
out to the very edge of the rock she poised herself on

one foot, and looked down the dizzy height to see if it were possible to descend.

"I can try at least," she said, and glancing at the pale face of the stranger unhesitatingly resolved to attempt it.

The descent was less difficult than she had antici-pated, and in an incredibly short space of time she was dipping her pretty velvet cap in the brook, whose sparkling foam had never before been disturbed by the touch of a hand as soft and fair as hers. To ascend was not so easy a matter; but, chamois-like, Maggie's feet trod safely the dangerous path, and she soon knelt by the unconscious man, bathing his forehead in the clear cold water, until he showed signs of re-turning life. His lips moved slowly at last, as if he would speak; and Maggie, bending low to catch the faintest sound, heard him utter the name of "Rose." In Maggie's bosom there was no feeling for the stran-ger save that of pity, and yet that one word "Rose" thrilled her with a strange undefinable emotion, awak-ing at once a yearning desire to know something of her who bore that beautiful name, and who to the young man was undoubtedly the one in all the world most dear.

"Rose," he said again, "is it you?" and his eyes, which opened slowly, scanned with an eager, question-ing look the face of Maggie, who, open-hearted and impulsive as usual, answered somewhat sadly: "I am nobody but Maggie Miller. I am not Rose, though I wish I was, if you would like to see her."

The tones of her voice recalled the stranger's wan-dering mind, and he answered: "Your voice is like Rose, but I would rather see you, Maggie Miller. I like your fearlessness, so unlike most of your sex. Rose is far more gentle, more feminine than you, and if her very life depended upon it she would never dare leap that gorge."

The young man intended no reproof; but Maggie took his words as such, and for the first time in her life began to think that possibly her manner was not always as womanly as might be. At all events, she was not like the gentle Rose, whom she instantly invested with every possible grace and beauty, wishing that she herself was like her instead of the wild madcap she was. Then, thinking that her conduct required some apology, she answered, as none save one as fresh and ingenuous as Maggie Miller would have answered: "I don't know any better than to behave as I do. I've always lived in the woods—have never been to school a day in my life—never been anywhere except to camp-meeting, and once to Douglas' store in Worcester!"

This was entirely a new phase of character to the man of the world, who laughed aloud, and at the mention of Douglas' store started so quickly that a spasm of pain distorted his features, causing Maggie to ask if he were badly hurt.

"Nothing but a broken leg," he answered; and Maggie, to whose mind broken bones conveyed a world of pain and suffering, replied: "Oh, I am so sorry for you! and it's my fault, too. Will you forgive me?" and her hands clasped his so pleadingly that, raising himself upon his elbow so as to obtain a better view of her bright face, he answered, "I'd willingly break a hundred bones for the sake of meeting a girl like you, Maggie Miller."

Maggie was unused to flattery, save as it came from her grandmother, Theo, or old Hagar, and now paying no heed to his remark she said: "Can you stay here alone while I go for help? Our house is not far away."

"I'd rather you would remain with me," he replied; "but as you cannot do both, I suppose you must go."

"I shan't be gone long, and I'll send old Hagar to keep you company." So saying, Maggie climbed the bank, and, mounting Gritty, who stood quietly awaiting her, seized the other horse by the bridle and rode swiftly away, leaving the young man to meditate upon the novel situation in which he had so suddenly been placed.

"Aint I in a pretty predicament!" said he, as he tried in vain to move his swollen limb, which was broken in two places, but which being partially benumbed did not now pain nim much. "But it serves me right for chasing a harum-scarum thing when I ought to have been minding my own business and collecting bills for Douglas & Co. And she says she's been there, too. I wonder who she is, the handsome sprite. I believe I made her more than half jealous talking of my golden-haired Rose; but she is far more beautiful than Rose, more beautiful than anyone I ever saw. I wish she'd come back again," and, shutting his eyes, he tried to recall the bright, animated face which had so lately bent anxiously above him. "She tarries long," he said at last, beginning to grow uneasy. "I wonder how far it is; and where the deuce can this old Hagar be, of whom she spoke?"

"She's here," answered a shrill voice, and looking up he saw before him the bent form of Hagar Warren, at whose door Maggie had paused for a moment while she told of the accident and begged of Hagar to hasten.

Accordingly, equipped with a blanket and pillow, a brandy bottle and camphor, old Hagar had come, but when she offered the latter for the young man's acceptance he pushed it from him, saying that camphor was his detestation, but he shouldn't object particularly to smelling of the other bottle!

"No, you don't," said Hagar, who thought him in not quite so deplorable a condition as she had expected to find him. "My creed is never to give young folks brandy except in cases of emergency." So saying, she made him more comfortable by placing a pillow beneath his head; and then, thinking possibly that this to herself was a "case of emergency," she withdrew to a little distance, and sitting down upon the gnarled roots of an upturned tree drank a swallow of the old Cognac, while the young man, maimed and disabled, looked wistfully at her.

Not that he cared for the brandy, of which he seldom tasted; but he needed something to relieve the deathlike faintness which occasionally came over him, and which old Hagar, looking only at his mischievous eyes, failed to observe. Only those who knew Henry Warner intimately gave him credit for many admirable qualities he really possessed—so full was he of fun. It was in his merry eyes and about his quizzically shaped mouth that the principal difficulty lay; and most persons, seeing him for the first time, fancied that in some way he was making sport of them. This was old Hagar's impression, as she sat there in dignified silence, rather enjoying, than otherwise, the occasional groans which came from his white lips. There were intervals, however, when he was comparatively free from pain, and these he improved by questioning her with regard to Maggie, asking who she was and where she lived.

" She is Maggie Miller, and she lives in a house," answered the old woman rather pettishly.

" Ah, indeed—snappish, are you? " said the young man, attempting to turn himself a little, the better to see his companion. " Confound that leg! " he continued, as a fierce twinge gave him warning not to try many experiments. " I know her name is Maggie Miller, and I supposed she lived in a house; but who is she, anyway, and what is she? "

" If you mean is she anybody, I can answer that question quick," returned Hagar. " She calls Madam Conway her grandmother, and Madam Conway came from one of the best families in England—that's who she is; and as to what she is, she's the finest, handsomest, smartest girl in America; and as long as old Hagar Warren lives no city chap with strapped-down pantaloons and sneering mouth is going to fool with her either! "

" Confound my mouth—it's always getting me into trouble! " thought the stranger, trying in vain to smooth down the corners of the offending organ, which in spite of him would curve with what Hagar called a sneer, and from which there finally broke a merry laugh, sadly at variance with the suffering expression of his face.

" Your leg must hurt you mightily, the way you go on," muttered Hagar; and the young man answered: " It does almost murder me, but when a laugh is in a fellow he can't help letting it out, can he? But where the plague can that witch of a—— I beg your pardon, Mrs. Hagar," he added hastily, as he saw the frown settling on the old woman's face, " I mean to say where can Miss Miller be? I shall faint away unless she comes soon, or you give me a taste of the brandy! "

This time there was something in the tone of his voice which prompted Hagar to draw near, and she was about to offer him the brandy when Maggie appeared, together with three men bearing a litter. The sight of her produced a much better effect upon him than Hagar's brandy would have done, and motioning the old woman aside he declared himself ready to be removed.

" Now, John, do pray be careful and not hurt him much! " cried Maggie, as she saw how pale and faint he was, while even Hagar forgot the curled lip, which the young man bit until the blood started through, so intense was his agony when they lifted him upon the litter. " The camphor, Hagar, the camphor! " said Maggie; and the stranger did not push it aside when her hand poured it on his head, but the laughing eyes, now dim with pain, smiled gratefully upon her, and the quivering lips once murmured as she walked beside him, " Heaven bless you, Maggie Miller! "

Arrived at Hagar's cottage, the old woman suggested that he be carried in there, saying as she met Maggie's questioning glance, " I can take care of him better than anyone else."

The pain by this time was intolerable, and scarcely knowing what he said the stranger whispered, " Yes, yes, leave me here."

For a moment the bearers paused, while Maggie,

bending over the wounded man, said softly: "Can't you bear it a little longer, until our house is reached? You'll be more comfortable there. Grandma has gone to England, and I'll take care of you myself!"

This last was perfectly in accordance with Maggie's frank, impulsive character, and it had the desired effect. Henry Warner would have borne almost death itself for the sake of being nursed by the young girl beside him, and he signified his willingness to proceed, while at the same time his hand involuntarily grasped that of Maggie, as if in the touch of her snowy fingers there were a mesmeric power to soothe his pain. In the meantime a hurried consultation had been held between Mrs. Jeffrey and Theo as to the room suitable for the stranger to be placed in.

"It's not likely he is much," said Theo; "and if grandma were here I presume she would assign him the chamber over the kitchen. The wall is low on one side, I know, but I dare say he is not accustomed to anything better."

Accordingly several articles of stray lumber were removed from the chamber, which the ladies arranged with care, and which when completed presented quite a respectable appearance. But Maggie had no idea of putting her guest, as she considered him, in the kitchen chamber; and when, as the party entered the house, Mrs. Jeffrey, from the head of the stairs, called out, "This way, Maggie; tell them to come this way," she waved her aside, and led the way to a large airy room over the parlor, where, in a high, old-fashioned bed, surrounded on all sides by heavy damask curtains, they laid the weary stranger. The village surgeon arriving soon after, the fractured bones were set, and then, as perfect quiet seemed necessary, the room was vacated by all save Maggie, who glided noiselessly around the apartment, while the eyes of the sick man followed her with eager, admiring glances, so beautiful she looked to him in her new capacity of nurse.

Henry Warner, as the stranger was called, was the junior partner of the firm of Douglas & Co., Worcester, and his object in visiting the Hillsdale neighborhood was to collect several bills which for a long time had been due. He had left the cars at the depot, and, hiring a livery horse, was taking the shortest route from the east side of town to the west, when he came accidentally upon Maggie Miller, and, as we have seen, brought his ride to a sudden close. All this he told to her on the morning following the accident, retaining until the last the name of the firm of which he was a member.

"And you were once at your store?" he said. "How long ago?"

"Five years," answered Maggie; "when I was eleven, and Theo thirteen;" then, looking earnestly at him, she exclaimed, "And you are the very one, the clerk with the saucy eyes whom grandma disliked so much because she thought he made fun of her; but we didn't think so—Theo and I," she added hastily, as she saw the curious expression on Henry's mouth, and fancied he might be displeased. "We liked them both very much, and knew they must of course be annoyed with grandma's English whims."

For a moment the saucy eyes studied intently the fair girlish face of Maggie Miller, then slowly closed, while a train of thought something like the following passed through the young man's mind: "A woman, and yet a perfect child—innocent and unsuspecting as little Rose herself. In one respect they are alike, knowing no evil and expecting none; and if I, Henry Warner, do aught by thought or deed to injure this young girl may I never again look on the light of day or breathe the air of heaven."

The vow had passed his lips. Henry Warner never broke his word, and henceforth Maggie Miller was as safe with him as if she had been an only and well-beloved sister. Thinking him to be asleep, Maggie started to leave the room, but he called her back, saying, " Don't go; stay with me, won't you? "

" Certainly," she answered, drawing a chair to the bedside. " I supposed you were sleeping."

" I was not," he replied. " I was thinking of you and of Rose. Your voices are much alike. I thought of it yesterday when I lay upon the rock."

" Who is Rose? " trembled on Maggie's lips, while at the sound of that name she was conscious of the same undefinable emotion she had once before experienced. But the question was not asked. " If she were his sister he would tell me," she thought; " and if she is not his sister——"

She did not finish the sentence, neither did she understand that if Rose to him was something dearer than a sister, she, Maggie Miller, did not care to know it.

" Is she beautiful as her name, this Rose? " she asked at last.

" She is beautiful, but not so beautiful as you. There are few who are," answered Henry; and his eyes fixed themselves upon Maggie to see how she would bear the compliment.

But she scarcely heeded it, so intent was she upon knowing something more of the mysterious Rose. " She is beautiful, you say. Will you tell me how she looks? " she continued; and Henry Warner answered, " She is a frail, delicate little creature, almost dwarfish in size, but perfect in form and feature."

Involuntarily Maggie shrunk back in her chair, wishing her own queenly form had been a very trifle shorter, while Mr. Warner continued, " She has a sweet, angel face, Maggie, with eyes of lustrous blue and curls of golden hair."

" You must love her very dearly," said Maggie, the tone of her voice indicating a partial dread of what the answer might be.

" I do indeed love her," was Mr. Warner's reply— " love her better than all the world beside. And she has made me what I am; but for her I should have been a worthless, dissipated fellow. It's my natural disposition; but Rose has saved me, and I almost worship her for it. She is my good angel—my darling —my——"

Here he paused abruptly, and leaning back upon his pillows rather enjoyed than otherwise the look of disappointment plainly visible on Maggie's face. She had fully expected to learn who Rose was; but this knowledge he purposely kept from her. It did not need a very close observer of human nature to read at a glance the ingenuous Maggie, whose speaking face betrayed all she felt. She was unused to the world. He was the first young gentleman whose acquaintance she had ever made, and he knew that she already felt for him a deeper interest than she supposed. To increase this interest was his object, and this he thought to do by withholding from her, for a time, a knowledge of the relation existing between him and the Rose of whom he had talked so much. The ruse was successful, for during the remainder of the day thoughts of the golden-haired Rose were running through Maggie's mind, and it was late that night ere she could compose herself to sleep, so absorbed was she in wondering what Rose was to Henry Warner. Not that she cared particularly, she tried to persuade herself; but she would very much like to be at ease upon the subject.

To Theo she had communicated the fact that their guest was a partner of Douglas & Co., and this tended greatly to raise the young man in the estimation of a young lady like Theo Miller. Next to rank and station, money was with her the one thing necessary to make a person " somebody." Douglas, she had heard, was an immensely wealthy man; possibly the junior partner was wealthy, too; and if so, the parlor chamber to which she had at first objected was none too good for his aristocratic bones. She would go herself and see him in the morning.

Accordingly, on the morning of the second day she went with Maggie to the sickroom, speaking to the stranger for the first time; but keeping still at a respectable distance, until she should know something definite concerning him.

" We have met before, it seems," he said, after the first interchange of civilities was over; " but I did not think our acquaintance would be renewed in this manner."

No answer from Theo, who, like many others, had

taken a dislike to his mouth, and felt puzzled to know whether he intended ridiculing her or not.

" I have a distinct recollection of your grandmother," he continued, " and now I think of it I believe Douglas has once or twice mentioned the elder of the two girls. That must be you? " and he looked at Theo, whose face brightened perceptibly.

" Douglas," she repeated. " He is the owner of the store; and the one I saw, with black eyes and black hair, was only a clerk."

" The veritable man himself! " cried Mr. Warner. " George Douglas, the senior partner of the firm, said by some to be worth two hundred thousand dollars, and only twenty-eight years old, and the best fellow in the world, except that he pretends to dislike women."

By this time Theo's proud blue eyes shone with delight, and when, after a little further conversation, Mr. Warner expressed a wish to write to his partner, she brought her own rosewood writing desk for him to use, and then, seating herself by the window, waited until the letter was written.

" What shall I say for you, Miss Theo? " he asked, near the close; and, coloring slightly, she answered, " Invite him to come out and see you."

" Oh, that will be grand! " cried Maggie, who was far more enthusiastic, though not more anxious, than her sister.

Of her Henry Warner did not ask any message. He would not have written it had she sent one; and folding the letter, after adding Theo's invitation, he laid it aside.

" I must write to Rose next," he said; " 'tis a whole

week since I have written, and she has never been so long without hearing from me."

Instantly there came a shadow over Maggie's face, while Theo, less scrupulous, asked who Rose was.

"A very dear friend of mine," said Henry; and, as Mrs. Jeffrey just then sent for Theo, Maggie was left with him alone.

"Wait one moment," she said, as she saw him about to commence the letter. "Wait till I bring you a sheet of gilt-edged paper. It is more worthy of Rose, I fancy, than the plainer kind."

"Thank you," he said. "I will tell her of your suggestion."

The paper was brought, and then seating herself by the window Maggie looked out abstractedly, seeing nothing, and hearing nothing save the sound of the pen, as it wrote down words of love for the gentle Rose. It was not a long epistle; and, as at the close of the Douglas letter he had asked a message from Theo, so now at the close of this he claimed one from Maggie.

"What shall I say for you?" he asked; and, coming toward him, Margaret answered, "Tell her I love her, though I don't know who she is!"

"Why have you never asked me?" queried Henry; and, coloring crimson, Maggie answered hesitatingly, "I thought you would tell me if you wished me to know."

"Read this letter, and that will explain who she is," the young man continued, offering the letter to Maggie, who, grasping it eagerly, sat down opposite, so that every motion of her face was clearly visible to him.

The letter was as follows:

" MY DARLING LITTLE ROSE: Do you fancy some direful calamity has befallen me, because I have not written to you for more than a week? Away with your fears, then, for nothing worse has come upon me than a badly broken limb, which will probably keep me a prisoner here for two months or more. Now don't be frightened, Rosa. I am not crippled for life, and even if I were I could love you just the same, while you, I'm sure, would love me more.

" As you probably know, I left Worcester on Tuesday morning for the purpose of collecting some bills in this neighborhood. Arrived at Hillsdale I procured a horse, and was sauntering leisurely through the woods, when I came suddenly upon a flying witch in the shape of a beautiful young girl. She was the finest rider I ever saw; and such a chase as she led me, until at last, to my dismay, she leaped across a chasm down which a nervous little creature like you would be afraid to look. Not wishing to be outdone, I followed her, and as a matter of course broke my bones.

" Were it not that the accident will somewhat incommode Douglas, and greatly fidget you, I should not much regret it, for to me there is a peculiar charm about this old stone house and its quaint surroundings. But the greatest charm of all, perhaps, lies in my fair nurse, Maggie Miller, for whom I risked my neck. You two would be fast friends in a moment, and yet you are totally dissimilar, save that your voices are much alike.

" Write to me soon, dear Rose, and believe me ever
" Your affectionate brother,
" HENRY."

"Oh!" said Maggie, catching her breath, which for a time had been partially suspended, "Oh!" and in that single monosyllable there was to the young man watching her a world of meaning. "She's your sister, this little Rose," and the soft dark eyes flashed brightly upon him.

"What did you suppose her to be?" he asked, and Maggie answered, "I thought she might be your wife, though I should rather have her for a sister if I were you."

The young man smiled involuntarily, thinking to himself how his fashionable city friends would be shocked at such perfect frankness, which meant no more than their own studied airs.

"You are a good girl, Maggie," he said at last, "and I wouldn't for the world deceive you; Rose is my step-sister. We are in no way connected save by marriage, still I love her all the same. We were brought up together by a lady who is aunt to both, and Rose seems to me like an own dear sister. She has saved me from almost everything. I once loved the wine cup; but her kindly words and gentle influence won me back, so that now I seldom taste it. And once I thought to run away to sea, but Rose found it out, and, meeting me at the gate, persuaded me to return. It is wonderful, the influence she has over me, keeping my wild spirits in check; and if I am ever anything I shall owe it all to her."

"Does she live in Worcester?" asked Maggie; and Henry answered: "No; in Leominster, which is not far distant. I go home once a month; and I fancy I can see Rose now, just as she looks when she comes tripping down the walk to meet me, her blue eyes shining like stars and her golden curls blowing over her pale forehead. She is very, very frail; and sometimes when I look upon her the dread fear steals over me that there will come a time, ere long, when I shall have no sister."

There were tears in Maggie's eyes, tears for the fair young girl whom she had never seen, and she felt a yearning desire to look on the beautiful face of her whom Henry called his sister. "I wish she would come here; I want to see her," she said at last; and Henry replied: "She does not go often from home. But I have her daguerreotype in Worcester. I'll write to Douglas to bring it," and opening the letter, which was not yet sealed, he added a few lines. "Come, Maggie," he said, when this was finished, "you need exercise. Suppose you ride over to the office with these letters?"

Maggie would rather have remained with him; but she expressed her willingness to go, and in a few moments was seated on Gritty's back with the two letters clasped firmly in her hand. At one of these, the one bearing the name of Rose Warner, she looked often and wistfully; it was a most beautiful name, she thought, and she who bore it was beautiful too. And then there arose within her a wish—shadowy and undefined to herself, it is true; but still a wish—that she, Maggie Miller, might one day call that gentle Rose her sister. "I shall see her sometimes, anyway," she thought, "and this George Douglas, too. I wish they'd visit us together;" and having by this time reached the post-office she deposited the letters and galloped rapidly toward home.

CHAPTER VII.

THE SENIOR PARTNER.

THE establishment of Douglas & Co. was closed for the night. The clerks had gone each to his own home; old Safford, the poor relation, the man-of-all-work, who attended faithfully to everything, groaning often and praying oftener over the careless habits of "the boys," as he called the two young men, his employers, had sought his comfortless bachelor attic, where he slept always with one ear open, listening for any burglarious sound which might come from the store below, and which had it come to him listening thus would have frightened him half to death. George Douglas, too, the senior partner of the firm, had retired to his own room, which was far more elegantly furnished than that of the old man in the attic, and now in a velvet easy-chair he sat reading the letter from Hillsdale, which had arrived that evening, and a portion of which we subjoin for the reader's benefit.

After giving an account of his accident, and the manner in which it occurred, Warner continued:

" They say 'tis a mighty bad wind which blows no one any good, and so, though I verily believe I suffer all a man can suffer with a broken bone, yet when I look at the fair face of Maggie Miller I feel that I would not exchange this high old bed, to enter which needs a short ladder, even for a seat by you on that three-legged stool behind the old writing-desk. I never saw anything like her in my life. Everything she thinks, she says, and as to flattering her, it can't be done. I've told her a dozen times at least that she was beautiful, and she didn't mind it any more than Rose does when I flatter her. Still, I fancy if I were to talk to her of love it might make a difference, and perhaps I shall ere I leave the place.

" You know, George, I have always insisted there was but one female in the world fit to be a wife, and as that one was my sister I should probably never have the pleasure of paying any bills for Mrs. Henry Warner; but I've half changed my mind, and I'm terribly afraid this Maggie Miller, not content with breaking my bones, has made sad work with another portion of the body, called by physiologists the heart. I don't know how a man feels when he is in love; but when this Maggie Miller looks me straight in the face with her sunshiny eyes, while her little soft white hand pushes back my hair (which, by the way, I slyly disarrange on purpose), I feel the blood tingle to the ends of my toes, and still I dare not hint such a thing to her. 'Twould frighten her off in a moment, and she'll send in her place either an old hag of a woman called Hagar, or her proud sister Theo, whom I cannot endure.

" By the way, George, this Theo will just suit you, who are fond of aristocracy. She's proud as Lucifer; thinks because she was born in England, and sprang from a high family, that there is no one in America worthy of her ladyship's notice, unless indeed they chance to have money. You ought to have seen how her eyes lighted up when I told her you were said to be worth two hundred thousand dollars! She told me directly to invite you out here, and this, I assure you, was a good deal for her to do. So don your best attire, not forgetting the diamond cross, and come for a day or two. Old Safford will attend to the store. It's what he was made for, and he likes it. But as I am a Warner, so shall I do my duty and warn you not to meddle with Maggie. She is my own exclusive property, and altogether too good for a worldly fellow like you. Theo will suit you better. She's just aristocratic enough in her nature. I don't see how the two girls come to be so wholly unlike as they are. Why, I'd sooner take Maggie for Rose's sister than for Theo's!

" Bless me, I had almost forgotten to ask if you remember that stiff old English woman with the snuff-colored satin who came to our store some five years ago, and found so much fault with Yankee goods, as she called them? If you have forgotten her, you surely remember the two girls in flats, one of whom seemed so much distressed at her grandmother's remarks. She, the distressed one, was Maggie; the other was Theo; and the old lady was Madam Conway, who, luckily for me, chances at this time to be in England, buying up goods, I presume. Maggie says that this trip to Worcester, together with a camp-meeting held in the Hillsdale woods last year, is the extent of her travels, and one would think so to see her. A perfect child of nature, full of fun, beautiful as a Hebe, and possessing the kindest heart in the world. If you wish to know more of her come and see for yourself; but again I warn you, hands off; nobody is to flirt with her but myself, and it is very doubtful whether even I can do it peaceably, for that old Hagar, who, by the way, is a curious specimen, gave me to understand when I lay on the rock, with her sitting by, as a sort of ogress, that so long as she lived no city chap with strapped pants (do pray, bring me a pair, George, without straps!) and sneering mouth was going to fool with Margaret Miller.

"So you see my mouth is at fault again. Hang it all, I can't imagine what ails it, that everybody should think I'm making fun of them. Even old Safford mutters about my making mouths at him when I haven't thought of him in a month! Present my compliments to the old gentleman and tell him one of 'the boys' thinks seriously of following his advice, which you know is 'to sow our wild oats and get a wife.' Do, pray, come, for I am only half myself without you.

"Yours in the brotherhood,

"HENRY WARNER."

For a time after reading the above George Douglas sat wrapped in thought, then bursting into a laugh as he thought how much the letter was like the jovial, light-hearted fellow who wrote it, he put it aside, and leaning back in his chair mused long and silently, not of Theo, but of Maggie, half wishing he were in Warner's place instead of being there in the dusty city. But as this could not be, he contented himself with thinking that at some time not far distant he would visit the old stone house—would see for himself this wonderful Maggie—and, though he had been warned against it, would possibly win her from his friend, who, unconsciously perhaps, had often crossed his path, watching him jealously lest he should look too often and too long upon the fragile **Rose, blooming** so sweetly in her bird's-nest of a home among the tall old trees of Leominster.

"But he need not fear," he said somewhat bitterly, "he need not fear for her, for it is over now. She has refused me, this Rose Warner, and though it touched my pride to hear her tell me no, I cannot hate her for it. She had given her love to another, she said, and Warner is blind or crazy that he does not see the truth. But it is not for me to enlighten him. He may call her sister if he likes, though there is no tie of blood between them. I'd far rather it would be thus, than something nearer;" and, slowly rising up, George Douglas retired to dream of a calm, almost heavenly face which but the day before had been bathed in tears as he told to Rose Warner the story of his love. Mingled, too, with that dream was another face, a laughing, sparkling, merry face, upon which no man ever yet had looked and escaped with a whole heart.

The morning light dispelled the dream, and when in the store old Safford inquired, "What news from the boy?" the senior partner answered gravely that he was lying among the Hillsdale hills, with a broken leg caused by a fall from his horse.

"Always was a careless rider," muttered old Safford, mentally deploring the increased amount of labor which would necessarily fall upon him, but which he performed without a word of complaint.

The fair May blossoms were faded, and the last June roses were blooming ere George Douglas found time or inclination to accept the invitation indirectly extended to him by Theo Miller. Rose Warner's refusal had affected him more than he chose to confess, and the wound must be slightly healed ere he could find pleasure in the sight of another. Possessed of many excellent qualities, he had unfortunately fallen into the error of thinking that almost anyone whom he should select would take him for his money. And when Rose Warner, sitting by his side in the shadowy twilight, had said, " I cannot be your wife," the shock was sudden and hard to bear. But the first keen bitterness was over now, and remembering " the wild girls of the woods," as he mentally styled both Theo and Maggie, he determined at last to see them for himself.

Accordingly, on the last day of June he started for Hillsdale, where he intended to remain until after the Fourth. To find the old house was an easy matter, for almost everyone in town was familiar with its locality, and towards the close of the afternoon he found himself upon its broad steps applying vigorous strokes to the ponderous brass knocker, and half hoping the summons would be answered by Maggie herself. But it was not, and in the bent, white-haired woman who came with measured footsteps we recognize old Hagar, who spent much of her time at the house, and who came to the door in compliance with the request of the young ladies, both of whom, from an upper window, were curiously watching the stranger.

" Just the old witch one would expect to find in this out-of-the-way place," thought Mr. Douglas, while at the same time he asked if that were Madam Conway's residence, and if a young man by the name of Warner were staying there.

" Another city beau ! " muttered Hagar, as she answered in the affirmative, and ushered him into the parlor. "Another city beau—there'll be high carry-ings-on now, if he's anything like the other one, who's come mighty nigh turning the house upside down.".

"What did you say?" asked George Douglas, catching the sound of her muttering, and thinking she was addressing himself.

"I wasn't speaking to you. I was talking to a like-lier person," answered old Hagar in an undertone, as she shuffled away in quest of Henry Warner, who by this time was able to walk with the help of a cane.

The meeting between the young men was a joyful one, for though George Douglas was a little sore on the subject of Rose, he would not suffer a matter like that to come between him and Henry Warner, whom he had known and liked from boyhood. Henry's first inquiries were naturally of a business character, and then George Douglas spoke of the young ladies, say-ing he was only anxious to see Maggie, for he knew of course he should dislike the other.

Such, however, is wayward human nature that the fair, pale face, and quiet, dignified manner of Theo Miller had greater attractions for a person of George Douglas' peculiar temperament than had the dashing, brilliant Maggie. There was a resemblance, he imagined, between Theo and Rose, and this of itself was sufficient to attract him towards her. Theo, too, was equally pleased; and when, that evening, Madam Jeffrey faintly interposed her fast-departing authority, telling her quondam pupils it was time they were asleep, Theo did not, as usual, heed the warning, but sat very still beneath the vine-wreathed portico, listen-ing while George Douglas told her of the world which she had never seen. She was not proud towards him,

for he possessed the charm of money, and as he looked
down upon her, conversing with him so familiarly, he
wondered how Henry could have called her cold and
haughty—she was merely dignified, high-bred, he
thought; and George Douglas liked anything which
savored of aristocracy.

Meanwhile Henry and Maggie had wandered to a
little summer-house, where, with the bright moonlight
falling upon them, they sat together, but not exactly
as of old, for Maggie did not now look up into his
face as she was wont to do, and if she thought his
eye was resting upon her she moved uneasily, while
the rich blood deepened on her cheek. A change has
come over Maggie Miller; it is the old story, too—old
to hundreds of thousands, but new to her, the blushing maiden. Theo calls her nervous—Mrs. Jeffrey
calls her sick—the servants call her mighty queer—
while old Hagar, hovering ever near, and watching
her with a jealous eye, knows she is in love.

Faithfully and well had Hagar studied Henry
Warner, to see if there were aught in him of evil;
and though he was not what she would have chosen
for the queenly Maggie she was satisfied if Margaret
loved him and he loved Margaret. But did he? He
had never told her so; and in Hagar Warren's wild
black eyes there was a savage gleam, as she thought,
" He'll rue the day that he dares trifle with Maggie
Miller."

But Henry Warner was not trifling with her. He
was only waiting a favorable opportunity for telling
her the story of his love; and now, as they sit together
in the moonlight, with the musical flow of the mill-
stream falling on his ear, he essays to speak—to tell

how she has grown into his heart; to ask her to go
with him where he goes; to make his home her home,
and so be with him always; but ere the first word was
uttered Maggie asked if Mr. Douglas had brought the
picture of his sister.

"Why, yes," he answered; "I had forgotten it entirely. Here it is;" and taking it from his pocket he
passed it to her.

It was a face of almost ethereal loveliness that
through the moonlight looked up to Maggie Miller,
and again she experienced the same undefinable emotion, a mysterious, invisible something drawing her
towards the original of the beautiful likeness.

"It is strange how thoughts of Rose always affect
me," she said, gazing earnestly upon the large eyes of
blue shadowed forth upon the picture. "It seems as
though she must be nearer to me than an unknown
friend."

"Seems she like a sister?" asked Henry Warner,
coming so near that Maggie felt his warm breath upon
her cheek.

"Yes, yes, that's it," she answered, with something
of her olden frankness. "And had I somewhere in
the world an unknown sister I should say it was Rose
Warner!"

There were a few low, whispered words, and when
the full moon, which for a time had hidden itself behind the clouds, again shone forth in all its glory,
Henry had asked Maggie Miller to be the sister of
Rose Warner, and Maggie had answered "Yes" !

That night in Maggie's dreams there was a strange
commingling of thoughts. Thoughts of Henry Warner, as he told her of his love—thoughts of the gentle

girl whose eyes of blue had looked so lovingly up to her, as if between them there was indeed a common bond of sympathy—and, stranger far than all, thoughts of the little grave beneath the pine where slept the so-called child of Hester Hamilton—the child defrauded of its birthright, and who, in the misty vagaries of dreamland, seemed to stand between her and the beautiful Rose Warner!

CHAPTER VIII.

STARS AND STRIPES.

ON the rude bench by her cabin door sat Hagar Warren, her black eyes peering out into the woods and her quick ear turned to catch the first sound of bounding footsteps, which came at last, and Maggie Miller was sitting by her side.

"What is it, darling?" Hagar asked, and her shriveled hand smoothed caressingly the silken hair, as she looked into the glowing face of the young girl, and half guessed what was written there.

To Theo Maggie had whispered the words, "I am engaged," and Theo had coldly answered: "Pshaw! Grandma will quickly break that up. Why, Henry Warner is comparatively poor! Mr. Douglas told me so, or rather I quizzed him until I found it out. He says, though, that Henry has rare business talents, and he could not do without him."

To the latter part of Theo's remark Maggie paid little heed; but the mention of her grandmother troubled her. She would oppose it, Maggie was sure of that, and it was to talk on this very subject that she had come to Hagar's cottage.

"Just the way I s'posed it would end," said Hagar, when Maggie, with blushing, half-averted face, told the story of her engagement. "Just the way I s'posed 'twould end, but I didn't think 'twould be so quick."

"Two months and a half is a great while, and then

we have been together so much," replied Maggie, at
the same time asking if Hagar did not approve her
choice.

"Henry Warner s well enough," answered Hagar.
" I've watched him close and see no evil in him; but
he isn't the one for you, nor are you the one for him.
You are both too wild, too full of fun, and if yoked
together will go to destruction, I know. You need
somebody to hold you back, and so does he."

Involuntarily Maggie thought of Rose, mentally resolving to be, if possible, more like her.

"You are not angry with me?" said Hagar, observing Maggie's silence. "You asked my opinion,
and I gave it to you. You are too young to know who
you like. Henry Warner is the first man you ever
knew, and in two years' time you'll tire of him."

"Tire of him, Hagar? Tire of Henry Warner?"
cried Maggie a little indignantly. "You do not know
me, if you think I'll ever tire of him; and then, too,
did I tell you grandma keeps writing to me about a
Mr. Carrollton, who she says is wealthy, fine-looking,
highly educated, and very aristocratic—and that last
makes me hate him! I've heard so much about aristocracy that I'm sick of it, and just for that reason I
would not have this Mr. Carrollton if I knew he'd
make me queen of England. But grandma's heart is
set upon it, I know, and she thinks of course he would
marry me—says he is delighted with my daguerreotype—that awful one, too, with the staring eyes. In
grandma's last letter he sent me a note. 'Twas beau-
tifully written, and I dare say he is a fine young man,
at least he talks common sense, but I shan't answer
it; and, if you'll believe me, I used part of it in light-

ing Henry's cigar, and with the rest I shall light fire-crackers on the Fourth of July; Henry has bought a lot of them, and we're going to have fun. How grandma would scold!—but I shall marry Henry Warner, any-way. Do you think she will oppose me, when she sees how determined I am?"

"Of course she will," answered Hagar. "I know those Carrolltons—they are a haughty race; and if your grandmother has one of them in view she'll turn you from her door sooner than see you married to an-other, and an American, too."

There was a moment's silence, and then, with an unnatural gleam in her eye, old Hagar turned towards Maggie, and, grasping her shoulder, said: "If she does this thing, Maggie Miller,—if she casts you off,—will you take me for your grandmother? Will you let me live with you? I'll be your drudge, your slave; say, Maggie, may I go with you? Will you call me grandmother? I'd willingly die if only once I could hear you speak to me thus, and know it was in love."

For a moment Maggie looked at her in astonish-ment; then thinking to herself, "She surely is half-crazed," she answered laughingly: "Yes, Hagar, if grandma casts me off, you may go with me. I shall need your care, but I can't promise to call you grandma, because you know you are not."

The corners of Hagar's mouth worked nervously, but her teeth shut firmly over the thin, white lip, forc-ing back the wild words trembling there, and the secret was not told.

"Go home, Maggie Miller," she said at last, rising slowly to her feet. "Go home now, and leave me alone. I am willing you should marry Henry Warner

—nay, I wish you to do it; but you must remember your promise."

Maggie was about to answer, when her thoughts were directed to another channel by the sight of George Douglas and Theo coming slowly down the shaded pathway which led past Hagar's door. Old Hagar saw them too, and, whispering to Maggie, said, " There's another marriage brewing, or the signs do not tell true, and madam will sanction this one, too, for there's money there, and gold can purify any blood."

Ere Maggie could reply Theo called out, " You here, Maggie, as usual? " adding, aside, to her companion: " She has the most unaccountable taste, so different from me, who cannot endure anything low and vulgar. Can you? But I need not ask," she continued, " for your associations have been of a refined nature."

George Douglas did not answer, for his thoughts were back in the brown farmhouse at the foot of the hill, where his boyhood was passed, and he wondered what the high-bred lady at his side would say if she could see the sunburned man and plain, old-fashioned woman who called him their son George Washington. He would not confess that he was ashamed of his parentage, for he tried to be a kind and dutiful child, but he would a little rather that Theo Miller should not know how democratic had been his early training. So he made no answer, but, addressing himself to Maggie, asked how she could find it in her heart to leave her patient so long.

" I'm going back directly," she said, and donning her hat she started for home, thinking she had gained but little satisfaction from Hagar, who, as Douglas and Theo passed on, resumed her seat by the door, and, listening to the sound of Margaret's retreating footsteps, muttered: "The old light-heartedness is gone. There are shadows gathering round her; for once in love, she'll never be as free and joyous again. But it can't be helped; it's the destiny of women, and I only hope this Warner is worthy of her. But he aint. He's too wild—too full of what Hagar Warren calls bedevilment. And Maggie does everything he tells her to do. Not content with tearing down his bed-curtains, which have hung there full twenty years, she's set things all cornerwise, because the folks do so in Worcester, and has turned the parlor into a smoking-room, till all the air of Hillsdale can't take away that tobacco scent. Why, it almost knocks me down!" and the old lady groaned aloud, as she recounted to herself the recent innovations upon the time-honored habits of her mistress' house.

Henry Warner was, indeed, rather a fast young man, but it needed the suggestive presence of George Douglas to bring out his true character; and for the four days succeeding the arrival of the latter there were rare doings at the old stone house, where the astonished and rather delighted servants looked on in amazement while the young men sang their jovial songs and drank of the rare old wine which Maggie, utterly fearless of what her grandmother might say, brought from the cellar below. But when, on the morning of the Fourth, Henry Warner suggested that they have a celebration, or at least hang out the American flag by way of showing their patriotism, there were signs of rebellion in the kitchen, while even Mrs. Jeffrey, who had long since ceased to interfere, felt it her duty to remonstrate. Accordingly, she descended to the parlor, where she found George Douglas and Maggie dancing to the tune of " Yankee Doodle," which Theo played upon the piano, while Henry Warner whistled a most stirring accompaniment! To be heard above that din was impossible, and involuntarily patting her own slippered foot to the lively strain the distressed little lady went back to her room, wondering what Madam Conway would say if she knew how her house was being desecrated.

But Madam Conway did not know. She was three thousand miles away, and with this distance between them Maggie dared do anything; so when the flag was again mentioned, she answered apologetically, as if it were something of which they ought to be ashamed: " We never had any, but we can soon make one, I know. 'Twill be fun to see it float from the housetop! " and, flying up the stairs to the dusty garret, she drew from a huge oaken chest a scarlet coat which had belonged to the former owner of the place, who little thought, as he sat in state, that his favorite coat would one day furnish material for the emblem of American freedom!

No such thought as this, however, obtruded itself upon Maggie as she bent over the chest. " The coat is of no use," she said, and gathering it up she ran back to the parlor, where, throwing it across Henry's lap, she told how it had belonged to her great-greatgrandfather, who at the time of the Revolution went home to England. The young men exchanged a meaning look, and then burst into a laugh, but the cause of their merriment they did not explain, lest the prejudices of the girls should be aroused.

"This is just the thing," said Henry, entering heart and soul into the spirit of the fun. "This is grand. Can't you find some blue for the groundwork of the stars?"

Maggie thought a moment, and then exclaimed: "Oh, yes—I have it; grandma has a blue satin bodice which she wore when she was a young lady. She once gave me a part of the back for my doll's dress. She won't care if I cut up the rest for a banner."

"Of course not," answered George Douglas. "She'll be glad to have it used for such a laudable purpose," and walking to the window he laughed heartily as he saw in fancy the wrath of the proud Englishwoman when she learned the use to which her satin bodice had been appropriated.

The waist was brought in a twinkling, and then, when Henry asked for some white, Maggie cried, "A sheet will be just the thing—one of grandma's small linen ones. It won't hurt it a bit," she added, as she saw a shadow on Theo's brow, and, mounting to the top of the high chest of drawers, she brought out a sheet of finest linen, which, with rose leaves and fragrant herbs, had been carefully packed away.

It was a long, delightful process, the making of that banner; and Maggie's voice rang out loud and clear as she saw how cleverly Henry Warner managed the shears, cutting the red coat into stripes. The arrangement of the satin fell to Maggie's lot; and while George Douglas made the stars, Theo looked on a little doubtfully—not that her nationality was in any way affected, for what George Douglas sanctioned was by this time right with her; but she felt some misgiving as to what her grandmother might say; and, thinking if she did nothing but look on and laugh the blame would fall on Maggie, she stood aloof, making occasionally a suggestion, and seeming as pleased as anyone when at last the flag was done. A quilting-frame served as a flagstaff, and Maggie was chosen to plant it upon the top of the house, where was a cupola, or miniature tower, overlooking the surrounding country. Leading to this tower was a narrow staircase, and up these stairs Maggie bore the flag, assisted by one of the servant girls, whose birthplace was green Erin, and whose broad, good-humored face shone with delight as she fastened the pole securely in its place, and then shook aloft her checked apron, in answer to the cheer which came up from below, when first the American banner waved over the old stone house.

Attracted by the noise, and wondering what fresh mischief they were doing, Mrs. Jeffrey went out into the yard just in time to see the flag of freedom as it shook itself out in the summer breeze.

" Heaven help me ! " she ejaculated ; " the ' Stars and Stripes ' on Madam Conway's house ! " and, resolutely shutting her eyes, lest they should look again on what to her seemed sacrilege, she groped her way back to the house ; and, retiring to her room, wrote to Madam Conway an exaggerated account of the proceedings, bidding her hasten home or everything would be ruined.

The letter being written, the good lady felt better—so much better, indeed, that after an hour's deliberation she concluded not to send it, inasmuch as it contained many complaints against the young lady Margaret, who she knew was sure in the end to find favor in her grandmother's eyes. This was the first time

Mrs. Jeffrey had attempted a letter to her employer, for Maggie had been the chosen correspondent, Theo affecting to dislike anything like letter-writing. On the day previous to Henry Warner's arrival at the stone house Maggie had written to her grandmother, and ere the time came for her to write again she had concluded to keep his presence there a secret: so Madam Conway was, as yet, ignorant of his existence; and while in the homes of the English nobility she bore herself like a royal duchess, talking to young Arthur Carrollton of her beautiful granddaughter, she little dreamed of the real state of affairs at home.

But it was not for Mrs. Jeffrey to enlighten her, and tearing her letter in pieces the governess sat down in her easy-chair by the window, mentally congratulating herself upon the fact that " the two young savages," as she styled Douglas and Warner, were to leave on the morrow. This last act of theirs, the hoisting of the banner, had been the culminating point; and, too indignant to sit with them at the same table, she resolutely kept her room throughout the entire day, poring intently over Baxter's " Saints' Rest," her favorite volume when at all flurried or excited. Occasionally, too, she would stop her ears with jeweler's cotton, to shut out the sound of " Hail, Columbia ! " as it came up to her from the parlor below, where the young men were doing their best to show their patriotism.

Towards evening, alarmed by a whizzing sound, which seemed to be often repeated, and wishing to know the cause, she stole halfway down the stairs, when the mischievous Maggie greeted her with a " serpent," which, hissing beneath her feet, sent her quickly back to her room, from which she did not venture again. Mrs. Jeffrey was very good-natured, and reflecting that " young folks must have fun," she became at last comparatively calm, and at an early hour sought her pillow. But thoughts of " stars and stripes " waving directly over her head, as she knew they were, made her nervous, and the long clock struck the hour of two, and she was yet restless and wakeful, notwithstanding the near approach of dawn.

" Maybe the ' Saints' Rest ' will quiet me a trifle," she thought; and, striking a light, she attempted to read; but in vain, for every word was a star, every line a stripe, and every leaf a flag. Shutting the book and hurriedly pacing the floor, she exclaimed: " It's of no use trying to sleep, or meditate either. Baxter himself couldn't do it with that thing over his head, and I mean to take it down. It's a duty I owe to King George's memory, and to Madam Conway; " and, stealing from her room, she groped her way up the dark, narrow stairway, until, emerging into the bright moonlight, she stood directly beneath the American banner, waving so gracefully in the night wind. " It's a clever enough device," she said, gazing rather admiringly at it. " And I'd let it be if I s'posed I could sleep a wink; but I can't. It's worse for my nerves than strong green tea, and I'll not lie awake for all the Yankee flags in Christendom." So saying, the resolute little woman tugged at the quilt-frame until she loosened it from its fastenings, and then started to return.

But, alas! the way was narrow and dark, the banner was large and cumbersome, while the lady that bore it was nervous and weak. It is not strange, then, that

Maggie, who slept at no great distance, was awakened by a tremendous crash, as of someone falling the entire length of the tower stairs, while a voice. frightened and faint, called out; " Help me, Margaret, do! I am dead! I know I am!"

Striking a light, Maggie hurried to the spot, while her merry laugh aroused the servants, who came together in a body. Stretched upon the floor, with one foot thrust entirely through the banner, which was folded about her so that the quilt-frame lay directly upon her bosom, was Mrs. Jeffrey, the broad frill of her cap standing up erect, and herself asserting with every breath that " she was dead and buried, she knew she was."

" Wrapped in a winding-sheet, I'll admit," said Maggie, " but not quite dead, I trust;" and, putting down her light, she attempted to extricate her governess, who continued to apologize for what she had done. " Not that I cared so much about your celebrating America; but I couldn't sleep with the thing over my head; I was going to put it back in the morning before you were up. There! there! careful! It's broken short off!" she screamed, as Maggie tried to release her foot from the rent in the linen sheet, a rent which the frightened woman persisted in saying she could darn as good as new, while at the same time she implored of Maggie to handle carefully her ankle, which had been sprained by the fall.

Maggie's recent experience in broken bones had made her quite an adept, and taking the slight form of Mrs. Jeffrey in her arms she carried her back to her room, where, growing more quiet, the old lady told her how she happened to fall, saying she never thought of stumbling, until she fancied that Washington and all his regiment were after her, and when she turned her head to see, she lost her footing and fell.

Forcing back her merriment, which in spite of herself would occasionally burst forth, Maggie made her teacher as comfortable as possible, and then stayed with her until morning, when, leaving her in charge of a servant, she went below to say farewell to her guests. Between George Douglas and Theo there were a few low-spoken words, she granting him permission to write, while he promised to visit her again in the early autumn. He had not yet talked to her of love, for Rose Warner had still a home in his heart, and she must be dislodged ere another could take her place. But his affection for her was growing gradually less. Theo suited him well, her family suited him better, and when at parting he took her hand in his he resolved to ask her for it when next he came to Hillsdale.

Meanwhile between Henry Warner and Maggie there was a far more affectionate farewell, he whispering to her of a time not far distant when he would claim her as his own, and she should go with him. He would write to her every week, he said, and Rose should write too. He would see Rose in a few days, and tell her of his engagement, which he knew would please her.

"Let me send her a line," said Maggie, and on a tiny sheet of paper she wrote: "Dear Rose: Are you willing I should be your sister Maggie?"

Half an hour later, and Hagar Warren, coming through the garden gate, looked after the carriage which bore the gentlemen to the depot, muttering to herself: " I'm glad the high bucks have gone. A good riddance to them both."

In her disorderly chamber, too, Mrs. Jeffrey hobbled on one foot to the window, where, with a deep sigh of relief, she sent after the young men a not very complimentary adieu, which was echoed in part by the servants below, while Theo, on the piazza, exclaimed against the lonesome old house, which was never so lonesome before, and Maggie seated herself upon the stairs and cried!

CHAPTER IX.

ROSE WARNER.

NESTLED among the tall old trees which skirt the borders of Leominster village was the bird's-nest of a cottage which Rose Warner called her home, and which, with its wealth of roses, its trailing vines and flowering shrubs, seemed fitted for the abode of one like her. Slight as a child twelve summers old, and fair as the white pond lily when first to the morning sun it unfolds its delicate petals, she seemed too frail for earth; and both her aunt and he whom she called brother watched carefully lest the cold north wind should blow too rudely on the golden curls which shaded her childish brow. Very, very beautiful was little Rose, and yet few ever looked upon her without a feeling of sadness; for in the deep blue of her eyes there was a mournful, dreamy look, as if the shadow of some great sorrow were resting thus early upon her.

And Rose Warner had a sorrow, too—a grief which none save one had ever suspected. To him it had come with the words, " I cannot be your wife, for I love another; one who will never know how dear he is to me."

The words were involuntarily spoken, and George Douglas, looking down upon her, guessed rightly that he who would never know how much he was beloved was Henry Warner. To her the knowledge that Henry was something dearer than a brother had come slowly, filling her heart with pain, for she well knew that whether he clasped her to his bosom, as he often did, or pressed his lips upon her brow, he thought of her only as a brother thinks of a beautiful and idolized sister. It had heretofore been some consolation to know that his affections were untrammeled with thoughts of another, that she alone was the object of his love, and hope had sometimes faintly whispered of what perchance might be; but from that dream she was waking now, and her face grew whiter still as there came to her from time to time letters fraught with praises of Margaret Miller; and if in Rose Warner's nature there had been a particle of bitterness, it would have been called forth toward one who, she foresaw, would be her rival. But Rose knew no malice, and she felt that she would sooner die than do aught to mar the happiness of Maggie Miller.

For nearly two weeks she had not heard from Henry, and she was beginning to feel very anxious, when one morning, two or three days succeeding the memorable Hillsdale celebration, as she sat in a small arbor so thickly overgrown with the Michigan rose as to render her invisible at a little distance, she was startled by hearing him call her name, as he came in quest of her down the garden walk. The next moment he held her in his arms, kissing her forehead, her lips, her cheek; then holding her off, he looked to see if there had been in her aught of change since last they met.

"You are paler than you were, Rose darling," he said, "and your eyes look as if they had of late been used to tears. What is it, dearest? What troubles you?"

Rose could not answer immediately, for his sudden coming had taken away her breath, and as he saw a faint blush stealing over her face he continued, " Can it be my little sister has been falling in love during my absence ? "

Never before had he spoken to her thus; but a change had come over him, his heart was full of a beautiful image, and fancying Rose might have followed his example he asked her the question he did, without, however, expecting or receiving a definite answer.

" I am so lonely, Henry, when you are gone and do not write to me ! " she said; and in the tones of her voice there was a slight reproof, which Henry felt keenly.

He had been so engrossed with Maggie Miller and the free joyous life he led in the Hillsdale woods, that for a time he had neglected Rose, who, in his absence, depended so much on his letters for comfort.

" I have been very selfish, I know," he said; " but I was so happy, that for a time I forgot everything save Maggie Miller."

An involuntary shudder ran through Rose's slender form; but, conquering her emotion, she answered calmly: " What of this Maggie Miller? Tell me of her, will you ? "

Winding his arm around her waist, and drawing her closely to his side, Henry Warner rested her head upon his bosom, where it had often lain, and, smoothing her golden curls, told her of Maggie Miller, of her queenly beauty, of her dashing, independent spirit, her frank, ingenuous manner, her kindness of heart; and last of all, bending very low, lest the vine leaves and

the fair blossoms of the rose should hear, he told her
of his love; and Rose, the fairest flower of all which
bloomed around that bower, clasped her hand upon her
heart, lest he should see its wild throbbings, and, forcing back the tears which moistened her long lashes,
listened to the knell of all her hopes.   Henceforth her
love for him must be an idle mockery, and the time
would come when to love him as she loved him then
would be a sin—a wrong to herself, a wrong to him,
and a wrong to Maggie Miller.

"You are surely not asleep," he said at last, as she
made him no reply, and bending forward he saw the
tear-drops resting on her cheek. "Not asleep, but
weeping!" he exclaimed. "What is it, darling?
What troubles you?"   And lifting up her head, Rose
Warner answered, "I was thinking how this new love
of yours would take you from me, and I should be
alone."

"No, not alone," he said, wiping her tears away.
"Maggie and I have arranged that matter. You are
to live with us, and instead of losing me you are to
gain another—a sister, Rose. You have often wished
you had one, and you could surely find none worthier
than Maggie Miller."

"Will she watch over you, Henry? Will she be
to you what your wife should be?" asked Rose; and
Henry answered: "She is not at all like you, my little
sister. She relies implicitly upon my judgment; so
you see I shall need your blessed influence all the
same, to make me what your brother and Maggie's
husband ought to be."

"Did she send me no message?" asked Rose; and
taking out the tiny note, Henry passed it to her, just

as his aunt called to him from the house, whither he
went, leaving her alone.

There were blinding tears in Rose's eyes as she read
the few lines, and involuntarily she pressed her lips
to the paper which she knew had been touched by
Maggie Miller's hands.

"My sister—sister Maggie," she repeated; and at
the sound of that name her fast-beating heart grew
still, for they seemed very sweet to her, those words
"my sister," thrilling her with a new and strange
emotion, and awakening within her a germ of the
deep, undying love she was yet to feel for her who had
traced those words and asked to be her sister. "I will
do right," she thought; "I will conquer this foolish
heart of mine, or break it in the struggle, and Henry
Warner shall never know how sorely it was wrung."

The resolution gave her strength, and, rising up,
she too sought the house, where, retiring to her room,
she penned a hasty note to Maggie, growing calmer
with each word she wrote.

"I grant your request [she said] and take you for
a sister well beloved. I had a half-sister once, they
say, but she died when a little babe. I never looked
upon her face, and connected with her birth there was
too much of sorrow and humiliation for me to think
much of her, save as of one who, under other circumstances, might have been dear to me. And yet as I
grow older I often find myself wishing she had lived,
for my father's blood was in her veins. But I do not
even know where her grave was made, for we only
heard one winter morning, years ago, that she was
dead with the mother who bore her. Forgive me,

Maggie dear, for saying so much about that little child. Thoughts of you, who are to be my sister, make me think of her, who, had she lived, would have been a young lady now nearly your own age. So in the place of her, whom, knowing, I would have loved, I adopt you, sweet Maggie Miller, my sister and my friend. May Heaven's choicest blessings rest on you forever, and no shadow come between you and the one you have chosen for your husband! To my partial eyes he is worthy of you, Maggie, royal in bearing and queenly in form though you be, and that you may be happy with him will be the daily prayer of

" ROSE."

The letter was finished, and Rose gave it to her brother, who, after its perusal, kissed her, saying: " It is right, my darling. I will send it to-morrow with mine; and now for a ride. I will see what a little exercise can do for you. I do not like the color of your face."

But neither the fragrant summer air, nor yet the presence of Henry Warner, who tarried several days, could rouse the drooping Rose; and when at last she was left alone she sought her bed, where for many weeks she hovered between life and death, while her brother and her aunt hung over her pillow, and Maggie, from her woodland home, sent many an anxious inquiry and message of love to the sick girl. In the close atmosphere of his counting-room George Douglas too again battled manfully with his olden love, listening each day to hear that she was dead. But not thus early was Rose to die, and with the waning summer days she came slowly back to life. More beautiful than ever, because more ethereal and fair, she walked the earth like one who, having struggled with a mighty sorrow, had won the victory at last; and Henry Warner, when he looked on her sweet, placid face, and listened to her voice as she made plans for the future, when Maggie would be his wife, dreamed not of the grave hidden in the deep recesses of her heart, where grew no flower of hope or semblance of earthly joy.

Thus little know mankind of each other!

CHAPTER X.

ON the Hillsdale hills the October sun was shining, and the forest trees were donning their robes of scarlet and brown, when again the old stone house presented an air of joyous expectancy. The large, dark parlors were thrown open, the best chambers were aired, the bright, autumnal flowers were gathered and in tastefully arranged bouquets adorned the mantels, while Theo and Maggie, in their best attire, flitted uneasily from room to room, running sometimes to the gate to look down the grassy road which led from the highway, and again mounting the tower stairs to obtain a more extended view.

In her pleasant apartment, where last we left her with a sprained ankle, Mrs. Jeffrey, too, fidgeted about, half sympathizing with her pupils in their happiness, and half regretting the cause of that happiness, which was the expected arrival of George Douglas and Henry Warner, who, true to their promise, were coming again to try for a week the Hillsdale air, and retrieve their character as fast young men. So, at least, they told Mrs. Jeffrey, who, mindful of her exploit with the banner, and wishing to make some amends, met them alone on the threshhold, Maggie having at the last moment run away, while Theo sat in a state of dignified perturbation upon the sofa.

A few days prior to their arrival letters had been re-

ceived from Madam Conway saying she should probably remain in England two or three weeks longer, and
thus the house was again clear to the young men, who,
forgetting to retrieve their characters, fairly outdid
all they had done before. The weather was remark-
ably clear and bracing, and the greater part of each
day was spent in the open air, either in fishing, riding,
or hunting; Maggie teaching Henry Warner how to
ride and leap, while he in turn taught her to shoot a
bird upon the wing, until the pupil was equal to her
master. In these outdoor excursions George Douglas and Theo did not always join, for he had something
to say which he would rather tell her in the silent
parlor, and which, when told, furnished food for many
a quiet conversation; so Henry and Maggie rode oftentimes alone; and old Hagar, when she saw them
dashing past her door, Maggie usually taking the lead,
would shake her head and mutter to herself: " 'Twill
never do—that match. He ought to hold her back,
instead of leading her on. I wish Madam Conway
would come home and end it."

Mrs. Jeffrey wished so too, as night after night her
slumbers were disturbed by the sounds of merriment
which came up to her from the parlor below, where
the young people were " enjoying themselves," as
Maggie said when reproved for the noisy revel. The
day previous to the one set for their departure chanced
to be Henry Warner's twenty-seventh birthday, and
this Maggie resolved to honor with an extra supper,
which was served at an unusually late hour in the
dining room, the door of which opened out upon a
closely latticed piazza.

" I wish we could think of something new to do,"

said Maggie, as she presided at the table—" something
real funny;" then, as her eyes fell upon the dark
piazza, where a single light was burning dimly, she exclaimed: " Why can't we get up tableaux? There are
heaps of the queerest clothes in the big oaken chest in
the garret. The servants can be audience, and they
need some recreation!"

The suggestion was at once approved, and in half
an hour's time the floor was strewn with garments
of every conceivable fashion, from long stockings and
smallclothes to scarlet cloaks and gored skirts, the
latter of which were immediately donned by Henry
Warner, to the infinite delight of the servants, who
enjoyed seeing the grotesque costumes, even if they
did not exactly understand what the tableaux were
intended to represent. The banner, too, was brought
out, and after bearing a conspicuous part in the performance was placed at the end of the dining room,
where it would be the first thing visible to a person
opening the door opposite. At a late hour the servants retired, and then George Douglas, who took
kindly to the luscious old wine, which Maggie again
had brought from her grandmother's choicest store,
filled a goblet to the brim, and, pledging first the
health of the young girls, drank to " the old lady across
the water" with whose goods they were thus making
free!

Henry Warner rarely tasted wine, for though miles
away from Rose her influence was around him—so,
filling his glass with water, he too drank to the wish
that " the lady across the sea" would remain there
yet a while, or at all events not " stumble upon us
to-night!"

" What if she should ! " thought Maggie, glancing around at the different articles scattered all over the floor, and laughing as she saw in fancy her grandmother's look of dismay should she by any possible chance obtain a view of the room, where perfect order and quiet had been wont to reign.

But the good lady was undoubtedly taking her morning nap on the shores of old England. There was no danger to be apprehended from her unexpected arrival, they thought; and just as the clock struck one the young men sought their rooms, greatly to the relief of Mrs. Jeffrey, who, in her long night robe, with streaming candle in hand, had more than a dozen times leaned over the banister, wondering if the " carouse " would ever end.

It did end at last; and, tired and sleepy, Theo went directly to her chamber, while Maggie stayed below, thinking to arrange matters a little, for their guests were to leave on the first train, and she had ordered an early breakfast. But it was a hopeless task, the putting of that room to rights; and trusting much to the good-nature of the housekeeper, she finally gave it up and went to bed, forgetting in her drowsiness to fasten the outer door, or yet to extinguish the lamp which burned upon the sideboard.

CHAPTER XI.

UNEXPECTED GUESTS.

At the delightful country seat of Arthur Carrollton Madam Conway had passed many pleasant days, and was fully intending to while away several more, when an unexpected summons from his father made it necessary for the young man to go immediately to London; and, as an American steamer was about to leave the port of Liverpool, Madam Conway determined to start for home at once. Accordingly, she wrote for Anna Jeffrey, whom she had promised to take with her, to meet her in Liverpool, and a few days previous to the arrival of George Douglas and Henry Warner at Hillsdale, the two ladies embarked with an endless variety of luggage, to say nothing of Miss Anna's guitar-case, bird-cage, and favorite lap-dog " Lottie."

Once fairly on the sea, Madam Conway became exceedingly impatient and disagreeable, complaining both of fare and speed, and at length came on deck one morning with the firm belief that something dreadful had happened to Maggie! She was dangerously sick, she knew, for never but once before had she been visited with a like presentiment, and that was just before her daughter died. Then it came to her just as this had done, in her sleep, and very nervously the lady paced the vessel's deck, counting the days as they passed, and almost weeping for joy when told Boston was in sight. Immediately after landing she made inquiries as to when the next train passing Hillsdale station would leave the city, and though it was midnight she resolved at all hazards to go on, for if Maggie were really ill there was no time to be lost!

Accordingly, when at four o'clock A. M. Maggie, who was partially awake, heard in the distance the shrill scream of the engine, as the night express thundered through the town, she little dreamed of the boxes, bundles, trunks, and bags which lined the platform of Hillsdale station, nor yet of the resolute woman in brown who persevered until a rude one-horse wagon was found in which to transport herself and her baggage to the old stone house. The driver of the vehicle, in which, under ordinary circumstances, Madam Conway would have scorned to ride, was a long, lean, half-witted fellow, utterly unfitted for his business. Still, he managed quite well until they turned into the grassy by-road, and Madam Conway saw through the darkness the light which Maggie had inadvertently left within the dining room!

There was no longer a shadow of uncertainty. " Margaret was dead! " and the lank Tim was ordered to drive faster, or the excited woman, perched on one of her traveling-trunks, would be obliged to foot it! A few vigorous strokes of the whip set the sorrel horse into a canter, and as the night was dark, and the road wound round among the trees, it is not at all surprising that Madam Conway, with her eye still on the beacon light, found herself seated rather unceremoniously in the midst of a brush heap, her goods and chattels rolling promiscuously around her, while lying across a log, her right hand clutching at the birdcage, and her left grasping the shaggy hide of Lottie,

who yelled most furiously, was Anna Jeffrey, half
blinded with mud, and bitterly denouncing American
drivers and Yankee roads! To gather themselves together was not an easy matter, but the ten pieces were
at last all told, and then, holding up her skirts, bedraggled with dew, Madam Conway resumed her seat
in the wagon, which was this time driven in safety to
her door. Giving orders for her numerous boxes to
be safely bestowed, she hastened forward and soon
stood upon the threshold.

"Great Heaven!" she exclaimed, starting backward
so suddenly that she trod upon the foot of Lottie, who
again sent forth an outcry, which Anna Jeffrey managed to choke down. "Is this bedlam, or what?"
And stepping out upon the piazza, she looked to see
if the blundering driver had made a mistake. But no;
it was the same old gray stone house she had left some
months before; and again pressing boldly forward,
she took the lamp from the sideboard and commenced
to reconnoiter. "My mother's wedding dress, as I
live! and her scarlet broadcloth, too!" she cried, holding to view the garments which Henry Warner had
thrown upon the arm of the long settee. A turban or
cushion, which she recognized as belonging to her
grandmother, next caught her view, together with the
smallclothes of her sire.

"The entire contents of the oaken chest," she continned, in a tone far from calm and cool. "What can
have happened! It's some of that crazy Hagar's
work, I know. I'll have her put in the——" But
whatever the evil was which threatened Hagar Warren it was not defined by words, for at that moment
the indignant lady caught sight of an empty bottle,

which she instantly recognized as having held her very oldest, choicest wine. "The Lord help me!" she cried, "I've been robbed;" and grasping the bottle by the neck, she leaned up against the banner which she had not yet descried.

"In the name of wonder, what's this?" she almost screamed, as the full blaze of the lamp fell upon the flag, revealing the truth at once, and partially stopping her breath.

Robbery was nothing to insult; and, forgetting the wine, she gasped: "'Stars and Stripes' in this house! In the house of my grandfather, as loyal a subject as King George ever boasted! What can Margaret be doing to suffer a thing like this?"

A few steps further on, and Margaret herself might have been seen peering out into the darkened upper hall, and listening anxiously to her grandmother's voice. The sound of the rattling old wagon had aroused her, and, curious to know who was stirring at this early hour, she had cautiously opened her window, which overlooked the piazza, and to her great dismay had recognized her grandmother as she gave orders concerning her baggage. Flying back to her room, she awoke her sister, who, springing up in bed, whispered faintly: "Will she kill us dead, Maggie? Will she kill us dead?"

"Pshaw! no," answered Maggie, her own courage rising with Theo's fears. "She'll have to scold a spell, I suppose; but I can coax her, I know!"

By this time the old lady was ascending the stairs, and closing the door Maggie applied her eye to the keyhole, listening breathlessly for what might follow. George Douglas and Henry Warner occupied separate rooms, and their boots were now standing outside their doors, ready for the chore boy, Jim, who thus earned a quarter every day. Stumbling first upon the pair belonging to George Douglas, the lady took them up, ejaculating: "Boots! boots! Yes, men's boots, as I'm a living woman! The like was never seen by me before in this hall. Another pair!" she continued, as her eye fell on those of Henry Warner. "Another pair, and in the best chamber, too! What will come next?" And setting down her light, she wiped the drops of perspiration from her face, at the same time looking around in some alarm lest the owners of said boots should come forth.

Just at that moment Mrs. Jeffrey appeared. Alarmed by the unusual noise, and fancying the young gentlemen might be robbing the house as a farewell performance, she had donned a calico wrapper, and tying a black silk handkerchief over her cap, had taken her scissors, the only weapon of defense she could find, and thus equipped for battle she had sallied forth. She was prepared for burglars—nay, she would not have been disappointed had she found the young men busily engaged in removing the ponderous furniture from their rooms; but the sight of Madam Conway, at that unseasonable hour, was wholly unexpected, and in her fright she dropped the lamp which she had lighted in place of her candle, and which was broken in fragments, deluging the carpet with oil and eliciting a fresh groan from Madam Conway.

"Jeffrey, Jeffrey!" she gasped; "what have you done?"

"Great goodness!" ejaculated Mrs. Jeffrey, remembering her adventure when once before she left

her room in the night. " I certainly am the most un-
fortunate of mortals. Catch me out of bed again, let
what will happen;" and turning, she was about to
leave the hall, when Madam Conway, anxious to know
what had been done, called her back, saying rather indignantly, " I'd like to know whose house I am in?"

" A body would suppose 'twas Miss Margaret's, the
way she's conducted," answered Mrs. Jeffrey; and
Madam Conway continued, pointing to the boots:
" Who have we here? These are not Margaret's,
surely?"

" No, ma'am, they belong to the young men who
have turned the house topsy-turvy with their tableaux,
their Revolution celebration, their banner, and carous-
ing generally," said Mrs. Jeffrey, rather pleased than
otherwise at being the first to tell the news.

" Young men!" repeated Madam Conway—" what
young men? Where did they come from, and why
are they here?"

" They are Douglas and Warner," said Mrs. Jeffrey,
" two as big scapegraces as there are this side of Old
Bailey—that's what they are. They came from
Worcester, and if I've any discernment they are after
your girls, and your girls are after them."

" After my girls! After Maggie! It can't be
possible!" gasped Mrs. Conway, thinking of Arthur
Carrollton.

" It's the very truth, though," returned Mrs. Jeffrey.
" Henry Warner, who, in my opinion, is the worst of
the two, got to chasing Margaret in the woods, as long
ago as last April. She jumped Gritty across the gorge,
and he, like a fool, jumped after, breaking his leg——"

" Pity it hadn't been his neck," interrupted Madam

Conway; and Mrs. Jeffrey continued: " Of course he
was brought here, and Margaret took care of him.
After a while his comrade Douglas came out, and of
all the carousals you ever thought of, I reckon they had
the worst. 'Twas the Fourth of July, and if you'll
believe it they made a banner, and Maggie planted it
herself on the housetop. They went off next morning; but now they've come again, and last night the
row beat all. I never got a wink of sleep till after
two o'clock."

Here, entirely out of breath, the old lady paused,
and, going to her room, brought out a basin of water
and a towel, with which she tried to wipe off the oil.
But Madam Conway paid little heed to the spoiled
carpet, so engrossed was she with what she had heard.

" I am astonished at Margaret's want of discretion,"
said she, " and I depended so much upon her, too."

" I always knew you were deceived by her," said
Mrs. Jeffrey, still bending over the oil; " but it wasn't
for me to say so, for you are blinded towards that
girl. She's got some of the queerest notions, and then
she's so high-strung. She won't listen to reason. But
I did my country good service once. I went up in
the dead of night to take down the flag, and I don't
regret it either, even if it did pitch me to the bottom
of the stairs, and sprained my ankle."

" Served you right," interposed Madam Conway,
who, not at all pleased at hearing Margaret thus censured, now turned the full force of her wrath upon
the poor little governess, blaming her for having suffered such proceedings. " What did Margaret and
Theo know, young things as they were? and what was
Mrs. Jeffrey there for if not to keep them circumspect!

But instead of doing this, she had undoubtedly encouraged them in their folly, and then charged it upon Margaret."

It was in vain that the greatly distressed and astonished lady protested her innocence, pleading her sleepless nights and lame ankle as proofs of having done her duty; Madam Conway would not listen. "Somebody was of course to blame," and as it is a long-established rule that a part of every teacher's duty is to be responsible for the faults of the pupils, so Madam Conway now continued to chide Mrs. Jeffrey as the prime-mover of everything, until that lady, overwhelmed with the sense of injustice done her, left the oil and retired to her room, saying as she closed the door: "I was never so injured in all my life— never. To think that after all my trouble she should charge it to me! It will break my heart, I know. Where shall I go for comfort or rest?"

This last word was opportune and suggestive. If rest could not be found in Baxter's "Saints' Rest," it was not by her to be found at all; and, sitting down by the window in the gray dawn of the morning, she strove to draw comfort from the words of the good divine; but in vain. It had never failed her before; but never before had she been so deeply injured; and, closing the volume at last, she paced the floor in a very perturbed state of mind.

Meantime, Madam Conway had sought her granddaughter's chamber, where Theo in her fright had taken refuge under the bed, while Maggie feigned a deep, sound sleep. A few vigorous shakes, however, aroused her, when, greatly to the amazement of her grandmother, she burst into a merry laugh, and, winding her arms around the highly scandalized lady's neck, said: "Forgive me, grandma, I've been awake ever since you came home. I did not mean to leave the dining room in such disorder, but I was so tired, and we had such fun! Hear me out," she continued, laying her hand over the mouth of her grandmother, who attempted to speak; "Mrs. Jeffrey told you how Mr. Warner broke his leg, and was brought here. He is a real nice young man, and so is Mr. Douglas, who came out to see him. They are partners in the firm of Douglas & Co., Worcester."

"Henry Warner is nothing but the Co., though; Mr. Douglas owns the store, and is worth two hundred thousand dollars!" cried a smothered voice under the bed; and Theo emerged into view, with a feather or two ornamenting her hair, and herself looking a little uneasy and frightened.

The two hundred thousand dollars produced a magical effect upon the old lady, exonerating George Douglas at once from all blame. But towards Henry Warner she was not thus lenient; for, coward-like, Theo charged him with having suggested everything, even to the cutting up of the ancestral red coat for Freedom's banner!

"What!" fairly screamed Madam Conway, who in her hasty glance at the flag had not observed the material; "not taken my grandfather's coat for a banner!"

"Yes, he did," said Theo, "and Maggie cut up your blue satin bodice for stars, and took one of your fine linen sheets for the foundation."

"The wretch!" exclaimed Madam Conway, stamping her foot in her wrath, and thinking only of Henry

Warner; "I'll turn him from my door instantly. My blue satin bodice, indeed!"

"'Twas I, grandma—'twas I," interrupted Maggie, looking reproachfully at Theo. "'Twas I who cut up the bodice. I who brought down the scarlet coat."

"And I didn't do a thing but look on," said Theo. "I knew you'd be angry, and I tried to make Maggie behave, but she wouldn't."

"I don't know as it is anything to you what Maggie does, and I think it would look quite as well in you to take part of the blame yourself, instead of putting it all upon your sister," was Madam Conway's reply; and, feeling almost as deeply injured as Mrs. Jeffrey herself, Theo began to cry, while Maggie, with a few masterly strokes, succeeded in so far appeasing the anger of her grandmother that the good lady consented for the young gentlemen to stay to breakfast, saying, though, that "they should decamp immediately after, and never darken her doors again."

"But Mr. Douglas is rich," sobbed Theo from behind her pocket handkerchief—"immensely rich, and of a very aristocratic family, I'm sure, else where did he get his money?"

This remark was timely, and when fifteen minutes later Madam Conway was presented to the gentlemen in the hall her manner was far more gracious towards George Douglas than it was towards Henry Warner, to whom she merely nodded, deigning no answer whatever to his polite apology for having made himself so much at home in her house. The expression of his mouth was as usual against him, and, fancying he intended adding insult to injury by laughing in her face, she coolly turned her back upon him ere he had finished speaking, and walked downstairs, leaving him to wind up his speech with "an old she-dragon"!

By this time both the sun and the servants had arisen, the former shining into the disorderly dining room, and disclosing to the latter the weary, jaded Anna, who, while Madam Conway was exploring the house, had thrown herself upon the lounge and had fallen asleep.

"Who is she, and where did she come from?" was anxiously inquired, and they were about going in quest of Margaret when their mistress appeared suddenly in their midst, and their noisy demonstrations of joyful surprise awoke the sleeping girl, who, rubbing her red eyelids, asked for her aunt, and why she did not come to meet her.

"She has been a little excited, and forgot you, perhaps," answered Madam Conway, at the same time bidding one of the servants to show the young lady to Mrs. Jeffrey's room.

The good lady had recovered her composure somewhat, and was just wondering why her niece had not come with Madam Conway, as had been arranged, when Anna appeared, and in her delight at once more beholding a child of her only sister, and her husband's brother, she forgot in a measure how injured she had felt. Ere long the breakfast bell rang; but Anna declared herself too weary to go down, and as Mrs. Jeffrey felt that she could not yet meet Madam Conway face to face, they both remained in their room, Anna again falling away to sleep, while her aunt, grown more calm, sought, and this time found, comfort in her favorite volume. Very cool, indeed, was that breakfast, partaken in almost unbroken silence below. Th toast was cold, the steak was cold, the coffee was cold, and frosty as an icicle was the lady who sat where the merry Maggie had heretofore presided. Scarcely a word was spoken by anyone; but in the laughing eyes of Maggie there was a world of fun, to which the mischievous mouth of Henry Warner responded by a curl exceedingly annoying to his stately hostess, who, in passing him his coffee, turned her head in another direction lest she should be too civil!

Breakfast being over, George Douglas, who began to understand Madam Conway tolerably well, asked of her a private interview, which was granted, when he conciliated her first by apologizing for anything ungentlemanly he might have done in her house, and startled her next by asking for Theo as his wife.

"You can," said he, "easily ascertain my character and standing in Worcester, where for the last ten years I have been known first as clerk, then as junior partner, and finally as proprietor of the large establishment which I now conduct."

Madam Conway was at first too astonished to speak. Had it been Maggie for whom he asked, the matter would have been decided at once, for Maggie was her pet, her pride, the intended bride of Arthur Carrollton; but Theo was a different creature altogether, and though the Conway blood flowing in her veins entitled her to much consideration, she was neither showy nor brilliant, and if she could marry two hundred thousand dollars, even though it were American coin, she would perhaps be doing quite as well as could be expected. So Madam Conway replied at last that she would consider the matter, and if she found that Theo's feelings were fully enlisted she would per-

haps return a favorable answer. " I know the firm of
Douglas & Co. by reputation," said she, " and I know
it to be a wealthy firm; but with me family is quite as
important as money."

" My family, madam, are certainly respectable," interrupted George Douglas, a deep flush overspreading
his face.

He was indignant at her presuming to question his
respectability, Madam Conway thought, and so she
hastened to appease him by saying: '' Certainly, I have
no doubt of it. There are marks by which I can always tell."

George Douglas bowed low to the far-seeing lady,
while a train of thought, not altogether complimentary
to her discernment in this case, passed through his
mind.

Not thus lenient would Madam Conway have been
towards Henry Warner had he presumed to ask her
that morning for Maggie, but he knew better than to
broach the subject then. He would write her, he said,
immediately after his return to Worcester, and in the
meantime Maggie, if she saw proper, was to prepare
her grandmother for it by herself announcing the engagement. This, and much more, he said to Maggie
as they sat together in the library, so much absorbed
in each other as not to observe the approach of Madam
Conway, who entered the door just in time to see
Henry Warner with his arm around Maggie's waist.
She was a woman of bitter prejudices, and had con-
ceived a violent dislike for Henry, not only on account
of the " Stars and Stripes," but because she read to
a certain extent the true state of affairs. Her suspicions were now confirmed, and rapidly crossing the

floor she confronted him, saying, "Let my grand-daughter alone, young man, both now and forever."

Something of Hagar's fiery spirit flashed from Maggie's dark eyes, but forcing down her anger she answered half earnestly, half playfully, " I am nearly old enough, grandma, to decide that matter for myself."

A fierce expression of scorn passed over Madam Conway's face, and harsh words might have ensued had not the carriage at that moment been announced. Wringing Maggie's hand, Henry arose and left the room, followed by the indignant lady, who would willingly have suffered him to walk; but thinking two hundred thousand dollars quite too much money to go on foot, she had ordered her carriage, and both the senior and junior partner of Douglas & Co. were ere long riding a second time away from the old house by the mill.

CHAPTER XII.

THE WATERS ARE TROUBLED.

"GRANDMA wishes to see you, Maggie, in her room," said Theo to her sister one morning, three days after the departure of their guests.

"Wishes to see me! For what?" asked Maggie; and Theo answered, "I don't know, unless it is to talk with you about Arthur Carrollton."

"Arthur Carrollton!" repeated Maggie. "Much good it will do her to talk to me of him. I hate the very sound of his name;" and, rising, she walked slowly to her grandmother's room, where in her stiff brown satin dress, her golden spectacles planted firmly upon her nose, and the Valenciennes border of her cap shading but not concealing the determined look on her face, Madam Conway sat erect in her high-backed chair, with an open letter upon her lap.

It was from Henry. Maggie knew his handwriting in a moment, and there was another too for her; but she was too proud to ask for it, and, seating herself by the window, she waited for her grandmother to break the silence, which she did ere long as follows:

"I have just received a letter from that Warner, asking me to sanction an engagement which he says exists between himself and you. Is it true? Are you engaged to him?"

"I am," answered Maggie, playing nervously with the tassel of her wrapper, and wondering why Henry

had written so soon, before she had prepared the way
by a little judicious coaxing.

"Well, then," continued Madam Conway, "the
sooner it is broken the better. I am astonished that
you should stoop to such an act, and I hope you are
not in earnest."

"But I am," answered Maggie; and in the same
cold, decided manner her grandmother continued:
"Then nothing remains for me but to forbid your
having any communication whatever with one whose
conduct in my house has been so unpardonably rude
and vulgar. You will never marry him, Margaret,
never! Nay, I would sooner see you dead than the
wife of that low, mean, impertinent fellow!"

In the large dark eyes there was a gleam decidedly
"Hagarish" as Maggie arose, and, standing before
her grandmother, made answer: "You must not, in
my presence, speak thus of Henry Warner. He is
neither low, mean, vulgar, nor impertinent. You are
prejudiced against him because you think him comparatively poor, and because he has dared to look at
me, who have yet to understand why the fact of my
being a Conway makes me any better. I have promised to be Henry Warner's wife, and Margaret Miller
never yet has broken her word."

"But in this instance you will," said Madam Conway, now thoroughly aroused. "I will never suffer
it; and to prove I am in earnest I will here, before
your face, burn the letter he has presumed to send
you; and this I will do to any others which may come
to you from him."

Maggie offered no remonstrance; but the fire of a
volcano burned within, as she watched the letter black-

ening upon the coals; and when next her eyes met
those of her grandmother there was in them a fierce,
determined look which prompted that lady at once to
change her tactics and try the power of persuasion
rather than of force. Feigning a smile, she said:
"What ails you, child? You look to me like Hagar.
It was wrong in me, perhaps, to burn your letter, and
had I reflected a moment I might not have done it;
but I cannot suffer you to receive any more. I have
other prospects in view for you, and have only waited
a favorable opportunity to tell you what they are. Sit
down by me, Margaret, while I talk with you on the
subject."

The burning of her letter had affected Margaret
strangely, and with a benumbed feeling at her heart
she sat down without a word and listened patiently to
praises long and praises loud of Arthur Carrollton,
who was described as being every way desirable, both
as a friend and a husband. "His father, the elder Mr.
Carrollton, was an intimate friend of my husband,"
said Madam Conway, "and wishes our families to be
more closely united, by a marriage between you and
his son Arthur, who is rather fastidious in his taste,
and though twenty-eight years old has never yet seen
a face which suited him. But he is pleased with you,
Maggie. He liked your picture, imperfect as it is, and
he liked the tone of your letters, which I read to him.
They were so original, he said, so much like what he
fancied you to be. He has a splendid country seat,
and more than one nobleman's daughter would gladly
share it with him; but I think he fancies you. He has
a large estate near Montreal, and some difficulty connected with it will ere long bring him to America. Of

course he will visit here, and with a little tact on your part you can, I'm sure, secure one of the best matches in England. He is fine-looking, too. I have his daguerreotype;" and opening her workbox she drew it forth and held it before Maggie, who resolutely shut her eyes lest she should see the face of one she was so determined to dislike.

"What do you think of him?" asked Madam Conway as her arm began to ache, and Maggie had not yet spoken.

"I haven't looked at him," answered Maggie; "I hate him, and if he comes here after me I'll tell him so, too. I hate him because he is an Englishman. I hate him because he is aristocratic. I hate him for everything, and before I marry him I'll run away!"

Here, wholly overcome, Maggie burst into tears, and precipitately left the room. An hour later, and Hagar, sitting by ner fire, which the coolness of the day rendered necessary, was startled by the abrupt entrance of Maggie, who, throwing herself upon the floor, and burying her face in the old woman's lap, sobbed bitterly.

"What is it, child? What is it, darling?" asked Hagar; and in a few words Maggie explained the whole. "I am persecuted, dreadfully persecuted! Nobody before ever had so much trouble as I. Grandma has burned a letter from Henry Warner, and would not give it to me. Grandma said, too, I should never marry him, should never write to him, nor see anything he might send to me. Oh, Hagar, Hagar, isn't it cruel?" and the eyes, whose wrathful, defiant expression was now quenched in tears, looked up in Hagar's face for sympathy.

The right chord was touched, and much as Hagar might have disliked Henry Warner she was his fast friend now. Her mistress' opposition and Maggie's tears had wrought a change, and henceforth all her energies should be given to the advancement of the young couple's cause.

"I can manage it," she said, smoothing the long silken tresses which lay in disorder upon her lap. "Richland post office is only four miles from here; I can walk double that distance easy. Your grandmother never thinks of going there, neither am I known to anyone in that neighborhood. Write your letter to Henry Warner, and before the sun goes down it shall be safe in the letter-box. He can write to the same place, but he had better direct to me, as your name might excite suspicion."

This plan seemed perfectly feasible; but it struck Maggie unpleasantly. She had never attempted to deceive in her life, and she shrunk from the first deception. She would rather, she said, try again to win her grandmother's consent. But this she found impossible; Madam Conway was determined, and would not listen.

"It grieves me sorely," she said, "thus to cross my favorite child, whom I love better than my life; but it is for her good, and must be done."

So she wrote a cold and rather insulting letter to Henry Warner, bidding him, as she had done before, "let her granddaughter alone," and saying it was useless for him to attempt anything secret, for Maggie would be closely watched, the moment there were indications of a clandestine correspondence.

This letter, which was read to Margaret, destroyed

all hope, and still she wavered, uncertain whether it would be right to deceive her grandmother. But while she was yet undecided, Hagar's fingers, of late unused to the pen, traced a few lines to Henry Warner, who, acting at once upon her suggestion, wrote to Margaret a letter which he directed to "Hagar Warren, Rich-land."

In it he urged so many reasons why Maggie should avail herself of this opportunity for communicating with him that she yielded at last, and regularly each week old Hagar toiled through sunshine and through storm to the Richland post office, feeling amply repaid for her trouble when she saw the bright expectant face which almost always greeted her return. Occasionally, by way of lulling the suspicions of Madam Conway, Henry would direct a letter to Hillsdale, knowing full well it would never meet the eyes of Margaret, over whom, for the time being, a spy had been set, in the person of Anna Jeffrey.

This young lady, though but little connected with our story, may perhaps deserve a brief notice. Older than either Theo or Margaret, she was neither remarkable for beauty nor talent. Dark-haired, dark-eyed, dark-browed, and, as the servants said, "dark in her disposition," she was naturally envious of those whose rank in life entitled them to more attention than she was herself accustomed to receive. For this reason Maggie Miller had from the first been to her an object of dislike, and she was well pleased when Madam Conway, enjoining the strictest secrecy, appointed her to watch that young lady, and see that no letter was ever carried by her to the post office which Madam Conway had not first examined. In the snaky

eyes there was a look of exultation as Anna Jeffrey
promised to be faithful to her trust, and for a time she
became literally Maggie Miller's shadow, following
her here, following her there, and following her everywhere, until Maggie complained so bitterly of the annoyance that Madam Conway at last, feeling tolerably
sure that no counterplot was intended, revoked her
orders, and bade Anna Jeffrey leave Margaret free to
do as she pleased.

Thus relieved from espionage, Maggie became a
little more like herself, though a sense of the injustice
done her by her grandmother, together with the deception she knew she was practicing, wore upon her;
and the servants at their work listened in vain for the
merry laugh they had loved so well to hear. In the
present state of Margaret's feelings Madam Conway
deemed it prudent to say nothing of Arthur Carrollton,
whose name was never mentioned save by Theo and
Anna, the latter of whom had seen him in England,
and was never so well pleased as when talking of his
fine country seat, his splendid park, his handsome
horses, and last, though not least, of himself. " He
is," she said, " without exception, the most elegant and
aristocratic young man I have ever seen;" and then
for more than an hour she would entertain Theo with
a repetition of the many agreeable things he had said
to her during the one day she had spent at his house
while Madam Conway was visiting there.

In perfect indifference, Maggie, who was frequently
present, would listen to these stories, sometimes listlessly turning the leaves of a book, and again smiling
scornfully as she thought how impossible it was that
the fastidious Arthur Carrolton should have been at

all pleased with a girl like Anna Jeffrey; and positive
as Maggie was that she hated him, she insensibly began to feel a very slight degree of interest in him; at
least, she would like to know how he looked; and one
day when her grandmother and Theo were riding she
stole cautiously to the box where she knew his picture
lay, and, taking it out, looked to see if he were so very
fine-looking.

Yes, he was,—Maggie acknowledged that; and, sure
that she hated him terribly, she lingered long over that
picture, admiring the classically shaped head, the finely
cut mouth, and more than all the large dark eyes which
seemed so full of goodness and truth. " Pshaw!" she
exclaimed at last, restoring the picture to its place; " if
Henry were only a little taller, and had as handsome
eyes, he'd be a great deal better-looking. Anyway, I
like him, and I hate Arthur Carrollton, who I know is
domineering, and would try to make me mind. He
has asked for my daguerreotype, grandma says—one
which looks as I do now. I'll send it too," and she
burst into a loud laugh at the novel idea which had
crossed her mind.

That day when Madam Conway returned from her
ride she was surprised at Maggie's proposing that
Theo and herself should have their likenesses taken for
Arthur Carrollton.

" If he wants my picture," said she, " I am willing
he shall have it. It is all he'll ever get."

Delighted at this unexpected concession, Madam
Conway gave her consent, and the next afternoon
found Theo and Maggie at the daguerrean gallery in
Hillsdale, where the latter astonished both her sister
and the artist by declaring her intention of not only

sitting with her bonnet and shawl on; but also of turning her back to the instrument! It was in vain that Theo remonstrated! "That position or none," she said; and the picture was accordingly taken, presenting a very correct likeness, when finished, of a bonnet, a veil, and a shawl, beneath which Maggie Miller was supposed to be.

Strange as it may seem, this freak struck Madam Conway favorably. Arthur Carrollton knew that Maggie was unlike any other person, and the joke, she thought, would increase, rather than diminish, the interest he already felt in her. So she made no objection, and in a few days it was on its way to England, together with a lock of Hagar's snow-white hair, which Maggie had coaxed from the old lady, and, unknown to her grandmother, placed in the casing at the last moment.

Several weeks passed away, and then there came an answer—a letter so full of wit and humor that Maggie confessed to herself that he must be very clever to write so many shrewd things and to be withal so perfectly refined. Accompanying the package was a small rosewood box, containing a most exquisite little pin made of Hagar's frosty hair, and richly ornamented with gold. Not a word was written concerning it, and as Maggie kept her own counsel, both Theo and her grandmother marveled greatly, admiring its beauty and wondering for whom it was intended.

"For me, of course," said Madam Conway. "The hair is Lady Carrollton's, Arthur's grandmother. I know it by its soft, silky look. She has sent it as a token of respect, for she was always fond of me;" and going to the glass she very complacently ornamented her Honiton collar with Hagar's hair, while Maggie, bursting with fun, beat a hasty retreat from the room, lest she should betray herself.

Thus the winter passed away, and early in the spring George Douglas, to whom Madam Conway had long ago sent a favorable answer, came to visit his betrothed, bringing to Maggie a note from Rose, who had once or twice sent messages in Henry's letters. She was in Worcester now, and her health was very delicate. " Sometimes," she wrote, " I fear I shall never see you, Maggie Miller—shall never look into your beautiful face, or listen to your voice; but whether in heaven or on earth I am first to meet with you, my heart claims you as a sister, the one whom of all the sisters in the world I would rather call my own."

" Darling Rose!" murmured Maggie, pressing the delicately traced lines to her lips, " how near she seems to me! nearer almost than Theo;" and then involuntarily her thoughts went backward to the night when Henry Warner first told her of his love, and when in her dreams there had been a strange blending together of herself, of Rose, and the little grave beneath the pine!

But not yet was that veil of mystery to be lifted. Hagar's secret must be kept a little longer; and, unsuspicious of the truth, Maggie Miller must dream on of sweet Rose Warner, whom she hopes one day to call her sister!

There was also a message from Henry, and this George Douglas delivered in secret, for he did not care to displease his grandmother-elect, who, viewing him through a golden setting, thought he was not to be equaled by anyone in America. "So gentlemanly," she said, "and so modest too," basing her last conclusion upon his evident unwillingness to say very much of himself or his family. Concerning the latter she had questioned him in vain, eliciting nothing save the fact that they lived in the country several miles from Worcester, and that his father always stayed at home, and consequently his mother went but little into society.

"Despises the vulgar herd, I dare say," thought Madam Conway, contemplating the pleasure she should undoubtedly derive from an acquaintance with Mrs. Douglas, senior!

"There was a sister, too," he said, and at this announcement Theo opened wide her blue eyes, asking her name, and why he had never mentioned her before.

"I call her Jenny," said he, coloring slightly, and adding playfully, as he caressed Theo's smooth, round cheek, "Wives do not usually like their husbands' sisters."

"But I shall like her, I know," said Theo. "She has a beautiful name, Jenny Douglas—much prettier than Rose Warner, about whom Maggie talks to me so much."

A gathering frown on her grandmother's face warned Theo that she had touched upon a forbidden subject, and as Mr. Douglas manifested no desire to continue the conversation it ceased for a time, Theo wishing she could see Jenny Douglas, and George wondering what she would say when she did see her!

For a few days longer he lingered, and ere his return it was arranged that early in July Theo should be his bride. On the morning of his departure, as he stood upon the steps alone with Madam Conway, she said, " I think I can rely upon you, Mr. Douglas, not to carry either letter, note, or message from Maggie to that young Warner. I've forbidden him in my house, and I mean what I say."

" I assure you, madam, she has not asked me to carry either." answered George; who, though he knew perfectly well of the secret correspondence, had kept it to himself. " You mistake Mr. Warner, I think," he continued, after a moment. " I have known him long, and esteem him highly."

" Tastes differ," returned Madam Conway coldly. " No man of good breeding would presume to cut up my grandfather's coat or drink up my best wine."

" He intended no disrespect, I'm sure," answered George. " He only wanted a little fun with the ' Stars and Stripes.' "

" It was fun for which he will pay most dearly, though," answered Madam Conway, as she bade Mr. Douglas good-by; then, walking back to the parlor, she continued speaking to herself: " ' Stars and Stripes '! I'll teach him to cut up my blue bodice for fun. I wouldn't give him Margaret if his life depended upon it; " and sitting down she wrote to Arthur Carrollton, asking if he really intended visiting America, and when.

CHAPTER XIII.

SOCIETY.

DURING the remainder of the spring matters at the old stone house proceeded about as usual, Maggie writing regularly to Henry, who as regularly answered, while old Hagar managed it so adroitly that no one suspected the secret correspondence, and Madam Conway began to hope her granddaughter had forgotten the foolish fancy. Arthur Carrollton had replied that his visit to America, though sure to take place, was postponed indefinitely, and so the good lady had nothing in particular with which to busy herself, save the preparations for Theo's wedding, which was to take place near the first of July.

Though setting a high value upon money, Madam Conway was not penurious, and the bridal trousseau far exceeded anything which Theo had expected. As the young couple were not to keep house for a time, a most elegant suite of rooms had been selected in a fashionable hotel; and determining that Theo should not, in point of dress, be rivaled by any of her fellow-boarders, Madam Conway spared neither time nor money in making the outfit perfect. So for weeks the old stone house presented a scene of great confusion. Chairs, tables, lounges, and piano were piled with finery, on which Anna Jeffrey worked industriously, assisted sometimes by her aunt, whom Madam Conway pronounced altogether too superannuated for a governess, and who, though really an excellent scholar, was herself far better pleased with muslin robes and satin bows than with French idioms and Latin verbs. Perfectly delighted, Maggie joined in the general excitement, wondering occasionally when and where her own bridal would be. Once she ventured to ask if Henry Warner and his sister might be invited to Theo's wedding; but Madam Conway answered so decidedly in the negative that she gave it up, consoling herself with thinking that she would some time visit her sister, and see Henry in spite of her grandmother.

The marriage was very quiet, for Madam Conway had no acquaintance, and the family alone witnessed the ceremony. At first Madam Conway had hoped that Mr. and Mrs. Douglas, senior, together with their daughter Jenny, would be present, and she had accordingly requested George to invite them, feeling greatly disappointed when she learned that they could not come.

"I wanted so much to see them," she said to Maggie, "and know whether they are worthy to be related to the Conways—but of course they are, as much so as any American family. George has every appearance of refinement and high-breeding."

"But his family, for all that, may be as ignorant as Farmer Canfield's," answered Maggie; to which her grandmother replied: "You needn't tell me that, for I'm not to be deceived in such matters. I can tell at a glance if a person is low-born, no matter what their education or advantages may have been. Who's that?" she added quickly, and turning round she saw old Hagar, her eyes lighted up and her lips moving with incoherent sounds.

Hagar had come up to the wedding, and had reached the door of Madam Conway's room just in time to hear the last remark, which roused her at once.

"Why don't she discover my secret, then," she muttered, "if she has so much discernment? Why don't she see the Hagar blood in her? for it's there, plain as day;" and she glanced proudly at Maggie, who, in her simple robe of white, was far more beautiful than the bride.

And still Theo, in her handsome traveling dress, was very fair to look upon, and George Douglas felt proud that she was his, resolving, as he kissed away the tears she shed at parting, that the vow he had just made should never be broken. A few weeks of pleasant travel westward, and then the newly wedded pair came back to what, for a time, was to be their home.

George Douglas was highly respected in Worcester, both as a man of honor and a man of wealth; consequently, every possible attention was paid to Theo, who was petted and admired, until she began to wonder why neither Maggie nor yet her all-discerning grandmother had discovered how charming and faultless she was!

Among George's acquaintance was a Mrs. Morton, a dashing, fashionable woman, who determined to honor the bride with a party, to which all the élite of Worcester were invited, together with many Bostonians. Madam Conway and Maggie were of course upon the list; and, as timely notice was given them by Theo, Madam Conway went twice to Springfield in quest of a suitable dress for Maggie. She wanted something becoming, she said; and a delicate rose-colored satin, with a handsome overskirt of lace, was at last decided upon.

" She must have some pearls for her hair," thought Madam Conway; and when next Maggie, who, girl-like, tried the effect of her first party dress at least a dozen times, stood before the glass to see if it were exactly the right length, she was presented with the pearls, which Anna Jeffrey, with a feeling of envy at her heart, arranged in the shining braids of her hair.

" Oh, isn't it perfectly splendid ! " cried Maggie, herself half inclined to compliment the beautiful image reflected in the mirror.

" You ought to see Arthur Carrollton's sister when she is dressed, if you think you look handsome," answered Anna, adding that diamonds were much more fashionable than pearls.

" You have attended a great many parties and seen a great deal of fashion, so I dare say you are right," Maggie answered ironically; and then, as through the open window she saw Hagar approaching, she ran out upon the piazza to see what the old woman would say.

Hagar had never seen her thus before, and now, throwing up her hands in astonishment, she involuntarily dropped upon her knees, and, while the tears rained over her timeworn face, whispered, " Hester's child—my granddaughter—Heaven be praised ! "

" Do I look pretty ? " Margaret asked; and Hagar answered : " More beautiful than anyone I ever saw. I wish your mother could see you now."

Involuntarily Maggie glanced at the tall marble gleaming through the distant trees, while Hagar's thoughts were down in that other grave—the grave beneath the pine. The next day was the party, and at an early hour Madam Conway was ready. Her rich purple satin and Valenciennes laces, with which she hoped to impress Mrs. Douglas, senior, were carefully packed up, together with Maggie's dress; and then, shawled and bonneted, she waited impatiently for her carriage, which she preferred to the cars. It came at last, but in place of John, the usual coachman, Mike, a rather wild youth of twenty, was mounted upon the box. His father, he said, had been taken suddenly ill, and had deputized him to drive.

For a time Madam Conway hesitated, for she knew Mike's one great failing, and she hardly dared risk herself with him, lest she should find a seat less desirable even than the memorable brush-heap. But Mike protested loudly to having joined the " Sons of Temperance " only the night before, and as in his new suit of blue, with shining brass buttons, he presented a more stylish appearance than his father, his mistress finally decided to try him, threatening all manner of evil if in any way he broke his pledge, either to herself or the " Sons," the latter of whom had probably never heard of him. He was perfectly sober now, and drove them safely to Worcester, where they soon found themselves in Theo's handsome rooms. Her wrappings removed and herself snugly ensconced in a velvet-cushioned chair, Madam Conway asked the young bride how long before Mrs. Douglas, senior, would probably arrive.

A slight shadow, which no one observed, passed over Theo's face as she answered, " George's father seldom goes into society, and consequently his mother will not come."

" Oh, I am so sorry ! " replied Madam Conway,

thinking of the purple satin, and continuing, " Nor the young lady, either? "

" None of them," answered Theo, adding hastily, as if to change the conversation, " Isn't my piano perfectly elegant? " and she ran her fingers over an exquisitely carved instrument, which had inscribed upon it simply " Theo "; and then, as young brides sometimes will, she expatiated upon the kindness and generosity of George, showing, withal, that her love for her husband was founded upon something far more substantial than family or wealth.

Her own happiness, it would seem, had rendered her less selfish and more thoughtful for others; for once that afternoon, on returning to her room after a brief absence, she whispered to Maggie that " someone in the parlor below wished to see her."

Then seating herself at her grandmother's feet, she entertained her so well with a description of her travels that the good lady failed to observe the absence of Maggie, who, face to face with Henry Warner, was making amends for their long separation. Much they talked of the past, and then Henry spoke of the future; but of this Maggie was less hopeful. Her grandmother would never consent to their marriage, she knew—the " Stars and Stripes " had decided that matter, even though there were no Arthur Carrollton across the sea, and Maggie sighed despondingly as she thought of the long years of single-blessedness in store for her.

" There is but one alternative left, then," said Henry. " If your grandmother refuses her consent altogether, I must take you without her consent."

" I shan't run away," said Maggie; " I shall live an

old maid, and you must live an old bachelor, until grandma——"

She did not have time to finish the sentence ere Henry commenced unfolding the following plan:

" It is necessary," he said, " for either myself or Mr. Douglas to go to Cuba; and as Rose's health makes a change of climate advisable for her, George has proposed to me to go and take my sister there for the winter. And, Maggie," he continued, " will you go, too? We are to sail the middle of October, stopping for a few weeks in Florida, until the unhealthy season in Havana is passed. I will see your grandmother to-morrow morning—will once more honorably ask her for your hand, and if she still refuses, as you think she will, it cannot surely be wrong in you to consult your own happiness instead of her prejudices. I will meet you at old Hagar's cabin at the time appointed. Rose and my aunt, who is to accompany her, will be in New York, whither we will go immediately. A few moments more and you will be my wife, and beyond the control of your grandmother. Do you approve my plan, Maggie, darling? Will you go?"

Maggie could not answer him then, for an elopement was something from which she instinctively shrunk, and with a faint hope that her grandmother might consent she went back to her sister's room, where she had not yet been missed. Very rapidly the remainder of the afternoon passed away, and at an early hour, wishing to know " exactly how she was going to look," Maggie commenced her toilet. Theo, too, desirous of displaying her white satin as long as possible, began to dress; while Madam Conway, in no haste to don her purple satin, which was uncomfortably tight, amused herself by watching the passers-by, nodding at intervals, in her chair.

While thus occupied, a perfumed note was brought to her, the contents of which elicited from her an exclamation of surprise.

"Can it be possible!" she said; and thrusting the note into her pocket she hastily left the room.

She was gone a long, long time; and when at last she returned, she was evidently much excited, paying no attention whatever to Theo, who, in her bridal robes, looked charming, but minutely inspecting Maggie, to see if in her adornings there was aught out of its place. Her dress was faultless, and she looked so radiantly beautiful, as she stood before her grandmother, that the old lady kissed her fondly, whispering, as she did so, "You are indeed beautiful!" It was a long time ere Madam Conway commenced her own toilet, and then she proceeded so slowly that George Douglas became impatient, and she finally suggested that he and Theo should go without her, sending the carriage back for herself and Maggie. To this proposition he at last yielded; and when they were left alone Madam Conway greatly accelerated her movements, dressing herself in a few moments, and then, much to Maggie's surprise, going below without a word of explanation. A few moments only elapsed ere a servant was sent to Maggie, saying that her presence was desired at No. 40, a small private parlor adjoining the public drawing rooms.

"What can it mean? Is it possible that Henry is there?" Maggie asked herself, as with a beating heart she descended the stairs.

A moment more, and Maggie stood on the thresh-

hold of No. 40. Seated upon the sofa was Madam
Conway, her purple satin seeming to have taken a
wide sweep, and her face betokening the immense degree of satisfaction she felt in being there with the
stylish, elegant-looking stranger who stood at her side,
with his deep, expressive eyes fixed upon the door ex-
pectantly. Maggie knew him in a moment—knew it
was Arthur Carrollton; and, turning pale, she started
backward, while he advanced forward, and, offering
her his hand, looked down upon her with a winning
smile, saying, as he did so: "Excuse my familiarity.
You are Maggie Miller, I am sure."

For an instant Maggie could not reply, but soon
becoming composed she received the stranger gracefully, and then taking the chair he politely brought her
she listened while her grandmother told that he
had arrived at Montreal two weeks before; that he had
reached Hillsdale that morning, an hour or two after
their departure, and, learning their destination, had followed them in the cars; that she had taken the liberty
of informing Mrs. Morton of his arrival, and that
lady had of course extended to him an invitation to be
present at her party.

"Which invitation I accept, provided Miss Maggie
allows me to be her escort," said the young man, and
again his large black eyes rested admiringly upon her.

Maggie had anticipated a long, quiet talk with
Henry Warner, and, wishing the Englishman anywhere but there, she answered coldly, "I cannot well
decline your escort, Mr. Carrollton, so of course I accept it."

Madam Conway bit her lip, but Mr. Carrollton, who
was prepared for anything from Maggie Miller, was

not in the least displeased, and, consulting his dia-
mond-set watch, which pointed to nearly ten, he asked
if it were not time to go.

"Certainly," said Madam Conway. "You remain
here, Maggie; I will bring down your shawl," and she
glided from the room, leaving them purposely alone.

Maggie was a good deal astonished, slightly embarrassed, and a little provoked, all of which Arthur
Carrollton readily saw; but this did not prevent his
talking to her, and during the few minutes of Madam
Conway's absence he decided that neither Margaret's
beauty, nor yet her originality, had been overrated by
her partial grandmother, while Maggie, on her part,
mentally pronounced him "the finest-looking, the most
refined, the most gentlemanly, the proudest, and the
hatefulest man she had ever seen!"

Wholly unconscious of her cogitation, he wrapped
her shawl very carefully about her, taking care to
cover her white shoulders from the night air; then
offering his arm to her grandmother, he led the way
to the carriage, whither she followed him, wondering
if Henry would be jealous, and thinking her first act
would be to tell him how she hated Arthur Carrollton,
and always should!

.   .   .   .   .

It was a gay, brilliant scene which Mrs. Morton's
drawing room presented; and, as yet the center of attraction, Theo, near the door, was bowing to the many
strangers who sought her acquaintance. Greatly
she marveled at the long delay of her grandmother and
Maggie, and she had just suggested to Henry that he
should go in quest of them, when she saw her sister
ascending the stairs.

On a sofa across the room sat a pale young girl arrayed in white, her silken curls falling around her neck like a golden shower, and her mournful eyes of blue scanning eagerly each newcomer, then a look of disappointment drooping beneath the long lashes which rested wearily upon her colorless cheek. It was Rose Warner, and the face she sought was Maggie Miller's. She had seen no semblance of it yet, for Henry had no daguerreotype. Still, she felt sure she would know it, and when at last, in all her queenly beauty, Maggie came, leaning on Arthur Carrollton's arm, Rose's heart made ready answer to the oft-repeated question, " Who is she? "

" Beautiful, gloriously beautiful! " she whispered softly, while from the grave of her buried hopes there came one wild heart-throb, one sudden burst of pain caused by the first sight of her rival, and then Rose Warner grew calm again, and those who saw the pressure of her hand upon her side dreamed not of the fierce pang within. She had asked her brother not to tell Maggie she was to be there. She would rather watch her a while, herself unknown; and now with eager, curious eyes she followed Maggie, who was quickly surrounded by a host of admirers.

It was Maggie's first introduction into s .ety, and yet so perfect was her intuition of what was proper that neither by word or deed did she do aught to shock the most fastidious. It is true her merry laugh more than once rang out above the din of voices; but it was so joyous that no one objected, particularly when they looked in her bright and almost childish face. Arthur Carrollton, too, acting as her escort, aided her materially, for it was soon whispered around that he was a wealthy Englishman, and many were the comments made upon the handsome couple, who seemed singularly adapted to each other. A glance had convinced Arthur Carrollton that Maggie was by far the most beautiful lady present, and feeling that on this her first introduction into society she needed someone to shield her, as it were, from the many foolish, flattering speeches which were sure to be made in her hearing, he kept her at his side, where she was nothing loath to stay; for, notwithstanding that she " hated " him so, there was about him a fascination she did not try to resist.

" They are a splen lid couple," thought Rose, and then she looked to see how Henry was affected by the attentions of the handsome foreigner.

But Henry was not jealous; and, standing a little aloof, he felt more pleasure than pain in watching Maggie as she received the homage of the gay throng. Thoughts similar to those of Rose, however, forced themselves upon him as he saw the dignified bearing of Mr. Carrollton, and for the first time in his life he was conscious of an uncomfortable feeling of inferiority to some thing or some body, he hardly knew what. This feeling, however, passed away when Maggie came at last to his side, with her winning smile and playful words.

Very closely Madam Conway watched her now; but Maggie did not heed it, and leaning on Henry's arm she seemed oblivious to all save him. After a time he led her out upon a side piazza, where they would be comparatively alone. Observing that she seemed a little chilly, he left her for a moment while he went in quest of her shawl. Scarcely was he gone when a slight, fairy form came flitting through the moonlight to where Maggie sat, and, twining its snow-white arms around her neck, looked lovingly into her eyes, whispering soft and low, " My sister ! "

" My sister ! " How Maggie's blood bounded at the sound of that name, which even the night wind, sighing through the trees, seemed to take up and repeat. " My sister ! " What was there in those words thus to affect her? Was that fair young creature, who hung so fondly over her, naught to her save a common stranger? Was there no tie between them, no bond of sympathy and love? We ask this of you, our reader, and not of Maggie Miller, for to her there came no questioning like this. She only knew that every pulsation of her heart responded to the name of sister, when breathed by sweet Rose Warner, and, folding her arms about her, she pillowed the golden head upon her bosom, and, pushing back the clustering curls, gazed long and earnestly into a face which seemed so heavenly and pure.

Few were the words they uttered at first, for a mysterious, invisible something prompted each to look into the other's eyes, to clasp the other's hands, to kiss the other's lips, and lovingly to whisper the other's name.

" I have wished so much to see you, to know if you are worthy of my noble brother," said Rose at last, thinking she must say something on the subject uppermost in both their minds.

" And am I worthy? " asked Maggie, the bright blushes stealing over her cheek. " Will you let me be your sister? "

" My heart would claim you for that, even though

I had no brother," answered Rose, and again her lips touched those of Maggie.

Seeing them thus together, Henry tarried purposely a long time, and when at last he rejoined them he proposed returning to the drawing room, where many inquiries were making for Maggie.

"I have looked for you a long time, Miss Maggie," said Mr. Carrollton. "I wish to hear you play;" and, taking her arm in his, he led her to the piano.

From the moment of her first introduction to him Maggie had felt that there was something commanding in his manner, something she could not disobey; and now, though she fancied it was impossible to play before that multitude, she seated herself mechanically, and while the keys swam before her eyes, went through with a difficult piece which she had never but once before executed correctly.

"You have done well; much better than I anticipated," said Mr. Carrollton, again offering her his arm; and though a little vexed, those few words of commendation were worth more to Maggie than the most flattering speech which Henry Warner had ever made to her.

Soon after leaving the piano a young man approached and invited her to waltz. This was something in which Maggie excelled; for two winters before Madam Conway had hired a teacher to instruct her granddaughters in dancing, and she was about to accept the invitation, when, drawing her arm still closer within his own, Mr. Carrollton looked down upon her, saying softly, "I wouldn't."

Maggie had often waltzed with Henry at home. He saw no harm in it, and now when Arthur Carroll•

ton objected, she was provoked, while at the same time she felt constrained to decline.

" Some time, when I know you better, I will explain to you why I do not think it proper for young girls to waltz with everyone," said Mr. Carrollton; and, leading her from the drawing room, he devoted himself to her for the remainder of the evening, making himself so perfectly agreeable that Maggie forgot everything, even Henry Warner, who in the meantime had tried to obtain recognition from Madam Conway as an acquaintance.

A cool nod, however, was all the token of recognition she had to give him. This state of feeling augured ill for the success of his suit; but when at a late hour that night, in spite of grandmother or Englishman, he handed Maggie to the carriage, he whispered to her softly, " I will see her to-morrow morning, and know the worst."

The words caught the quick ear of Madam Conway; but, not wishing Mr. Carrollton to know there was anything particular between her granddaughter and Henry Warner, she said nothing, and when, arrived at last at the hotel, she asked an explanation, Maggie, who hurried off to bed, was too sleep v to give her any answer.

" I shall know before long, anyway, if he sees me in the morning," she thought, as she heard a distant clock strike two, and settling her face into the withering frown with which she intended to annihilate Henry Warner, the old lady was herself ere long much faster asleep than the young girl at her side, who was thinking of Henry Warner, wishing he was three inches taller, or herself three inches shorter, and wondering if his square shoulders would not be somewhat improved by braces!

"I never noticed how short and crooked he was," she thought, "until I saw him standing by the side of Mr. Carrollton, who is such a splendid figure, so tall and straight; but big, overgrown girls like me always get short husbands, they say;" and satisfied with this conclusion she fell asleep.

CHAPTER XIV.

MADAM CONWAY'S DISASTERS.

At a comparatively early hour Madam Conway arose, and going to the parlor found there Arthur Carrollton, who asked if Margaret were not yet up. " Say that I wish her to ride with me on horseback," said he. " The morning air will do her good ; " and, quite delighted, Madam Conway carried the message to her granddaughter.

" Tell him I shan't do it," answered the sleepy Maggie, adjusting herself for another nap. Then, as she thought how his eyes probably looked as he said, " I wish her to ride," she felt impelled to obey, and greatly to her grandmother's surprise she commenced dressing.

Theo's riding dress was borrowed, and though it did not fit her exactly she looked unusually well when she met Mr. Carrollton in the lower hall, and once mounted upon the gay steed, and galloping away into the country, she felt more than repaid for the loss of her morning slumber.

" You ride well," said Mr. Carrollton, when at last they paused upon the brow of a hill overlooking the town, " but you have some faults which, with your permission, I will correct," and in the most polite and gentlemanly manner he proceeded to speak of a few points wherein her riding might be improved.

Among other things, he said she rode too fast for a lady; and, biting her lip, Maggie thought, " If I only had Gritty here, I'd lead him such a race as would either break his bones or his neck, I'm not particular which."

Still, she .followed his directions implicitly, and when, ere they reached home, he told her that she excelled many who had been for years to riding schools, she felt repaid for his criticisms, which she knew were just, even if they were not agreeable. Breakfast being over, he announced his intention of going down to Boston, telling Maggie he should probably return that evening and go with her to Hillsdale on the morrow.

Scarcely had he gone when Henry Warner appeared, asking an interview with Madam Conway, who haughtily led the way into a private room. Very candidly and honorably Henry made known to her his wishes, whereupon a most stormy scene ensued, the lady so far forgetting herself as to raise her voice several notes above its usual pitch, while Henry, angered by her insulting words, bade her take the consequences of her refusal, hinting that girls had been known to marry without their guardian's consent.

"An elopement, hey? He threatens me with an elopement, does he?" said Madam Conway, as the door closed after him. " I am glad he warned me in time," and then, trembling in every limb lest Maggie should be spirited away before her very eyes, she determined upon going home immediately and leaving Arthur Carrollton to follow in the cars.

Accordingly, Maggie was bidden to pack her things at once, the excited old lady keeping her eye constantly upon her to see that she did not disappear through the

window or some other improbable place. In silence
Maggie obeyed, pouting the while a very little, partly
because she should not again see Henry, partly because she had confidently expected to ride home with
Mr. Carrollton, and partly because she wished to stay
to the firemen's muster, which had long been talked
about, and was to take place on the morrow. They
were ready at last, and then in a very perturbed state
of feeling Madam Conway waited for her carriage,
which was not forthcoming, and upon inquiry George
Douglas learned that, having counted upon another
day in the city, Mike was now going through with a
series of plunge-baths, by way of sobering himself ere
appearing before his mistress. This, however, George
kept from Madam Conway, not wishing to alarm her;
and when after a time Mike appeared, sitting bolt up-
right upon the box, with the lines grasped firmly in
his hands, she did not suspect the truth, nor know that
he too was angry for being thus compelled to go home
before he saw the firemen.

Thinking him sober enough to be perfectly safe,
George Douglas felt no fear, and, bowing to his new
relatives, went back to comfort Theo, who as a matter
of course cried a little when the carriage drove away.
Worcester was left behind, and they were far out in
the country ere a word was exchanged between
Madam Conway and Maggie; for while the latter was
pouting behind her veil, the former was wondering
what possessed Mike to drive into every rut and over
every stone.

"You, Mike!" she exclaimed at last, leaning from
the window. "What ails you?"

"Nothing, as I'm a living man," answered Mike,

halting so suddenly as to jerk the lady backwards and mash the crown of her bonnet.

Straightening herself up, and trying in vain to smooth the jam, Madam Conway continued: " In liquor, I know. I wish I had stayed home." But Mike loudly denied the charge, declaring he had spent the blessed night at a meeting of the " Sons," where they passed around nothing stronger than lemons and water, and if the horses chose to run off the track it wasn't his fault—he couldn't help it; and with the air of one deeply injured he again started forward, turning off ere long into a cross road, which, as they advanced, grew more stony and rough, while the farmhouses, as a general thing, presented a far less respectable appearance than those on the Hillsdale route.

" Mike, you villain! " ejaculated the lady, as they ran down into a ditch, and she sprang to one side to keep the carriage from going over.

But ere she had time for anything further, one of the axletrees snapped asunder, and to proceed further in their present condition was impossible. Alighting from the carriage, and setting her little feet upon the ground with a vengeance, Madam Conway first scolded Mike unmercifully for his carelessness, and next chided Maggie for manifesting no more concern.

" You'd as lief go to destruction as not, I do believe! " said she, looking carefully after the bandbox containing her purple satin.

" I'd rather go there first," answered Maggie, pointing to a brown old-fashioned farmhouse about a quarter of a mile away.

At first Madam Conway objected, saying she preferred sitting on the bank to intruding herself upon

strangers; but as it was now noonday, and the warm
September sun poured fiercely down upon her, she
finally concluded to follow Maggie's advice, and gathering up her box and parasol started for the house,
which, with its tansy patch on the right, and its single
poplar tree in front, presented rather an uninviting
appearance.

" Some vulgar creatures live there, I know. Just
hear that old tin horn ! " she exclaimed, as a blast, loud
and shrill, blown by practiced lips, told the men in a
distant field that dinner was ready.

A nearer approach disclosed to view a slanting-
roofed farmhouse such as is often found in New England, with high, narrow windows, small panes of glass,
and the most indispensable paper curtains of blue
closely shading the windows of what was probably
the " best room." In the apartment opposite, however, they were rolled up, so as to show the old-fashioned drapery of dimity, bordered with a netted fringe.
Half a dozen broken pitchers and pots held gerani-
ums, verbenas, and other plants, while the well-kept
beds of hollyhocks, sunflowers, and poppies indicated
a taste for flowers in someone. Everything about the
house was faultlessly neat. The doorsill was scrubbed
to a chalky white, while the uncovered floor wore the
same polished hue.

All this Madam Conway saw at a glance, but it did
not prevent her from holding high her aristocratic
skirts, lest they should be contaminated, and when, in
answer to her knock, an odd-looking, peculiarly
dressed woman appeared, she uttered an exclamation
of disgust, and, turning to Maggie, said, " You talk
—I can't ! "

But the woman did not stand at all upon ceremony. For the last ten minutes she had been watching the strangers as they toiled over the sandy road, and when sure they were coming there had retreated into her bedroom, donning a flaming red calico, which, guiltless of hoops, clung to her tenaciously, showing her form to good advantage, and rousing at once the risibility of Maggie. A black lace cap, ornamented with ribbons of the same fanciful color as the dress, adorned her head; and, with a dozen or more pins in her mouth, she now appeared, hooking her sleeve and smoothing down the black collar upon her neck.

In a few words Maggie explained to her their misfortune, and asked permission to tarry there until the carriage was repaired.

"Certing, certing," answered the woman, courtesying almost to the floor. "Walk right in, if you can git in. It's my cheese day, or I should have been cleared away sooner. Here, Betsy Jane, you have prinked long enough; come and hist the winders in t'other room, and wing 'em off, so the ladies can set in there out of this dirty place;" then turning to Madam Conway, who was industriously freeing her French kids from the sand they had accumulated during her walk, she continued, "Have some of my shoes to rest your feet a spell"; and diving into a recess or closet she brought forth a pair of slippers large enough to hold both of Madam Conway's feet at once.

With a haughty frown the lady declined the offer, while Maggie looked on in delight, pleased with an adventure which promised so much fun. After a moment Betsy Jane appeared, attired in a dress similar to that of her mother, for whose lank appearance she made ample amends, in the wonderful expansion of her robes, which, minus gather or fold at the bottom, set out like a miniature tent, upsetting at once the bandbox, which Madam Conway had placed upon a chair, and which, with its contents, rolled promiscuously over the floor!

"Betsy Jane! How can you wear them abominable things!" exclaimed the distressed woman, stooping to pick up the 'purple sati_ which had tumbled out.,

A look from the more fashionable daughter, as with a swinging sweep she passed on into the parlor, silenced the mother on the subject of hoops, and thinking her guests must necessarily be thirsty after their walk she brought them a pitcher of water, asking if they'd " chuse it clear, or with a little ginger and molasses," at the same time calling to Betsy Jane to know if them windows was " wung " off!

The answer was in the affirmative, whereupon the ladies were invited to enter, which they did the more willingly as through the open door they had caught glimpses of what proved to be a very handsome Brussels carpet, which in that room seemed a little out of place, as did the sofa, and handsome haircloth rocking-chair. In this last Madam Conway seated herself, while Maggie reclined upon a lounge, wondering at the difference in the various articles of furniture, some of which were quite expensive, while others were of the most common kind.

"Who can they be? She looks like someone I have seen," said Maggie as Betsy Jane left the room. "I mean to ask their names;" but this her grandmother would not suffer. "It was too much like familiarity," she said, "and she did not believe in putting one's self on a level with such people."

Another loud blast from the horn was blown, for the bustling woman of the house was evidently getting uneasy, and ere long three or four men appeared, washing themselves from the spout of the pump, and wiping upon a coarse towel which hung upon a roller near the back door.

"I shan't eat at the same table with those creatures," said Madam Conway, feeling intuitively that she would be invited to dinner.

"Why, grandma, yes you will, if she asks you," answered Maggie. "Only think how kind they are to us—perfect strangers!"

What else she might have said was prevented by the entrance of Betsy Jane, who informed them that dinner was ready, and with a mental groan, as she thought how she was about to be martyred, Madam Conway followed her to the dining room, where a plain, substantial farmer's meal was spread. Standing at the head of the table, with her good-humored face all in a glow, was the hostess, who, pointing Madam Conway to a chair, said: "Now set right by, and make yourselves to hum. Mebby I orto have set the table over, and I guess I should if I had anything fit to eat. Be you fond of biled victuals?" and taking it for granted they were, she loaded both Madam Conway's and Maggie's plate with every variety of vegetables used in the preparation of the dish known everywhere as "boiled victuals."

By this time the men had ranged themselves in respectful silence upon the opposite side of the table, each stealing an admiring though modest glance at

Maggie; for the masculine heart, whether it beats beneath a homespun frock or coat of finest cloth, is alike susceptible to glowing, youthful beauty like that of Maggie Miller. The head of the house was absent—"had gone to town with a load of wood," so his spouse informed the ladies, at the same time pouring out a cup of tea, which she said she had tried to make strong enough to bear up an egg. "Betsy Jane," she continued, casting a deprecating glance, first at the blue sugar bowl and then at her daughter, "what possessed you to put on this brown sugar, when I told you to get crush? Have some of the apple sass? It's new—made this morning. Dew have some," she continued, as Madam Conway shook her head. "Mebby it's better than it looks. Seem's ef you wan't goin' to eat nothin'. Betsy Jane, now you're up after the crush, fetch them china sassers for the cowcumbers. Like enough she'll eat some of them."

But, affecting a headache, Madam Conway declined everything save the green tea and a Boston cracker, which, at the first mention of headache, the distressed woman had brought her. Suddenly remembering Mike, who, having fixed the carriage, was fast asleep on a wheelbarrow under the woodshed, she exclaimed: "For the land of massy, if I hain't forgot that young gentleman! Go, William, and call him this minute. Are you sick at your stomach?" she asked, turning to Madam Conway, who at the thought of eating with her drunken coachman had uttered an exclamation of disgust. "Go, Betsy Jane, and fetch the camphire, quick!"

But Madam Conway did not need the camphor, and so she said, adding that Mike was better where he

was. Mike thought so too, and refused to come,
whereupon the woman insisted that he must. " There
was room enough," she said, " and no kind of sense
in Betsy Jane's taking up the hull side of the table
with them rattans. She could set nearer the young
lady."

" Certainly," answered Maggie, anxious to see how
the " rattans " would manage to squeeze in between
herself and the table-leg, as they would have to do if
they came an inch nearer.

This feat could not be done, and in attempting it
Betsy Jane upset Maggie's tea upon her handsome
traveling dress, eliciting from her mother the exclamation, " Betsy Jane Douglas, you allus was the blun-
derin'est girl!"

This little accident diverted the woman's mind from
Mike, while Madam Conway, starting at the name of
Douglas, thought to herself: " Douglas!—Douglas!
I did not suppose 'twas so common a name. But then
it don't hurt George any, having these creatures bear
his name."

Dinner being over, Madam Conway and Maggie returned to the parlor, where, while the former resumed
her chair, the latter amused herself by examining the
books and odd-looking daguerreotypes which lay upon
the table.

" Oh, grandmother!" she almost screamed, bounding to that lady's side, " as I live, here's a picture of
Theo and George Douglas taken together," and she
held up a handsome casing before the astonished old
lady, who, donning her golden spectacles in a twinkling, saw for herself that what Maggie said was true.

" They stole it!" she gasped. " We are in a den

of thieves! Who knows what they'll take from my bandbox?" and she was about to leave the room when Maggie, whose quick mind saw farther ahead, bade her stop.

"I may discover something more," said she, and taking up a handsomely bound volume of Lamb, she turned to the fly-leaf, and read, "Jenny Douglas, from her brother George, Worcester, January 8."

It was plain to her now; but any mortification she might otherwise have experienced was lost in the one absorbing thought, "What will grandma say?"

"Grandmother," said she, showing the book, "don't you remember the mother of that girl called her Betsy Jane Douglas?"

"Yes, yes!" gasped Madam Conway, raising both hands, while an expression of deep, intense anxiety was visible upon her face.

"And don't you know, too," continued Maggie, "that George always seemed inclined to say as little as possible of his parents? Now, in this country it is not unusual for the sons of just such people as these to be among the most wealthy and respectable citizens."

"Maggie, Maggie!" hoarsely whispered Madam Conway, grasping Maggie's arm, "do you mean to insinuate—am I to understand that you believe that odious woman and hideous girl to be the mother and sister of George Douglas?"

"I haven't a doubt of it," answered Maggie. "'Twas the resemblance between Betsy Jane and George which I observed at first."

Out of her chair to the floor tumbled Madam Conway, fainting entirely away, while Maggie, stepping to the door, called for help.

"I mistrusted she was awful sick at dinner," said Mrs. Douglas, taking her hands from the dish-water, and running to the parlor. "I wish she'd smelt of the camphire, as I wanted her to do. Does she have such spells often?"

By this time Betsy Jane brought a basin of water, which she dashed in the face of the unconscious woman, who soon began to revive.

"Pennyr'yal tea 'll settle her stomach quicker'n anything else," said Mrs. Douglas. "I'll clap a little right on the stove;" and, helping Madam Conway to the sofa, she left the room.

"There may possibly be a mistake, after all," thought Maggie. "I'll question the girl;" and, turning to Betsy Jane, she said, taking up the book which had before attracted her attention, "Is this 'Jenny Douglas' intended for you?"

"Yes, ma'am," answered the girl, coloring slightly. "Brother George calls me Jenny, because he thinks Betsy so old-fashioned."

An audible groan from the sofa, and Maggie continued, "Where does your brother live?"

"In Worcester, ma'am. He keeps a store there," answered Betsy, who was going to say more, when her mother, re-entering the room, took up the conversation by saying, "Was you tellin' 'em about George Washington? Waal, he's a boy no mother need to be ashamed on, though my old man sometimes says he's ashamed of us, we are so different. But, then, he orto consider the advantages he's had. We only brung him up till he was ten years old, and then an uncle he was named after took him and gin him a college schoolin', and then put him into his store in Worcester.

Your head aches wus, don't it? Poor thing! The
pennyryal will be steeped directly," she added, in an
aside to Madam Conway, who had groaned aloud as if
in pain. Then resuming her story, she continued,
"Better'n six year ago Uncle George, who was a
bachelor, died, leaving the heft of his property, sev-
enty-five thousand dollars or more, to my son, who
is now top of the heap in the store, and worth one
hundred thousand dollars, I presume; some say two
hundred thousand dollars; but that's the way some
folks have of agitatin' things."

"Is he married?" asked Maggie, and Mrs. Douglas, mistaking the motive which prompted the question,
answered: "Yes, dear, he is. If he wan't, I know of
no darter-in-law I'd as soon have as you. I don't
believe in finding fault with my son's wife; but there's
a proud look in her face I don't like. This is her
picter," and she passed to Maggie the daguerreotype
of Theo.

"I've looked at it before," said Maggie; and the
good woman proceeded: "I hain't seen her yet; but
he's going to bring her to Charlton bime-by. He's a
good boy, George is, free as water—gave me this carpet, the sofy and chair, and has paid Betsy Jane's
schoolin' one winter at Leicester. But Betsy don't take
to books much. She's more like me, her father says.
They had a big party for George last night, but I
wan't invited. Shouldn't 'a' gone if I had been; but
for all that a body don't want to be slighted, even if
they don't belong to the quality. If I'm good enough
to be George's mother I'm good enough to go to a
party with his wife. But she wan't to blame, and I
shan't lay it up against her. I shall see her to-mor-

row, pretty likely, for Sam Babbit's wife and I are goin' down to the firemen's muster. You've heard on't, I suppose. The different engines are goin' to see which will shute water the highest over a 180-foot pole. I wouldn't miss goin' for anything, and of course I shall call on Theodoshy. I calkerlate to like her, and when they go to housekeepin' I've got a hull chest full of sheets and piller-biers and towels I'm goin' to give her, besides three or four bedquilts I pieced myself, two in herrin'-bone pattern, and one in risin' sun. I'll show 'em to you," and leaving the room, she soon returned with three patchwork quilts, wherein were all possible shades of color, red and yellow predominating, and in one the " rising sun " forming a huge centerpiece.

"Heavens!" faintly articulated Madam Conway, pressing her hands upon her head, which was supposed to be aching dreadfully. The thought of Theo reposing beneath the " risin' sun," or yet the " herrin'-bone," was intolerable; and looking beseechingly at Maggie, she whispered, " Do see if Mike is ready."

" If it's the carriage you mean," chimed in Mrs. Douglas, " it's been waiting quite a spell, but I thought you warn't fit to ride yet, so I didn't tell you."

Starting to her feet, Madam Conway's bonnet went on in a trice, and taking her shawl in her hand she walked outdoors, barely expressing her thanks to Mrs. Douglas, who, greatly distressed at her abrupt departure, ran for the herb tea, and taking the tin cup in her hand followed her guest to the carriage, urging her to " take a swaller just to keep from vomiting."

" She is better without it," said Maggie. " She seldom takes medicine," and politely expressing her grati-

tude to Mrs. Douglas for her kindness she bade Mike
drive on.

"Some crazy critter just out of the asylum, I'll bet,"
said Mrs. Douglas, walking back to the house with her
pennyroyal tea. "How queer she acted! but that
girl's a lady, every inch of her, and so handsome too—
I wonder who she is?"

"Don't you believe the old woman felt a little above
us?" suggested Betsy Jane, who had more discernment than her mother.

"Like enough she did, though I never thought on't.
But she needn't. I'm as good as she is, and I'll warrant as much thought on, where I'm known;" and
quite satisfied with her own position, Mrs. Douglas
went back to her dish-washing, while Betsy Jane stole
away upstairs to try the experiment of arranging her
hair after the fashion in which Margaret wore hers.

In the meantime Mike, perfectly sobered, had
turned his horses' heads in the direction of Hillsdale,
when Madam Conway called out, "To Worcester,
Mike—to Worcester, as fast as you can drive."

"To Worcester! For what?" asked Maggie, and
the excited woman answered: "To stop it! To forbid the banns! I should think you'd ask for what!"

"To stop it," repeated Maggie. "I'd like to see
you stop it, when they've been married two months!"

"So they have! so they have!" said Madam Conway, wringing her hands in her despair, and crying
out that a Conway should be so disgraced. "What
shall I do? What shall I do?"

"Make the best of it, of course," answered Maggie. "I don't see that George is any worse for his
parentage. He is evidently greatly respected in Wor-

cester, where his family are undoubtedly known. He is educated and refined, if they are not. Theo loves him, and that is sufficient, unless I add that he has money."

"But not as much as I supposed," moaned Madam Conway. "Theo told me two hundred thousand dollars; but that woman said one. Oh, what will become of me! Give me the hartshorn, Maggie. I feel so faint!"

The hartshorn was handed her, but it could not quiet her distress. Her family pride was sorely wounded, and had Theo been dead she would hardly have felt worse than she did.

"How will she bear it when it comes to her knowledge, as it necessarily must? It will kill her, I know!" she exclaimed, after Maggie had exhausted all her powers of reasoning in vain; then, as she remembered the woman's avowed intention of visiting her daughter-in-law on the morrow, she felt that she must turn back; she must see Theo and break it to her gently, or the first sight of that odious creature, claiming her for a daughter, might be of incalculable injury.

"Stop, Mike," she was about to say; but ere the words passed her lips she reflected that to take Maggie back to Worcester was to throw her again in Henry Warner's way, and this she could not do. There was but one alternative. She could stop at the Charlton depot, not far distant, and wait for the downward train, while Mike drove Maggie home; and this she resolved to do. Mike was accordingly bidden to take her at once to the depot, which he did, while she explained to Maggie her reason for returning.

" Theo is much better alone, and George will not thank you for interfering," said Maggie, not at all pleased with her grandmother's proceedings.

But the old lady was determined. It was her duty, she said, to stand by Theo in trouble; and if a visit from that horrid creature wasn't trouble, she could not well define it.

" When will you come home? " asked Maggie.

" Not before to-morrow night. Now I have undertaken the matter, I intend to see it through," said Madam Conway, referring to the expected visit of Mrs. Douglas, senior.

But Mike did not thus understand it, and thinking her only object in turning back was to " see the doin's," as he designated the firemen's muster, he muttered long and loud about being thus sent home while his mistress went to see the fun.

In the meantime, on a hard settee, at the rather uncomfortable depot, Madam Conway awaited the arrival of the train, which came at last, and in a short time she found herself again in Worcester. Once in a carriage, and on her way to the " Bay State," she began to feel a little nervous, half wishing she had followed Maggie's advice, and left Theo alone. But it could not now be helped, and while trying to think what she should say to her astonished granddaughter she was set down at the door of the hotel, slightly bewildered and a good deal perplexed, a feeling which was by no means diminished when she learned that Mr. and Mrs. Douglas were both out of town.

" Where have they gone, and when will they return? " she gasped, untying her bonnet strings for easier respiration.

To these queries the clerk replied that he believed
Mr. Douglas had gone to Boston on business, that he
might be home that night; at all events, he would
probably return in the morning; she could find Mr.
Warner, who would tell her all about it. " Shall I
send for him? " he continued, as he saw the scowl
upon her face.

" Certainly not," she answered; and taking the key,
which had been left in his charge, she repaired to
Theo's rooms, and sinking into a large easy-chair
fanned herself furiously, wondering if they would return that night, and what they would say when they
found her there. " But I don't care," she continued,
speaking aloud and shaking her head very decidedly
at the excited woman whose image was reflected by
the mirror opposite, and who shook her head as de--
cidedly in return. " George Douglas has deceived us
shamefully, and I'll tell him so, too. I wish he'd come
this minute! "

But George Douglas knew well what he was doing.
Very gradually was he imparting to Theo a knowledge
of his parents, and Theo, who really loved her husband, was learning to prize him for himself, and not
for his family. Feeling certain that the firemen's muster would bring his mother to town, and knowing that
Theo was not yet prepared to see her, he was greatly
relieved at Madam Conway's sudden departure, and
had himself purposely left home, with the intention of
staying away until Friday night. This, however,
Madam Conway did not know, and very impatiently
she awaited his coming, until the lateness of the hour
precluded the possibility of his arrival, and she retired to bed, but not to sleep, for the city was full of

firemen, and one company, failing of finding lodgings
elsewhere, had taken refuge in an empty carriage-shop
near by.   The hard, bare floor was not the most comfortable bed imaginable, and preferring the bright
moonlight and open air they made the night hideous
with their noisy shouts, which the watchmen tried in
vain to hush.   To sleep in that neighborhood was impossible, and all night long Madam Conway vibrated
between her bed and the window, from which latter
point she frowned wrathfully down upon the red coats
below, who, scoffing alike at law and order as dis-
pensed by the police, kept up their noisy revel, shout-
ing lustily for " Chelsea, No. 4" and " Washington,
No. 2," until the dawn of day.

" I wish to mercy I'd gone home! " sighed Madam
Conway, as weak and faint she crept down to the
breakfast table, doing but little justice to anything, and
returning to her room pale, haggard, and weary.

Ere long, however, she became interested in watching the crowds of people who at an early hour filled
the streets; and when at last the different fire com-
panies of the State paraded the town, in a seemingly
never-ending procession, she forgot in a measure her
trouble, and drawing her chair to the window sat down
to enjoy the brilliant scene, involuntarily nodding her
head to the stirring music, as company after company
passed.   Up and down the street, far as the eye could
reach, the sidewalks were crowded with men, women,
and children, all eager to see the sight.   There were
people from the city and people from the country, the
latter of whom, having anticipated the day for weeks
and months, were now unquestionably enjoying it to
the last degree.

Conspicuous among these was a middle-aged woman, who elicited remarks from all who beheld her,
both from the peculiarity of her dress and the huge
blue cotton umbrella she persisted in hoisting, to the
great annoyance of those in whose faces it was thrust,
and who forgot in a measure their vexation when they
read the novel device it bore. Like many other people,
who can sympathize with the good woman, she was
always losing her umbrella, and at last, in self-defense,
had embroidered upon the blue in letters of white:

> " Steal me not, for fear of shame,
> For here you see my owner's name :
> " CHARITY DOUGLAS."

As the lettering was small and not very distinct, it
required a close observation to decipher it; but the
plan was a successful one, nevertheless, and for four
long years the blue umbrella had done good service to
its mistress, shielding her alike from sunshine and
from storm, and now in the crowded city it performed
a double part, preventing those standing near from
seeing, while at the same time it kept the dust from
settling on the thick green veil and leghorn bonnet of
its owner. At Betsy Jane's suggestion she wore a
hoop to-day on Theo's account, and that she was painfully conscious of the fact was proved by the many
anxious glances she cast at her chocolate-colored
muslin, through the thin folds of which it was plainly
visible.

" I wish I had left the pesky thing to hum," she
thought, feeling greatly relieved when at last, as the
crowd became greater, it was broken in several pieces
and ceased to do its duty.

From her seat near the window Madam Conway caught sight of the umbrella as it swayed up and down amid the multitude, but she had no suspicion that she who bore it thus aloft had even a better right than herself to sit where she was sitting. In her excitement she had forgotten Mrs. Douglas' intended visit, to prepare Theo for which she had returned to Worcester, but it came to her at length, when, as the last fire company passed, the blue umbrella was closed, and the leghorn bonnet turned in the direction of the hotel. There was no mistaking the broad, good-humored face which looked so eagerly up at " George's window," and involuntarily Madam Conway glanced under the bed with the view of fleeing thither for refuge!

"What shall I do?" she cried, as she heard the umbrella on the stairs. "I'll lock her out," she continued; and in an instant the key was in her pocket, while, trembling in every limb, she awaited the result.

Nearer and nearer the footsteps came; there was a knock upon the door, succeeded by a louder one, and then, as both these failed to elicit a response, the handle of the umbrella was vigorously applied. But all in vain, and Madam Conway heard the discomfited outsider say, " They told me Theodoshy's grandmarm was here, but I guess she's in the street. I'll come agin bime-by," and Mrs. Douglas, senior, walked disconsolately down the stairs, while Madam Conway thought it doubtful whether she gained access to the room that day, come as often as she might.

Not long after, the gong sounded for dinner, and unlocking the door Madam Conway was about descending to the dining room, when the thought burst upon her: "What if she should be at the table! It's just like her."

The very idea was overwhelming, taking from her at once all desire for dinner; and returning to her room she tried, by looking over the books and examining the carpet, to forget how hungry and faint she was. Whether she would have succeeded is doubtful, had not an hour or two later brought another knock from the umbrella, and driven all thoughts of eating from her mind. In grim silence she waited until her tormentor was gone, and then wondering if it was not time for the train she consulted her watch. But alas! 'twas only four; the cars did not leave until six; and so another weary hour went by. At the end of that time, however, thinking the depot preferable to being a prisoner there, she resolved to go; and leaving the key with the clerk, she called a carriage and was soon on her way to the cars.

As she approached the depot she observed an immense crowd of people gathered together, among which the red coats of the firemen were conspicuous. A fight was evidently in progress, and as the horses began to grow restive she begged of the driver to let her alight, saying she could easily walk the remainder of the way. Scarcely, however, was she on terra-firma when the yelling crowd made a precipitate rush towards her, and in much alarm she climbed for safety into an empty buggy, whereupon the horse, equally alarmed, began to rear, and without pausing an instant the terrified lady sprang out on the side opposite to that by which she had entered, catching her dress upon the seat, and tearing half the gathers from the waist.

"Heaven help me!" she cried, picking herself up, and beginning to wish she had never troubled herself with Theo's mother-in-law.

To reach the depot was now her great object, and, as the two belligerent parties occupied the front, she thought to effect an entrance at the rear. But the doors were locked, and as she turned the corner of the building she suddenly found herself in the thickest of the fight. To advance was impossible, to turn back equally so, and while meditating some means of escape she lost her footing and fell across a wheelbarrow which stood upon the platform, crumpling her bonnet, and scratching her face upon a nail which protruded from the vehicle. Nearer dead than alive, she made her way at last into the depot, and from thence into the cars, where, sinking into a seat, and drawing her shawl closely around her, the better to conceal the sad condition of her dress, she indulged in meditations not wholly complimentary to firemen in general and her late comrades in particular.

For half an hour she waited impatiently, but though the cars were filling rapidly there were no indications of starting; and it was almost seven ere the long and heavily loaded train moved slowly from the depot. About fifteen minutes previous to their departure, as Madam Conway was looking ruefully out upon the multitude, she was horrified at seeing directly beneath her window the veritable woman from whom, through the entire day, she had been hiding. Involuntarily she glanced at the vacant seat in front of her, which, as she feared, was soon occupied by Mrs. Douglas and her companion, who, as Madam Conway divined, was "Sam Babbit's wife."

Trembling nervously lest she should be discovered, she drew her veil closely over her face, keeping very quiet, and looking intently from the window into the gathering darkness without. But her fears were groundless, for Mrs. Douglas had no suspicion that the crumpled bonnet and sorry figure, sitting so disconsolately in the corner, was the same which but the day before had honored her with a call. She was in high spirits, having had, as she informed her neighbor, "a tip-top time." On one point, however, she was disappointed. She meant as much as could be to have seen "Theodoshy," but she "wan't to hum." "Her grandmarm was in town," said she, "but if she was in the room she must have been asleep, or dreadful deaf, for I pounded with all my might. I'm sorry, for I'd like to scrape acquaintance with her, bein' we're connected."

An audible groan came from beneath the thick brown veil, whereupon both ladies turned their heads. But the indignant woman made no sign; and, in a whisper loud enough for Madam Conway to hear, Mrs. Douglas said, "Some Irish critter in liquor, I presume. Look at her jammed bonnet."

This remark drew from Mrs. Babbit a very close inspection of the veiled figure, who, smothering her wrath, felt greatly relieved when the train started and prevented her from hearing anything more. At the next station, however, Mrs. Douglas showed her companion a crochet collar, which she had purchased for two shillings, and which, she said, was almost exactly like the one worn by the woman who stopped at her house the day before.

Leaning forward, Madam Conway glanced con-

temptuously at the coarse knit thing, which bore about
the same resemblance to her own handsome collar as
cambric does to satin.

"Vulgar, ignorant creatures!" she muttered, while
Mrs. Babbit, after duly praising the collar, proceeded
to make some inquiries concerning the strange lady
who had shared Mrs. Douglas' hospitality.

"I've no idee who she was," said Mrs. Douglas;
"but I think it's purty likely she was some crazy critter they was takin' to the hospital."

Another groan from beneath the brown veil, and
turning around the kind-hearted Mrs. Douglas asked
if she was sick, adding in an aside, as there came no
answer, "Been fightin', I'll warrant!"

Fortunately for Madam Conway, the cars moved on,
and when they stopped again, to her great relief, the
owner of the blue umbrella, together with "Sam Babbit's wife," alighted, and amid the crowd assembled
on the platform she recognized Betsy Jane, who had
come down to meet her mother. The remainder of the
way seemed tedious enough, for the train moved but
slowly, and it was near ten o'clock ere they reached
the Hillsdale station, where, to her great delight,
Madam Conway found Margaret awaiting her, together with Arthur Carrollton. The moment she saw
the former, who came eagerly forward to meet her,
the weary, worn-out woman burst into tears; but at
the sight of Mr. Carrollton she forced them back, saying, in reply to Maggie's inquiries, that Theo was not
at home, and that she had spent a dreadful day, and
been knocked down in a fight at the depot, in proof of
which she pointed to her torn dress, her crumpled
bonnet, and scratched face. Maggie laughed aloud

in spite of herself, and though Mr. Carrollton's eyes were several times turned reprovingly upon her she continued to laugh at intervals at the sorry, forlorn appearance presented by her grandmother, who for several days was confined to her bed from the combined effects of fasting, fright, firemen's muster, and her late encounter with Mrs. Douglas, senior!

CHAPTER XV.

ARTHUR CARROLLTON AND MAGGIE.

MR. CARROLLTON had returned from Boston on Thursday afternoon, and, finding them all gone from the hotel, had come on to Hillsdale on the evening train, surprising Maggie as she sat in the parlor alone, wishing herself in Worcester, or in some place where it was not as lonely as there. With his presence the loneliness disappeared, and in making his tea and listening to his agreeable conversation she forgot everything, until, observing that she looked weary, he said: " Maggie, I would willingly talk to you all night, were it not for the bad effect it would have on you to-morrow. You must go to bed now," and he showed her his watch, which pointed to the hour of midnight.

Exceedingly mortified, Maggie was leaving the room, when, noticing her evident chagrin, Mr. Carrollton came to her side, and laying his hand very respectfully on hers, said kindly: " It is my fault, Maggie, keeping you up so late, and I only send you away now because those eyes are growing heavy, and I know that you need rest. Good-night to you, and pleasant dreams."

He went with her to the door, watching her until she disappeared up the stairs; then, half wishing he had not sent her from him, he too sought his chamber; but not to sleep, for Maggie, though absent, was with him still in fancy. For more than a year he had been haunted by a bright, sunshiny face, whose owner embodied the dashing, independent spirit and softer qualities which made Maggie Miller so attractive. Of this face he had often thought, wondering if the real would equal the ideal, and now that he had met with her, had looked into her truthful eyes, had gazed upon her sunny face, which mirrored faithfully every thought and feeling, he was more than satisfied, and to love that beautiful girl seemed to him an easy matter. She was so childlike, so artless, so different from anyone whom he had ever known, that he was interested in her at once. But Arthur Carrollton never did a thing precipitately. She might have many glaring faults; he must see her more, must know her better, ere he lavished upon her the love whose deep fountains had never yet been stirred.

After this manner he reasoned as he walked up and down his chamber, while Maggie, on he sleepless pillow, was thinking, too, of him, wondering if she did hate him as much as she intended, and if Henry would be offended at her sitting up with him until after twelve o'clock.

It was nearly half-past nine when Maggie awoke next morning, and making a hasty toilet she descended to the dining room, where she found Mr. Carrollton awaiting her. He had been up a long time; but when Anna Jeffrey, blessed with an uncommon appetite, fretted at the delay of breakfast, and suggested calling Margaret, he objected, saying she needed rest, and must not be disturbed. So, in something of a pet, the young lady breakfasted alone with her aunt, Mr. Carrollton preferring to wait for Maggie.

"I am sorry I kept you waiting," said Maggie, seating herself at the table and continuing to apologize for her tardiness.

But Mr. Carrollton felt more than repaid by having her thus alone with him, and many were the admiring glances he cast toward her, as, with her shining hair, her happy face, her tasteful morning gown of pink, and her beautiful white hands which handled so gracefully the silver coffee-urn, she made a living, glowing picture such as any man might delight to look upon. Breakfast being over, Mr. Carrollton proposed a ride, and as Anna Jeffrey at that moment entered the parlor he invited her to accompany them. There was a shadow on Maggie's brow as she left the room to dress, a shadow which had not wholly disappeared when she returned; and, observing this, Mr. Carrollton said, " Were I to consult my own wishes, Maggie, I should leave Miss Jeffrey at home; but she is a poor girl whose enjoyments are far less than ours, consequently I invited her for this once, knowing how fond she is of riding."

" How thoughtful you are of other people's happiness ! " said Maggie, the shadow leaving her brow at once.

" I am glad that wrinkle has gone, at all events," returned Mr. Carrollton laughingly, and laying his hand upon her forehead he continued: " Were you my sister Helen I should probably kiss you for having so soon got over your pet; but as you are Maggie Miller, I dare not," and he looked earnestly at her, to see if he had spoken the truth.

Coloring crimson, as it became the affianced bride of Henry Warner to do, Maggie turned away, thinking Helen must be a happy girl, and half wishing she too were Arthur Carrollton's sister. It was a long, delightful excursion they took, and Maggie, when she saw how Anna Jeffrey enjoyed it, did not altogether regret her presence. On their way home she proposed calling upon Hagar, whom she had not seen for " three whole days."

"And who, pray, is Hagar?" asked Mr. Carrollton; and Maggie replied, " She is my old nurse—a strange, crazy creature, whom they say I somewhat resemble."

By this time they were near the cottage, in the door of which old Hagar was standing, with her white hair falling round her face.

" I see by your looks you don't care to call, but I shall," said Maggie; and, bounding from her saddle, she ran up to Hagar, pressing her hand and whispering that it would soon be time to hear from Henry.

" Kissed her, I do believe!" said Anna Jeffrey. " She must have admirable taste!"

Mr. Carrollton said nothing, but with · a halfcomical, half-displeased expression he watched the interview between that weird old woman and the fair young girl, little suspecting how nearly they were allied.

"Why didn't you come and speak to her?" said Maggie, as he alighted to assist her in again mounting Gritty. "She used to see you in England, when you were a baby, and if you won't be angry I'll tell you what she said. It was that you were the crossest, ugliest young one she ever saw! There, there; don't set me down so hard!" and the saucy eyes looked mischievously at the proud Englishman, who, truth to say, did place her in the saddle with a little more force than was at all necessary.

Not that he was angry. He was only annoyed at
what he considered Maggie's undue familiarity with
a person like Hagar, but he wisely forbore making any
comments in Anna Jeffrey's presence, except, indeed,
to laugh heartily at Hagar's complimentary description
of himself when a baby. Arrived at home, and alone
again with Maggie, he found her so very good-natured
and agreeable that he could not chide her for anything, and Hagar was for a time forgotten.

That evening, as the reader knows, they went together to the depot, where they waited four long
hours, but not impatiently; for sitting there in the
moonlight, with the winding Chicopee full in view,
and Margaret Miller at his side, Arthur Carrollton
forgot the lapse of time, especially when Maggie,
thinking it no harm, gave a most ludicrous description
of her call upon Mrs. Douglas, senior, and of her
grandmother's distress at finding herself so nearly connected with what she termed "a low, vulgar family."

Arthur Carrollton was very proud, and had Theo
been his sister he might to some extent have shared in
Madam Conway's chagrin; and so he said to Maggie,
at the same time fully agreeing with her that George
Douglas was a refined, agreeable man, and as such
entitled to respect. Still, had Theo known of his
parentage, he said, it would probably have made some
difference; but now that it could not be helped it was
wise to make the best of it.

These words were little heeded then by Maggie, but
with most painful distinctness they recurred to her in
the after time, when, humbled in the very dust, she
had no hope that the highborn, haughty Carrollton
would stoop to a child of Hagar Warren! But no

sh.dow of the dark future was over her now, and very eagerly she drank in every word and look of Arthur Carrollton, who, all unconsciously, was trampling on another's rights and gradually weakening the fancied love she bore for Henry Warner.

The arrival of the train brought their pleasant conversation to a close, and for a day or two Maggie's time was wholly occupied with her grandmother, to whom she frankly acknowledged having told Mr. Carrollton of Mrs. Douglas and her daughter Betsy Jane. The fact that he knew of her disgrace and did not despise her was of great benefit to Madam Conway, and after a few days she resumed her usual spirits, and actually told of the remarks made by Mrs. Douglas concerning herself and the " fight " she had been in! As time passed on she became reconciled to the Douglases, having, as she thought, some well-founded reasons for believing that for Theo's disgrace Maggie would make amends by marrying Mr. Carrollton, whose attentions each day became more and more marked, and were not apparently altogether disagreeable to Maggie. On the contrary, his presence at Hillsdale was productive of much pleasure to her, as well as a little annoyance.

From the first he seemed to exercise over her an influence she could not well resist—a power to make her do whatever he willed that she should do; and though she sometimes rebelled she was pretty sure in the end to yield the contest, and submit to one who was evidently the ruling spirit. As yet nothing had been said of the hair ornament which, out of compliment to him, her grandmother wore every morning in her collar, but at last one day Madam Conway

spoke of it herself, asking if it were, as she had supposed, his grandmother's hair.

"Why, no," he answered involuntarily; "it is a
lock Maggie sent me in that wonderful daguerreotype!"

"The stupid thing!" thought Maggie, while her eyes
fairly danced with merriment as she anticipated the
question she fancied was sure to follow, but did not.

One glance at her tell-tale face was sufficient for
Madam Conway. In her whole household there was
but one head with locks as white as that, and whatever
her thoughts might have been, she said nothing, but
from that day forth Hagar's hair was never again seen
ornamenting her person! That afternoon Mr. Carrollton and Maggie went out to ride, and in the course
of their conversation he referred to the pin, asking
whose hair it was, and seeming much amused when
told that it was Hagar's.

"But why did you not tell her when it first came?"
he said; and Maggie answered: "Oh, it was such fun
to see her sporting Hagar's hair, when she is so proud!
It didn't hurt her either, for Hagar is as good as anybody. I don't believe in making such a difference because one person chances to be richer than another."

"Neither do I," returned Mr. Carrollton. "I
would not esteem a person for wealth alone, but there
are points of difference which should receive consideration. For instance, this old Hagar may be well
enough in her way, but suppose she were nearly connected with you—your grandmother, if you like—it
would certainly make some difference in your po-
sitiou. You would not be Maggie Miller, and I——"

"Wouldn't ride with me, I dare say," interrupted

Maggie; to which he replied, " I presume not," adding, as he saw slight indications of pouting, "And
therefore I am glad you are Maggie Miller, and not
Hagar's grandchild."

Mentally pronouncing him a " proud, hateful thing,"
Maggie rode on a while in silence. But Mr. Carrollton knew well how to manage her, and he too was
silent until Maggie, who could never refrain from
talking any length of time, forgot herself and began
chatting away as gayly as before. During their excursion they came near to the gorge of Henry Warner
memory, and Maggie, who had never quite forgiven
Mr. Carrollton for criticising her horsemanship, resolved to show him what she could do. The signal
was accordingly given to Gritty, and ere her companion was aware of her intention she was tearing
over the ground at a speed he could hardly equal.
The ravine was just on the border of the wood, and
without pausing for an instant Gritty leaped across
it, landing safely on the other side, where he stopped,
while half fearfully, half exultingly, Maggie looked
back to see what Mr. Carrollton would do. At first
he fancied Gritty beyond her control, and when he
saw her directly over the deep chasm he shuddered,
involuntarily stretching out his arms to save her; but
the look she gave him as she turned around convinced
him that the risk she had run was done on purpose.
Still he had no intention of following her, for he
feared his horse's ability as well as his own to clear
that pass.

" Why don't you jump? Are you afraid?" and
Maggie's eyes looked archly out from beneath her
tasteful riding cap.

For half a moment he felt tempted to join her, but his better judgment came to his aid, and he answered: " Yes, Maggie, I am afraid, having never tried such an experiment. But I wish to be with you in some way, and as I cannot come to you I ask you to come to me. You seem accustomed to the leap!"

He did not praise her. Nay, she fancied there was more of censure in the tones of his voice; at all events, he had asked her rather commandingly to return, and she "wouldn't do it." For a moment she made no reply, and he said again, " Maggie, will you come?" then half playfully, half reproachfully, she made answer, " A gallant Englishman indeed! willing I should risk my neck where you dare not venture yours. No, I shan't try the leap again to-day, I don't feel like it; but I'll cross the long bridge half a mile from here— good-by;" and fully expecting him to meet her, she galloped off, riding ere long quite slowly, " so he'd have a nice long time to wait for her!"

How, then, was she disappointed, when, on reaching the bridge, there was nowhere a trace of him to be seen, neither could she hear the sound of his horse's footsteps, though she listened long and anxiously!

" He is certainly the most provoking man I ever saw!" she exclaimed, half crying with vexation. " Henry wouldn't have served me so, and I'm glad I was engaged to him before I saw this hateful Carrollton, for grandma might possibly have coaxed me into marrying him, and then wouldn't Mr. Dog and Mrs. Cat have led a stormy life! No, we wouldn't," she continued; " I should in time get accustomed to minding him, and then I think he'd be splendid, though no better than Henry. I wonder if Hagar has a letter

for me!" and, chirruping to Gritty, she soon stood at
the door of the cabin.

"Have you two been quarreling?" asked Hagar,
noticing Maggie's flushed cheeks. "Mr. Carrollton
passed here twenty minutes or more ago, looking
mighty sober, and here you are with your face as
red—— What has happened?"

"Nothing," answered Maggie, a little testily, "only
he's the meanest man! Wouldn't follow me when I
leaped the gorge, and I know he could if he had
tried."

"Showed his good sense," interrupted Hagar, adding that Maggie mustn't think every man was going
to risk his neck for her.

"I don't think so, of course," returned Maggie;
"but he might act better—almost commanded me to
come back and join him, as though I was a little child;
but I wouldn't do it. I told him I'd go down to the
long bridge and cross, expecting, of course, he'd meet
me there; and instead of that he has gone off home.
How did he know what accident would befall me?"

"Accident!" repeated Hagar; "accident befall you,
who know every crook and turn of these woods so
much better than he does!"

"Well, anyway, he might have waited for me," returned Maggie. "I don't believe he'd care if I were
to get killed. I mean to scare him and see;" and,
springing from Gritty's back, she gave a peculiar
whistling sound, at which the pony bounded away towards home, while she followed Hagar into the cottage, where a letter from Henry awaited her.

They were to sail for Cuba on the 15th of October,
and he now wrote asking if Maggie would go without

her grandmother's consent. But, though irresolute when he before broached the subject, Maggie was decided now. She would not run away; and so she said to Hagar, to whom she confided the whole affair.

"I do not think it would be right to elope," she said. "In three years more I shall be twenty-one, and free to do as I like; and if grandma will not let me marry Henry now, he must wait. I can't run away. Rose would not approve of it, I'm sure, and I almost know Mr. Carrollton would not."

"I can't see how his approving or not approving can affect you," said Hagar; then bending down, so that her wild eyes looked full in Maggie's eyes, she said, "Are you beginning to like this Englishman?"

"Why, no, I guess I aint," answered Maggie, coloring slightly. "I dislike him dreadfully, he's so proud. Why, he did the same as to say that if I were your grandchild he would not ride with me!"

"My grandchild, Maggie Miller!—my grandchild!" shrieked Hagar. "What put that into his head?"

Thinking her emotion caused by anger at Arthur Carrollton, Maggie mentally chided herself for having inadvertently said what she did, while at the same time she tried to soothe old Hagar, who rocked to and fro, as was her custom when her "crazy spells" were on. Growing a little more composed, she said at last, "Marry Henry Warner, by all means, Maggie; he aint as proud as Carrollton—he would not care as much if he knew it."

"Knew what?" asked Maggie; and, remembering herself in time, Hagar answered adroitly: "Knew of your promise to let me live with you. You remem-

ber it, don't you?" and she looked wistfully towards
Maggie, who, far more intent upon something else,
answered: "Yes, I remember. But hußh! don't I
hear horses' feet coming rapidly through the woods?"
and, running to the window, she saw Mr. Carrollton
mounted upon Gritty, and riding furiously towards the
house.

"You go out, Hagar, and see if he is looking for
me," whispered Maggie, stepping back, so he could not
see.

"Henry Warner must snare the bird quick, or he
will lose it," muttered Hagar, as she walked to the
door, where, evidently much excited, Mr. Carrollton
asked if she knew aught of Miss Miller, and why
Gritty had come home alone. "It is such an unusual
occurrence," said he, "that we felt alarmed, and I have
come in quest of her."

From her post near the window Maggie could
plainly see his face, which was very pale, and expressive of much concern, while his voice, she fancied,
trembled as he spoke her name.

"He does care," she thought; woman's pride was
satisfied, and ere Hagar could reply she ran out, saying
laughingly: "And so you thought maybe I was killed,
but I'm not. I concluded to walk home and let Gritty
go on in advance. I did not mean to frighten
grandma."

"She was not as much alarmed as myself," said Mr.
Carrollton, the troubled expression of his countenance
changing at once. "You do not know how anxious
I was when I saw Gritty come riderless to the door,
nor yet how relieved I am in finding you thus un-
harmed."

Maggie knew she did not deserve this, and blushing like a guilty child she offered no resistance when he lifted her into the saddle gently—tenderly—as if she had indeed escaped from some great danger.

"It is time you were home," said he, and throwing the bridle across his arm he rested his hand upon the saddle and walked slowly by her side.

All his fancied coldness was forgotten; neither was the leap nor yet the bridge once mentioned, for he was only too happy in having her back alive, while she was doubting the propriety of an experiment which, in the turn matters had taken, seemed to involve deception. Observing at last that he occasionally pressed his hand upon his side, she asked the cause, and was told that he had formerly been subject to a pain in his side, which excitement or fright greatly augmented. "I hoped I was free from it," he said, "but the sight of Gritty dashing up to the door without you brought on a slight attack; for I knew if you were harmed the fault was mine for having rather unceremoniously deserted you."

This was more than Maggie could endure in silence. The frank ingenuousness of her nature prevailed, and turning towards him her dark, beautiful eyes, in which tears were shining, she said: "Forgive me, Mr. Carrollton. I sent Gritty home on purpose to see if you would be annoyed, for I felt vexed because you would not humor my whim and meet me at the bridge. I am sorry I caused you any uneasiness," she continued, as she saw a shadow flit over his face. "Will you forgive me?"

Arthur Carrollton could not resist the pleading of those lustrous eyes, nor yet refuse to take the ungloved

hand she offered him; and if, in token of reconcilia-
tion, he did press it a little more fervently than Henry
Warner would have thought at all necessary, he only
did what, under the circumstances, it was very natural
he should do. From the first Maggie Miller had been
a puzzle to Arthur Carrollton; but he was fast learning to read her—was beginning to understand how
perfectly artless she was—and this little incident in·
creased, rather than diminished, his admiration.

" I will forgive you, Maggie," he said, " on one con·
dition. You must promise never again to experiment
with my feelings in a similar manner."

The promise was readily given, and then they pro·
ceeded on as leisurely as if at home there was no anxious grandmother vibrating between her high-backed
chair and the piazza, nor yet an Anna Jeffrey watching them enviously as they came slowly up the road.

That night there came to Mr. Carrollton a letter
from Montreal, saying his immediate presence was
necessary there, on a business matter of some impor-
tance; and he accordingly decided to go on the morrow.

" When may we expect you back? " asked Madam
Conway, as in the morning he was preparing for his
journey.

" It will, perhaps, be two months at least, before I
return," said he, adding that there was a possibility
of his being obliged to go immediately to England.

In the recess of the window Maggie was standing,
thinking how lonely the house would be without him,
and wishing there was no such thing as parting from
those she liked—even as little as she did Arthur Carrollton.

"I won't let him know that I care, though," she thought, and forcing a smile to her face she was about turning to bid him good-by, when she heard him tell her grandmother of the possibility there was that he would be obliged to go directly to England from Montreal.

"Then I may never see him again," she thought; and the tears burst forth involuntarily at the idea of parting with him forever.

Faster and faster they came, until at last, fearing lest he should see them, she ran away upstairs, and, mounting to the roof, sat down behind the chimney, where, herself unobserved, she could watch him far up the road. From the half-closed door of her chamber Anna Jeffrey had seen Maggie stealing up the tower stairs; had seen, too, that she was weeping, and, suspecting the cause, she went quietly down to the parlor to hear what Arthur Carrollton would say. The carriage was waiting, his trunk was in its place, his hat was in his hand; to Madam Conway he said good-by, to Anna Jeffrey too; and still he lingered, looking wistfully round in quest of something which evidently was not there.

"Where's Margaret?" he asked at last, and Madam Conway answered: "Surely, where can she be? Have you seen her, Anna?"

"I saw her on the stairs some time ago," said Anna, adding that possibly she had gone to see Hagar, as she usually visited her at this hour.

A shade of disappointment passed over Mr. Carrollton's face as he replied, "Tell her I am sorry she thinks more of Hagar than of me."

The next moment he was gone, and leaning against

the chimney Maggie watched with tearful eyes the carriage as it wound up the grassy road. On the brow of the hill, just before it would disappear from sight, it suddenly stopped. Something was the matter with the harness, and while John was busy adjusting it Mr. Carrollton leaned from the window, and, looking back, started involuntarily as he caught sight of the figure so clearly defined upon the housetop. A slight suspicion of the truth came upon him, and kissing his hand he waved it gracefully towards her. Maggie's handkerchief was wet with tears, but she shook it out in the morning breeze, and sent to Arthur Carrollton, as she thought, her last good-by.

Fearing lest her grandmother should see her swollen eyes, she stole down the stairs, and taking her shawl and bonnet from the table in the hall ran off into the woods, going to a pleasant, mossy bank not far from Hagar's cottage, where she had more than once sat with Arthur Carrollton, and where she fancied she would never sit with him again.

" I don't believe it's for him that I am crying," she thought, as she tried in vain to stay her tears; " I always intended to hate him, and I almost know I do; I'm only feeling badly because I won't run away, and Henry and Rose will go without me so soon!" And fully satisfied at having discovered the real cause of her grief, she laid her head upon the bright autumn grass and wept bitterly, holding her breath, and listening intently as she heard in the distance the sound of the engine which was bearing Mr. Carrollton away.

It did not occur to her that he could not yet have reached the depot, and as she knew nothing of a change in the time of the trains she was taken wholly

by surprise when, fifteen minutes later, a manly form
bent over her, as she lay upon the bank, and a voice,
earnest and thrilling in tones, murmured softly,
" Maggie, are those tears for me? "

When about halfway to the station Mr. Carrollton
had heard of the change of time, and knowing he
should not be in season had turned back with the intention of waiting for the next train, which would pass
in a few hours. Learning that Maggie was in the
woods, he had started in quest of her, going naturally
to the mossy bank, where, as we have seen, he found
her weeping on the grass. She was weeping for him
—he was sure of that. He was not indifferent to her,
as he had sometimes feared, and for an instant he felt
tempted to take her in his arms and tell her how dear
she was to him.

" I will speak to her first," he thought, and so he
asked if the tears were for him.

Inexpressibly astonished and mortified at having
him see her thus, Maggie started to her feet, while
angry words at being thus intruded upon trembled on
her lips. But winding his arm around her, Mr. Carrollton drew her to his side, explaining to her in a few
words how he came to be there, and continuing: " I
do not regret the delay, if by its means I have discovered what I very much wish to know. Maggie, do
you care for me? Were you weeping because I had
left you? "

He drew her very closely to him—looking anxiously
into her face, which she covered with her hands. She
knew he was in earnest, and the knowledge that he
loved her thrilled her for an instant with indescribable
happiness. A moment, however, and thoughts of her

engagement with another flashed upon her. " She must not sit there thus with Arthur Carrollton—she would be true to Henry," and with mingled feelings of sorrow, regret, and anger—though why she should experience either she did not then understand—she drew herself from him; and when he said again: "Will Maggie answer? Are those tears for me?" she replied petulantly: " No; can't a body cry without being bothered for a reason? I came down here to be alone! "

" I did not mean to intrude, and I beg your pardon for having done so," said Mr. Carrollton sadly, adding, as Maggie made no reply: " I expected a different answer, Maggie. I almost hoped you liked me, and I believe now that you do."

In Maggie's bosom there was a fierce struggle of feeling. She did like Arthur Carrollton—and she thought she liked Henry Warner—at all events she was engaged to him, and half angry at the former for having disturbed her, and still more angry at herself for being thus disturbed, she exclaimed, as he again placed his arm around her: " Leave me alone, Mr. Carrollton. I don't like you. I don't like anybody! " and gathering up her shawl, which lay upon the grass, she ran away to Hagar's cabin, hoping he would follow her. But he did not. It was his first attempt at love-making, and very much disheartened he walked slowly back to the house; and while Maggie, from Hagar's door, was looking to see if he were coming, he, from the parlor window, was watching, too, for her, with a shadow on his brow and a load upon his heart. Madam Conway knew that something was wrong, but it was in vain that she sought an explanation. Mr. Carrollton kept his own secret; and consoling herself with his volunteered assurance that in case it became necessary for him to return to England he should, before embarking, visit Hillsdale, she bade him a second adieu.

In the meantime Maggie, having given up all hopes of again seeing Mr. Carrollton, was waiting impatiently the coming of Hagar, who was absent, having, as Maggie readily conjectured, gone to Richland. It was long past noon when she returned, and by that time the stains had disappeared from Maggie's face, which looked nearly as bright as ever. Still, it was with far less eagerness than usual that she took from Hagar's hand the expected letter from Henry. It was a long, affectionate epistle, urging her once more to accompany him, and saying if she still refused she must let him know immediately, as they were intending to start for New York in a few days.

" I can't go," said Maggie; " it would not be right." And going to the time-worn desk, where, since her secret correspondence, she had kept materials for writing, she wrote to Henry a letter telling him she felt badly to disappoint him, but she deemed it much wiser to defer their marriage until her grandmother felt differently, or at least until she was at an age to act for herself. This being done, she went slowly back to the house, which to her seemed desolate indeed. Her grandmother saw readily that something was the matter, and, rightly guessing the cause, she forebore questioning her, neither did she once that day mention Mr. Carrollton, although Anna Jeffrey did, telling her what he had said about her thinking more of Hagar than of himself, and giving as her opinion that he was much displeased with Maggie for her rudeness in running away.

" Nobody cares for his displeasure," answered Maggie, greatly vexed at Anna, who took especial delight in annoying her.

Thus a week went by, when one evening, as Madam Conway and Maggie sat together in the parlor, they were surprised by the sudden appearance of Henry Warner. He had accompanied his aunt and sister to New York, where they were to remain for a few days, and then impelled by a strong desire to see Margaret once more he had come with the vain hope that at the last hour she would consent to fly with him, or her grandmother consent to give her up. All the afternoon he had been at Hagar's cottage waiting for Maggie, and at length determining to see her he had ventured to the house. With a scowling frown Madam Conway looked at him through her glasses, while Maggie, half joyfully, half fearfully, went forward to meet him. In a few words he explained why he was there, and then again asked of Madam Conway if Margaret could go.

" I do not believe she cares to go," thought Madam Conway, as she glanced at Maggie's face; but she did not say so, lest she should awaken within the young girl a feeling of opposition.

She had watched Maggie closely, and felt sure that her affection for Henry Warner was neither deep nor lasting. Arthur Carrollton's presence had done much towards weakening it, and a few months more would suffice to wear it away entirely. Still, from what had passed, she fancied that opposition alone would only make the matter worse by rousing Maggie at once. She knew far more of human nature than either of the young people before her; and after a little reflection she suggested that Henry should leave Maggie with her for a year, during which time no communication whatever should pass between them, while she would promise faithfully not to influence Margaret either way.

"If at the end of the year," said she, "you both retain for each other the feelings you have now, I will no longer object to the marriage, but will make the best of it."

At first Henry spurned the proposition, and when he saw that Margaret thought well of it he reproached her with a want of feeling, saying she did not love him as she had once done.

"I shall not forget you, Henry," said Maggie, coming to his side and taking his hand in hers, "neither will you forget me; and when the year has passed away, only think how much pleasanter it will be for us to be married here at home, with grandma's blessing on our union!"

"If I only knew you would prove true!" said Henry, who missed something in Maggie's manner.

"I do mean to prove true," she answered sadly, though at that moment another face, another form, stood between her and Henry Warner, who, knowing that Madam Conway would not suffer her to go with him on any terms, concluded at last to make a virtue of necessity, and accordingly expressed his willingness to wait, provided Margaret were allowed to write occasionally either to himself or Rose.

But to this Madam Conway would not consent. She wished the test to be perfect, she said, and unless he accepted her terms he must give Maggie up, at once and forever.

As there seemed no alternative, Henry rather ungraciously yielded the point, promising to leave Maggie free for a year, while she too promised not to write either to him or to Rose, except with her grandmother's consent. Maggie Miller's word once passed, Madam Conway knew it would not be broken, and she unhesitatingly left the young people together while they said their parting words. A message of love from Maggie to Rose—a hundred protestations of eternal fidelity, and then they parted; Henry, sad and disappointed, slowly wending his way back to the spot where Hagar impatiently awaited his coming, while Maggie, leaning from her chamber window, and listening to the sound of his retreating footsteps, brushed away a tear, wondering the while why it was that she felt so relieved.

CHAPTER XVI.

PERPLEXITY.

HALF in sorrow, half in joy, old Hagar listened to the story which Henry told her, standing at her cottage door. In sorrow because she had learned to like the young man, learned to think of him as Maggie's husband, who would not wholly cast her off, if her secret should chance to be divulged; and in joy because her idol would be with her yet a little longer.

" Maggie will be faithful quite as long as you," she said, when he expressed his fears of her forgetfulness; and, trying to console himself with this assurance, he sprang into the carriage in which he had come, and was driven rapidly away.

He was too late for the night express, but taking the early morning train he reached New York just as the sun was setting.

" Alone! my brother, alone? " queried Rose, as he entered the private parlor of the hotel where she was staying with her aunt.

" Yes, alone; just as I expected," he answered somewhat bitterly.

Then very briefly he related to her the particulars of his adventure, to which she listened eagerly, one moment chiding herself for the faint, shadowy hope which whispered that possibly Maggie Miller would never be his wife, and again sympathizing in his disappointment.

"A year will not be very long," she said, "and in the new scenes to which you are going it will pass rapidly away;" and then, in her childlike, guileless manner, she drew a glowing picture of the future, when, her own health restored, they would return to their old home in Leominster, where, after a few months more, he would bring to them his bride.

"You are my comforting angel, Rose," he said, folding her lovingly in his arms and kissing her smooth white cheek. "With such a treasure as you for a sister, I ought not to repine, even though Maggie Miller should never be mine."

The words were lightly spoken, and by him soon forgotten, but Rose remembered them long, dwelling upon them in the wearisome nights, when in her narrow berth she listened to the swelling sea as it dashed against the vessel's side. Many a fond remembrance, too, she gave to Maggie Miller, who, in her woodland home, thought often of the travelers on the sea, never wishing that she was with them; but experiencing always a feeling of pleasure in knowing that she was Maggie Miller yet, and should be until next year's autumn leaves were falling.

Of Arthur Carrollton she thought frequently, wishing she had not been so rude that morning in the woods, and feeling vexed because in his letters to her grandmother he merely said, "Remember me to Margaret."

"I wish he would write something besides that," she thought, "for I remember him now altogether too much for my own good;" and then she wondered what he would have said that morning, if she had not been so cross.

Very little was said to her of him by Madam Conway, who, having learned that he was not going to
England, and would ere long return to them, concluded for a time to let the matter rest, particularly as
she knew how much Maggie was already interested
in one whom she had resolved to hate.   Feeling thus
confident that all would yet end well, Madam Conway
was in unusually good spirits save when thoughts of
Mrs. Douglas, senior, obtruded themselves upon her.
Then, indeed, in a most unenviable state of mind, she
repined at the disgrace which Theo had brought upon
them, and charged Maggie repeatedly to keep it a secret from Mrs. Jeffrey and Anna, the first of whom
made many inquiries concerning the family, which she
supposed of course was very aristocratic.

One day towards the last of November there came
to Madam Conway a letter from Mrs. Douglas, senior,
wonderful alike in composition and appearance. Directed wrong side up, sealed with a wafer, and
stamped with a thimble, it bore an unmistakable resemblance to its writer, who expressed many regrets
that she had not known "in the time on't" who her
illustrious visitors were.

"If I had known [she wrote] I should have sot the
table in the parlor certing, for though I'm plain and
homespun I know as well as the next one what good
manners is, and do my endeavors to practice it. But
do tell a body [she continued] where you was muster
day in Wooster. I knocked and pounded enough to
raise the dead, and nobody answered. I never noticed you was deaf when you was here, though Betsy
Jane thinks she did. If you be, I'll send you up a

receipt for a kind of intment which Miss Sam Babbit invented, and which cures everything.

" Theodoshy has been to see us, and though in my way of thinkin' she aint as handsome as Margaret, she looks as well as the ginerality of women. I liked her, too, and as soon as the men's winter clothes is off my hands I calkerlate to have a quiltin', and finish up another bed quilt to send her, for, man-like, George has furnished up his rooms with all sorts of nicknacks, and got only two blankets, and two Marsales spreads for his bed. So I've sent 'em down the herrin'-bone and risin'-sun quilts for everyday wear, as I don't believe in usin' your best things all the time. My old man says I'd better let 'em alone; but he's got some queer ideas, thinks you'll sniff your nose at my letter, and all that, but I've more charity for folks, and well I might have, bein' that's my name.

" CHARITY DOUGLAS."

To this letter were appended three different postscripts. In the first Madam Conway and Maggie were cordially invited to visit Charlton again; in the second Betsy Jane sent her regrets; while in the third Madam Conway was particularly requested to excuse haste and a bad pen.

" Disgusting creature! " was Madam Conway's exclamation as she finished the letter, then tossing it into the fire without a passing thought, she took up another one, which had come by the same mail, and was from Theo herself.

After dwelling at length upon the numerous calls she made, the parties she attended, the compliments she received, and her curiosity to know why her grand-

mother came back that day, she spoke of her recent
visit in Charlton.

"You have been there, it seems [she wrote], so I
need not particularize, though I know how shocked
and disappointed you must have been; and I think it
was kind in you to say nothing upon the subject except that you had called there, for George reads all my
letters, and I would not have his feelings hurt. He
had prepared me in a measure for the visit, but the
reality was even worse than I anticipated. And still
they are the kindest-hearted people in the world, while
Mr. Douglas is a man, they say, of excellent sense.
George never lived at home much, and their heathenish
ways mortify him, I know, though he never says a
word except that they are his parents.

"People here respect George, too, quite as much as
if he were a Conway, and I sometimes think they like
him all the better for being so kind to his old father,
who comes frequently to the store. Grandma, I be-
gin to think differently of some things from what I
did. Birth and blood do not make much difference,
in this country, at least; and still I must acknowledge
that I should feel dreadfully if I did not love George
and know that he is the kindest husband in the world."

The letter closed with a playful insinuation that as
Henry Warner had gone, Maggie might possibly
marry Arthur Carrollton, and so make amends for the
disgrace which Theo had unwittingly brought upon
the Conway line.

For a long time after finishing the above, Madam
Conway sat wrapped in thought. Could it be possi-

ble that all her life she had labored under a mistake?
Were birth and family rank really of no consequence?
Was George just as worthy of respect as if he had descended directly from the Scottish race of Douglas,
instead of belonging to that vulgar woman? " It may
be so in America," she sighed, " but it is not true of
England," and, sincerely hoping that Theo's remark
concerning Mr. Carrollton might prove true, she laid
aside the letter, and for the remainder of the day
busied herself with preparations for the return of
Arthur Carrollton, who had written that he should
be with them on the 1st of December.

The day came, and, unusually excited, Maggie flitted from room to room, seeing that everything was in
order, and wondering how he would meet her and if
he had forgiven her for having been so cross at their
last interview in the woods. The effect of every suitable dress in her wardrobe was tried, and she decided
at last upon a crimson and black merino, which har-
monized well with her dark eyes and hair. The dress
was singularly becoming, and feeling quite well satisfied with the face and form reflected by her mirror
she descended to the parlor, where any doubts she
might have had concerning her personal appearance
were put to flight by Anna Jeffrey, who, with a feeling of envy, asked if she had the scarlet fever, referring to her bright color, and saying she did not think
too red a face becoming to anyone, particularly to Margaret, to whom it gave a " blowsy " look, such as she
had more than once heard Mr. Carrollton say he did
not like to see.

Margaret knew well that the dark-browed girl
would give almost anything for the roses blooming on

her cheeks; so she made no reply, but simply wished Anna would return to England, as for the last two months she had talked of doing. It was not quite dark, and Mr. Carrollton, if he came that night, would be with them soon. The car whistle had sounded some time before, and Maggie's quick ear caught at last the noise of the bells in the distance. Nearer and nearer they came; the sleigh was at the door, and forgetting everything but her own happiness Maggie ran out to meet their guest, nor turned her glowing face away when he stooped down to kiss her. He had forgiven her ill-nature, she was certain of that, and very joyfully she led the way to the parlor, where as the full light of the lamp fell upon him she started involuntarily, he seemed so changed.

"Are you sick?" she asked; and her voice expressed the deep anxiety she felt.

Forcing back a slight cough, and smiling down upon her, he answered cheerfully, "Oh, no, not sick! Canada air does not agree with me, that's all. I took a severe cold soon after my arrival in Montreal," and the cough he had attempted to stifle now burst forth, sounding to Maggie, who thought only of consumption, like an echo from the grave.

"Oh, I am so sorry!" she answered sadly, and her eyes filled with tears, which she did not try to conceal, for looking through the window across the snow-clad field, on which the winter moon was shining, she saw instinctively another grave beside that of her mother.

Madam Conway had not yet appeared, and, as Anna Jeffrey just then left the room, Mr. Carrollton was for some moments alone with Maggie. Winding his arm around her waist, and giving her a most expressive look, he said, "Maggie, are those tears for me?"

Instantly the bright blushes stole over Maggie's face and neck, for she remembered the time when once before he had asked her a similar question. Not now, as then, did she turn away from him, but she answered frankly: "Yes, they are. You look so pale and thin, I'm sure you must be very ill."

Whether Mr. Carrollton liked "blowsy" complexions or not, he certainly admired Maggie's at that moment, and drawing her closer to his side, he said, half playfully, half earnestly: "To see you thus anxious for me, Maggie, more than atones for your waywardness when last we parted. You are forgiven, but you are unnecessarily alarmed. *I* shall be better soon. Hillsdale air will do me good, and I intend remaining here until I am well again. Will you nurse me, Maggie, just as my sister Helen would do were she here?"

The right chord was touched, and all the soft, womanly qualities of Maggie Miller's nature were called forth by Arthur Carrollton's failing health. For several weeks after his arrival at Hillsdale he was a confirmed invalid, lying all day upon the sofa in the parlor, while Maggie read to him from books which he selected, partly for the purpose of amusing himself, and more for the sake of benefiting her and improving her taste for literature. At other times he would tell her of his home beyond the sea, and Maggie, listening to him while he described its airy halls, its noble parks, its shaded walks, and musical fountains, would sometimes wish aloud that she might one day see that spot which seemed to her so much like paradise. He wished so too, and oftentimes when, with half-closed eyes, his mind was wandering amid the scenes of his youth, he saw at his side a queenly figure with features like those of Maggie Miller, who each day was stealing more and more into his heart, where love for other than his nearest friends had never before found entrance. She had many faults, he knew, but these he possessed both the will and the power to correct, and as day after day she sat reading at his side he watched her bright, animated face, thinking what a splendid woman she would make, and wondering if an American rose like her would bear transplanting to English soil.

Very complacently Madam Conway looked on, reading aright the admiration which Arthur Carrollton evinced for Margaret, who in turn was far from being uninterested in him. Anna Jeffrey, too, watched them jealously, pondering in her own mind some means by which she could, if possible, annoy Margaret. Had she known how far matters had gone with Henry Warner, she would unhesitatingly have told it to Arthur Carrollton; but so quietly had the affair been managed that she knew comparatively little. This little, however, she determined to tell him, together with any embellishments she might see fit to use. Accordingly, one afternoon, when he had been there two months or more, and Maggie had gone with her grandmother to ride, she went down to the parlor under pretense of getting a book to read. He was much better now, but, feeling somewhat fatigued from a walk he had taken in the yard, he was reclining upon the sofa. Leaning over the rocking-chair which stood near by, Anna inquired for his health, and then asked how long since he had heard from home.

He liked to talk of England, and as there was nothing to him particularly disagreeable in Anna Jeffrey he bade her be seated. Very willingly she complied with his request, and, after talking a while of England, announced her intention of returning home the last of March. "My aunt prefers remaining with Madam Conway, but I don't like America," said she, "and I often wonder why I am here."

"I supposed you came to be with your aunt, who, I am told, has been to you a second mother," answered Mr. Carrollton; and Anna replied: "You are right. She could not be easy until she got me here, where I know I am not wanted—at least not altogether."

Mr. Carrollton looked inquiringly at her, and Anna continued, "I fully supposed I was to be a companion for Margaret; but instead of that she treats me with the utmost coolness, making me feel keenly my position as a dependent."

"That does not seem at all like Maggie," said Mr. Carrollton; and, with a meaning smile far more expressive than words, Anna answered: "She may not always be alike. But hush! don't I hear bells?" and she ran to the window, saying as she resumed her seat: "I thought they had come: but I was mistaken. I dare say Maggie has coaxed her grandmother to drive by the post office, thinking there might be a letter from Henry Warner."

Her manner affected Mr. Carrollton perceptibly, but he made no reply; and Anna asked if he knew Mr. Warner.

"I saw him in Worcester, I believe," he said; and Anna continued, "Do you think him a suitable husband for a girl like Maggie?"

There was a deep flush on Arthur Carrollton's cheek, and his lips were whiter than their wont as he answered, "I know nothing of him, neither did I suppose Miss Miller ever thought of him for a husband."

"I know she did at one time," said his tormentor, turning the leaves of her book with well-feigned indifference. "It was not any secret, or I should not speak of it; of course Madam Conway was greatly opposed to it too, and forbade her writing to him; but how the matter is now I do not positivel know, though I am quite sure they are engaged."

"Isn't it very close here? Will you please to open the hall door?" said Mr. Carrollton suddenly, panting for breath; and, satisfied with her work, Anna did as desired and then left him alone.

"Maggie engaged!" he said; "engaged!—when I hoped to win her for myself!" and a sharp pang shot through his heart as he thought of giving to another the beautiful girl who had grown so into his love. "But I am glad I learned it in time," he continued, hurriedly walking the floor, "knew it ere I had done Henry Warner a wrong by telling her of my love, and asking her to go with me to my English home, which will be desolate without her. This is why she repulsed me in the woods. She knew I ought not to speak of love to her. Why didn't I see it before, or why has not Madam Conway told me the truth! She at least has deceived me;" and with a feeling of keen disappointment he continued to pace the floor, one moment resolving to leave Hillsdale at once, and again thinking how impossible it was to tear himself away.

Arthur Carrollton was a perfectly honorable man, and once assured •of Maggie's engagement he would neither by word nor deed do aught to which the most fastidious lover could object, and Henry Warner's rights were as safe with him as with the truest of friends. But was Maggie really engaged? Might there not be some mistake? He hoped so at least, and alternating between hope and fear he waited impatiently the return of Maggie, who, with each thought of losing her, seemed tenfold dearer to him than she had ever been before; and when at last she came bounding in, he could scarcely refrain from folding her in his arms and asking of her to think again ere she gave another than himself the right of calling her his bride. But she is not mine, he thought; and so he merely took her cold hands within his own, rubbing them until they were warm. Then seating himself by her side upon the sofa he spoke of her ride, asking casually if she called at the post office.

"No, we did not drive that way," she answered readily, adding that the post office had few attractions for her now, as no one wrote to her save Theo.

She evidently spoke the truth, and with a feeling of relief Mr. Carrollton thought that possibly Miss Jeffrey might have been mistaken; but he would know at all hazards, even though he ran the risk of being thought extremely rude. Accordingly, that evening, after Mrs. Jeffrey and Anna had retired to their room, and while Madam Conway was giving some household directions in the kitchen, he asked her to come and sit by him as he lay upon the sofa, himself placing her chair where the lamplight would fall full upon her face and reveal its every expression. Closing the piano, she complied with his request, and then waited in silence for what he was to say.

"Maggie," he began, "you may think me bold, but there is something I very much wish to know, and which you, if you choose, can tell me. From what I have heard, I am led to think you are engaged. Will you tell me if this is true?"

The bright color faded from Maggie's cheek, while her eyes grew darker than before, and still she did not speak. Not that she was angry with him for asking her that question; but because the answer, which, if made at all, must be yes, was hard to utter. And yet why should she hesitate to tell him the truth at once?

Alas, for thee, Maggie Miller! The fancied love you feel for Henry Warner is fading fast away. Arthur Carrollton is a dangerous rival, and even now you cannot meet the glance of his expressive eyes without a blush! Your better judgment acknowledged his superiority to Henry long ago, and now in your heart there is room for none save him.

"Maggie," he said, again stretching out his hand to take the unresisting one which lay upon her lap, "you need not make me other answer save that so plainly written on your face. You are engaged, and may Heaven's blessing attend both you and yours!"

At this moment Madam Conway appeared, and fearing her inability to control her feelings longer Maggie precipitately left the room. Going to her chamber, she burst into a passionate fit of weeping, one moment blaming Mr. Carrollton for having learned her secret, and the next chiding herself for wishing to withhold from him a knowledge of her engagement.

"It is not that I love Henry less, I am sure," she thought; and laying her head upon her pillow she recalled everything which had passed between herself and her affianced husband, trying to bring back the olden· happiness with which she had listened to his words of love. But it would not come; there was a barrier in the way—Arthur Carrollton, as he looked when he said so sadly, " You need not tell me, Maggie."

" Oh, I wish he had not asked me that question!" she sighed. " It has put such dreadful thoughts into my head. And yet I love Henry as well as ever—I know I do; I am sure of it, or if I do not, I will," and repeating to herself again and again the words, " I will, I will," she fell asleep.

Will, however, is not always subservient to one's wishes, and during the first few days succeeding the in-eident of that night Maggie often found herself wishing Arthur Carrollton had never come to Hillsdale, he made her so wretched, so unhappy. Insensibly, too, she became a very little unamiable, speaking pettishly to her grandmother, disrespectfully to Mrs. Jeffrey, haughtily to Anna, and rarely to Mr. Carrollton, who after the lapse of two or three weeks began to talk of returning home in the same vessel with Anna Jeffrey, at which time his health would be fully restored. Then, indeed, did Maggie awake to the reality that while her hand was plighted to one, she loved another —not as in days gone by she had loved Henry War-ner, but with a deeper, more absorbing love. With this knowledge, too, there came the thought that Arthur Carrollton had once loved her, and but for the engagement now so much regretted he would ere this have told her so. But it was too late! too late! He would never feel toward her again as he once had felt, and bitter tears she shed as she contemplated the fast-coming future, when Arthur Carrollton would be gone, or shudderingly thought of the time when Henry Warner would return to claim her promise.

" I cannot, cannot marry him," she cried, " until I've torn that other image from my heart!" and then for many days she strove to recall the olden love in vain; for, planted on the sandy soil of childhood, as it were, it had been outgrown, and would never again spring into life. " I will write to him exactly how it is," she said at last; " will tell him that the affection I felt for him could not have been what a wife should feel for her husband. I was young, had seen nothing of the world, knew nothing of gentlemen's society, and when he came with his handsome face and winning ways my interest was awakened. Sympathy, too, for his misfortune increased that interest, which grandma's opposition tended in no wise to diminish. But it has died out, that fancied love, and I cannot bring it back. Still, if he insists, I will keep my word, and when he comes next autumn I will not tell him ' No.' "

Maggie was very calm when this deeision was reached, and opening her writing desk she wrote just as she said she would, begging him to forgive her if she had done him wrong, and beseeching Rose to comfort him as only a sister like her could do. " And remember," she wrote at the close, " remember that sooner than see you very unhappy, I will marry you, will try to be a faithful wife; though, Henry, I would rather not—oh, so much rather not!"

The letter was finished, and then Maggie took it to her grandmother, who read it eagerly, for in it she saw a fulfillment of her wishes. Very closely had she watched both Mr. Carrollton and Maggie, readily divining the truth that something was wrong between them. But from past experience she deemed it wiser not to interfere directly. Mr. Carrollton's avowed intention of returning to England, however, startled her, and she was revolving some method of procedure when Margaret brought to her the letter.

"I am happier than I can well express," she said, when she had finished reading it. "Of course you have my permission to send it. But what has changed you, Maggie? Has another taken the place of Henry Warner?"

"Don't ask me, grandma," cried Maggie, covering her face with her hands; "don't ask me, for indeed I can only tell you that I am very unhappy."

A little skillful questioning on Madam Conway's part sufficed to explain the whole—how constant association with Arthur Carrollton had won for him a place in Maggie's heart which Henry Warner had never filled; how the knowledge that she loved him as she could love no other one had faintly revealed itself to her on the night when he asked if she were engaged, and had burst upon her with overwhelming power when she heard that he was going home.

"He will never think of me again, I know," she said; "but, with my present feelings, I cannot marry Henry, unless he insists upon it."

"Men seldom wish to marry a woman who says she does not love them, and Henry Warner will not prove an exception," answered Madam Conway; and, comforted with this assurance, Maggie folded up her letter, which was soon on its way to Cuba.

The next evening, as Madam Conway sat alone with

Mr. Carrollton, she spoke of his return to England, expressing her sorrow, and asking why he did not remain with them longer.

"I will deal frankly with you, madam," said he, "and say that if I followed my own inclination I should stay, for Hillsdale holds for me an attraction which no other spot possesses. I refer to your granddaughter, who, in the little time I have known her, has grown very dear to me—so dear that I dare not stay longer where she is, lest I should love her too well, and rebel against yielding her to another."

For a moment Madam Conway hesitated; but, thinking the case demanded her speaking, she said: "Possibly Mr. Carrollton, I can make an explanation which will show some points in a different light from that in which you now see them. Margaret is engaged to Henry Warner, I will admit; but the engagement has become irksome, and yesterday she wrote asking a release, which he will grant, of course."

Instantly the expression of Mr. Carrollton's face was changed, and very intently he listened while Madam Conway frankly told him the story of Margaret's engagement up to the present time, withholding from him nothing, not even Maggie's confession of the interest she felt in him, an interest which had weakened her girlish attachment for Henry Warner.

"You have made me very happy," Mr. Carrollton said to Madam Conway, as, at a late hour, he bade her good-night—"happier than I can well express; for without Margaret life to me would be dreary indeed."

The next morning, at the breakfast table, Anna Jeffrey, who was in high spirits with the prospect of having Mr. Carrollton for a fellow-traveler, spoke of

their intended voyage, saying she could hardly wait
for the time to come, and asking if he were not equally
impatient to leave so horrid a country as America.

"On the contrary," he replied, "I should be sorry
to leave America just yet. I have therefore decided
to remain a little longer;" and his eyes sought the
face of Maggie, who, in her joyful surprise, dropped
the knife with which she was helping herself to but-
ter; while Anna Jeffrey, quite as much astonished, upset her coffee, exclaiming: "Not going home! What
has changed your mind?"

Mr. Carrollton made her no direct reply, and she
continued her breakfast in no very amiable mood;
while Maggie, too much overjoyed to eat, managed
ere long to find an excuse for leaving the table. Mr.
Carrollton wished to do everything honorably, and
so he decided to say nothing to Maggie of the cause
of this sudden change in his plan until Henry Warner's
answer was received, as she would then feel freer to
act as she felt. His resolution, however, was more
easily made than kept, and during the succeeding
weeks, by actions, if not by words, he more than once
told Maggie Miller how much she was beloved; and
Maggie, trembling with fear lest the cup of happiness
just within her grasp should be rudely dashed aside,
waited impatiently for the letter which was to set her
free. But weeks went by, and Maggie's heart grew
sick with hope deferred, for there came to her no message from the distant Cuban shore, which in another
chapter we shall visit.

CHAPTER XVII.

BROTHER AND SISTER.

BRIGHTLY shone the moonlight on the sunny isle of Cuba, dancing lightly on the wave, resting softly on the orange groves, and stealing gently through the casement, into the room where a young girl lay, whiter far than the flowers strewn upon her pillow. From the commencement of the voyage Rose had drooped, growing weaker every day, until at last all who looked upon her felt that the home of which she talked so much would never again be gladdened by her presence. Very tenderly Henry Warner nursed her, bearing her often in his arms up on the vessel's deck, where she could breathe the fresh morning air as it came rippling o'er the sea. But neither the ocean breeze, nor yet the fragrant breath of Florida's aromatic bowers, where for a time they stopped, had power to rouse her; and when at last Havana was reached she laid her weary head upon her pillow, whispering to no one of the love which was wearing her life away. With untold anguish at their hearts, both her aunt and Henry watched her, the latter shrinking ever from the thought of losing one who seemed a part of his very life.

"I cannot give you up, my Rose. I cannot live without you," he said, when once she talked to him of death. "You are all the world to me;" and, laying

his head upon her pillow, he wept as men will sometimes weep over their one great sorrow.

".Don't, Henry," she said, laying her tiny hand
upon his hair. " Maggie will comfort you when I am
gone. She will talk to you of me, standing at my
grave, for, Henry, you must not leave me here alone.
You must carry me home and bury me in dear old Leominster, where my childhood was passed, and where
I learned to love you so much—oh, so much!"

There was a mournful pathos in the tone with which
the last words were uttered, but Henry Warner did
not understand it, and covering the little blue-veined
hand with kisses he promised that her grave should be
made at the foot of the garden in their far-off home,
where the sunlight fell softly and the moonbeams
gently shone. That evening Henry sat alone by Rose,
who had fallen into a disturbed slumber. For a time
he took no notice of the disconnected words she uttered in her dreams, but when at last he heard the
sound of his own name he drew near, and, bending
low, listened with mingled emotions of joy, sorrow,
and surprise to a secret which, waking, she would
never have told him, above all others. She loved him,
—the fair girl he called his sister,—but not as a sister
loves; and now, as he stood by her, with the knowledge thrilling every nerve, he remembered many bygone scenes, when but for his blindness he would have
seen how every pulsation of her heart throbbed alone
for him whose hand was plighted to another, and that
other no unworthy rival. Beautiful, very beautiful,
was the shadowy form which at that moment seemed
standing at his side, and his heart went out towards
her as the one above all others to be his bride.

"Had I known it sooner," he thought, "known it before I met the peerless Maggie, I might have taken Rose to my bosom and loved her—it may be with a deeper love than that I feel for Maggie Miller, for Rose is everything to me. She has made and keeps me what I am, and how can I let her die when I have the power to save her?"

There was a movement upon the pillow. Rose was waking, and as her soft blue eyes unclosed and looked up in his face he wound his arms around her, kissing her lips as never before he had kissed her. She was not his sister now—the veil was torn away—a new feeling had been awakened, and as days and weeks went by there gradually crept in between him and Maggie Miller a new love—even a love for the fair-haired Rose, to whom he was kinder, if possible, than he had been before, though he seldom kissed her lips or caressed her in any way.

"It would be wrong," he said, "a wrong to myself —a wrong to her—and a wrong to Maggie Miller, to whom my troth is plighted;" and he did not wish it otherwise, he thought; though insensibly there came over him a wish that Maggie herself might weary of the engagement and seek to break it. Not that he loved her the less, he reasoned, but that he pitied Rose the more.

In this manner time passed on, until at last there came to him Maggie's letter, which had been a long time on the sea.

"I expected it," he thought, as he finished reading it, and though conscious for a moment of a feeling of disappointment the letter brought him far more pleasure than pain.

Of Arthur Carrollton no mention had been made, but he readily guessed the truth; and thinking, "It is well," he laid the letter aside and went back to Rose, deciding to say nothing to her then. He would wait until his own feelings were more perfectly defined. So a week went by, and again, as he had often done before, he sat with her alone in the quiet night, watching her as she slept, and thinking how beautiful she was, with her golden hair shading her childish face, her long eyelashes resting on her cheek, and her little hands folded meekly upon her bosm.

"She is too beautiful to die," he murmured, pressing a kiss upon her lips.

This act awoke her, and, turning towards him she said, "Was I dreaming, Henry, or did you kiss me as you used to do?"

"Not dreaming, Rose," he answered—then rather hurriedly he added: "I have a letter from Maggie Miller, and ere I answer it I would read it to you. Can you hear it now?"

"Yes, yes," she whispered faintly; "read it to me, Henry;" and, turning her face away, she listened while he read that Maggie Miller, grown weary of her troth, asked a release from her engagement.

He finished reading, and then waited in silence to hear what Rose would say. But for a time she did not speak. All hope for herself had long since died away, and now she experienced only sorrow for Henry's disappointment.

"My poor brother," she said at last, turning her face towards him and taking his hand in hers; "I am sorry for you—to lose us both, Maggie and me. What will you do?"

" Rose," he said, bending so low that his brown locks mingled with the yellow tresses of her hair—" Rose, I do not regret Maggie Miller's decision, neither do I blame her for it. She is a noble, true-hearted girl, and so long as I live I shall esteem her highly; but I too have changed—have learned to love another. Will you sanction this new love, dear Rose? Will you say that it is right?"

The white lids closed over the eyes of blue, but they could not keep back the tears which rolled down her face, as she asked somewhat sadly, "Who is it, Henry?"

There was another moment of silence, and then he whispered in her ear: " People call her Rose; I once called her sister; but my heart now claims her for something nearer. My Rose," he continued, " shall it be? Will you live for my sake? Will you be my wife?"

The shock was too sudden—too great; and neither on that night, nor yet the succeeding day, had Rose the power to answer. But as the dew of heaven is to the parched and dying flower, so were these words of love to her, imparting at once new life and strength, making her as it were another creature. The question asked that night so unexpectedly was answered at last; and then with almost perfect happiness at her heart, she too added a few lines to the letter which Henry sent to Maggie Miller, over whose pathway, hitherto so bright, a fearful shadow was falling.

CHAPTER XVIII.

THE PEDDLER.

IT was a rainy April day—a day which precluded all outdoor exercise, and Hagar Warren, from the window of her lonely cabin, watched in vain for the coming of Maggie Miller. It was now more than a week since she had been there, for both Arthur Carrollton and herself had accompanied the disappointed Anna Jeffrey to New York, going with her on board the vessel which was to take her from a country she affected so to dislike.

"I dare say you'll be Maggie somebody else ere I meet you again," she said to Maggie, at parting, and Mr. Carrollton, on the journey home, found it hard to keep from asking her if for the " somebody else " she would substitute his name, and so be " Maggie Carrollton."

This, however, he did not do; but his attentions were so marked, and his manner towards her so affectionate, that ere Hillsdale was reached there was in Maggie's mind no longer a doubt as to the nature of his feelings toward her. Arrived at home, he kept her constantly at his side, while Hagar, who was suffering from a slight attack of rheumatism, and could not go up to the stone house, waited and watched, thinking herself almost willing to be teased for the secret, if she could once more hear the sound of Maggie's voice. The secret, however, had been forgotten in the exciting scenes through which Maggie had passed since first she learned of its existence; and it was now a long time since she had mentioned it to Hagar, who each day grew more and more determined never to reveal it.

"My life is almost ended," she thought, "and the secret shall go with me to my grave. Margaret will be happier without it, and it shall not be revealed."

Thus she reasoned on that rainy afternoon, when she sat waiting for Maggie, who, she heard, had returned the day before. Slowly the hours dragged on, and the night shadows fell at last upon the forest trees, creeping into the corners of Hagar's room, resting upon the hearthstone, falling upon the window pane, creeping up the wall, and affecting Hagar with a nameless fear of some impending evil. This fear not even the flickering flame of the lamp, which she lighted at last and placed upon the mantel, was able to dispel, for the shadows grew darker, folding themselves around her heart, until she covered her eyes with her hands, lest some goblin shape should spring into life before her.

The sound of the gate latch was heard, and footsteps were approaching the door—not the bounding step of Maggie, but a tramping tread, followed by a heavy knock, and next moment a tall, heavy-built man appeared before her, asking shelter for the night. The pack he carried showed him at once to be a peddler, and upon a nearer view Hagar recognized in him a stranger who, years before, had craved her hospitality. He had been civil to her then; she did not fear him now, and she consented to his remaining, thinking his presence there might dispel the mysterious terror hanging around her. But few words passed between them that night, for Martin, as he called himself, was tired, and after partaking of the supper that she prepared he retired to rest. The next morning, however, he was more talkative, kindly enlightening her with regard to his business, his family, and his place of residence, which last he said was in Meriden, Conn.

It was a long time since Hagar had heard that name, and now, turning quickly towards him, she said, " Meriden? That is where my Hester lived, and where her husband died."

" I want to know!" returned the Yankee peddler. " What might have been his name?"

" Hamilton—Nathan Hamilton. Did you know him? He died nineteen years ago this coming summer."

" Egzactly!" ejaculated the peddler, setting down his pack and himself taking a chair, preparatory to a long talk. " Egzactly; I knowed him like a book. Old Squire Hampleton, the biggest man in Meriden, and you don't say his last wife, that tall, handsome gal, was your darter?"

" Yes, she was my daughter," answered Hagar, her whole face glowing with the interest she felt in talking for the first time in her life with one who had known her daughter's husband, Maggie's father. " You knew her. You have seen her?" she continued; and Martin answered, " Seen her a hundred times, I'll bet. Anyhow, I sold her the weddin' gown; and now, I think on't, she favored you. She was a likely person, and I allus thought that proud sister of his'n, the Widder Warner, might have been in better business than takin' them children away as she did, because he married his hired gal.

But it's as well for them, I s'pose, particularly for the boy, who is one of the fust young men in Wooster now. Keeps a big store!"

"Warner, Warner!" interrupted old Hagar, the nameless terror of the night before creeping again into her heart. "Whose name did you say was Warner?"

"The hull on 'em, boy, girl, and all, is called Warner now—one Rose, and t'other Henry," answered the peddler, perfectly delighted with the interest manifested by his auditor, who, grasping at the bedpost and moving her hand rapidly before her eyes, as if to clear away a mist which had settled there, continued, "I remember now, Hester told me of the children; but one, she said, was a stepchild—that was the boy, wasn't it?" and her wild, black eyes had in them a look of unutterable anxiety, wholly incomprehensible to the peddler, who, instead of answering her question said: "What ails you woman? Your face is as white as a piece of paper?"

"Thinking of Hester always affects me so," she answered; and stretching her hands beseechingly towards him, she entreated him to say if Henry were not the stepchild.

"No marm, he warn't," answered the peddler, who, like a great many talkative people, pretended to know more than he really did, and who in this particular instance was certainly mistaken. "I can tell you egzactly how that is: Henry was the son of Mr. Hampleton's first marriage—Henry Hampleton. The second wife, the one your darter lived with, was the Widder Warner, and had a little gal, Rose, when she married Mr. Hampleton. This Widder Warner's husband's brother married Mr. Hampleton's sister, the woman who took the children, and had Henry change his name to Warner. The Hampletons and Warners were mighty big-feelin' folks, and the old squire's match mortified 'em dreadfully."

"Where are they now?" gasped Hagar, hoping there might be some mistake.

"There you've got me!" answered Martin. "I haven't seen 'em this dozen year; but the last I heard, Miss Warner and Rose was livin' in Leominster, and Henry was in a big store in Wooster. But what the plague is the matter?" he continued, alarmed at the expression of Hagar's face, as well as at the strangeness of her manner.

Wringing her hands as if she would wrench her fingers from their sockets, she clutched at her long white hair, and, rocking to and fro, moaned, " Woe is me, and woe the day when I was born!"

From everyone save her grandmother Margaret had kept the knowledge of her changed feelings towards Henry Warner; and looking upon a marriage between the two as an event surely to be expected, old Hagar was overwhelmed with grief and fear. Falling at last upon her knees, she cried: " Had you cut my throat from ear to ear, old man, you could not have hurt me more! Oh, that I had died years and years ago! But I must live now—live!" she screamed, springing to her feet—"live to prevent the wrong my own wickedness has caused!"

Perfectly astonished at what he saw and heard, the peddler attempted to question her, but failing to obtain any satisfactory answers he finally left, mentally pronouncing her " as crazy as a loon." This opinion was confirmed by the people on whom he next called, for, chancing to speak of Hagar, he was told that noth-ing which she did or said was considered strange, as she had been called insane for years. This satisfied Martin, who made no further mention of her, and thus the scandal which his story might otherwise have pro-duced was prevented.

In the meantime on her face lay old Hagar, moan-ing bitterly. "My sin has found me out; and just when I thought it never need be known! For myself I do not care; but Maggie, Maggie—how can I tell her that she is bone of my bone, blood of my blood, flesh of my flesh—and me old Hagar Warren!"

It would be impossible to describe the scorn and intense loathing concentrated in the tones of Hagar's voice as she uttered these last words, "and me old Hagar Warren!" Had she indeed been the veriest wretch on earth, she could not have hated herself more than she did in that hour of her humiliation, when, with a loud voice, she cried, "Let me die, oh, let me die, and it will never be known!" Then, as she reflected upon the terrible consequence which would ensue were she to die and make no sign, she wrung her hands despairingly, crying: "Life, life—yes, give me life to tell her of my guilt; and then it will be a blessed rest to die. Oh, Margaret, my precious child, I'd give my heart's blood, drop by drop, to save you; but it can't be; you must not wed your father's son; oh, Maggie, Maggie, Maggie!"

Fainter and fainter grew each succeeding word, and when the last was spoken she fell again upon her face, unconscious and forgetful of her woe. Higher and higher in the heavens rose the morning sun, stealing across the window sill, and shining aslant the floor, where Hagar still lay in a deep, deathlike swoon. An hour passed on, and then the wretched woman came slowly back to life, her eyes lighting up with joy, as she whispered, " It was a dream, thank Heaven, 'twas a dream!" and then growing dim with tears, as the dread reality came over her. The first fearful burst of grief was passed, for Hagar now could weep, and tears did her good, quelling the feverish agony at her heart. Not for herself did she suffer so much as for Maggie, trembling for the effect the telling of the secret would have on her. For it must be told. She knew that full well, and as the sun fast neared the western horizon, she murmured, " Oh, will she come to-night, will she come to-night? "

Yes, Hagar, she will. Even now her feet, which, when they backward turn, will tread less joyously, are threading the woodland path. The halfway rock is reached—nearer and nearer she comes—her shadow falls across the floor—her hand is on your arm—her voice in your ear—Maggie Miller is at your side—Heaven help you both!

CHAPTER XIX.

THE TELLING OF THE SECRET.

"HAGAR! Hagar!" exclaimed Maggie, playfully bounding to her side, and laying her hand upon her arm. "What aileth thee, Hagar?"

The words were meet, for never Hagar in the desert, thirsting for the gushing fountain, suffered more than did she who sat with covered face and made no word of answer. Maggie was unusually happy that day, for but a few hours before she had received Henry's letter making her free—free to love Arthur Carrollton, who she well knew only waited a favorable opportunity to tell her of his love; so with a heart full of happiness she had stolen away to visit Hagar, reproaching herself as she came for having neglected her so long. "But I'll make amends by telling her what I'm sure she must have guessed," she thought, as she entered the cottage, where, to her surprise, she found her weeping. Thinking the old woman's distress might possibly be occasioned by her neglect, she spoke again. "Are you crying for me, Hagar?"

"Yes, Maggie Miller, for you—for you!" answered Hagar, lifting up a face so ghastly white that Maggie started back in some alarm.

"Poor Hagar, you are ill," she said, and advancing nearer she wound her arms around the trembling form, and, pillowing the snowy head upon her bosom, continued soothingly: "I did not mean to stay away long.

I will not do it again, but I am so happy, Hagar, so happy that I half forgot myself."

For a moment Hagar let her head repose upon the bosom of her child, then murmuring softly, " It will never lie there again," she arose, and, confronting Maggie, said, " Is it love which makes you so happy?"

" Yes, Hagar, love," answered Margaret, the deep blushes stealing over her glowing face.

" And is it your intention to marry the man you love?'" continued Hagar, thinking only of Henry Warner, while Margaret, thinking only of Arthur Carrollton, replied, " If he will marry me, I shall most surely marry him."

" It is enough. I must tell her," whispered Hagar; while Maggie asked, " Tell me what? "

For a moment the wild eyes fastened themselves upon her with a look of yearning anguish, and then Hagar answered slowly, " Tell you what you've often wished to know—my secret! " the last word dropping from her lips more like a warning hiss than like a human sound. It was long since Maggie had teased for the secret, so absorbed had she been in other matters, but now that there was a prospect of knowing it her curiosity was reawakened, and while her eyes glistened with expectation, she said, " Yes, tell it to me, Hagar, and then I'll tell you mine; " and all over her beautiful face there shone a joyous light as she thought how Hagar, who had once pronounced Henry Warner unworthy, would rejoice in her new love.

" Not here, Maggie—not here in this room can I tell you," said old Hagar; " but out in the open air, where my breath will come more freely; " and, leading the way, she hobbled to the mossy bank where

Maggie had sat with Arthur Carrollton on the morning of his departure for Montreal.

Here she sat down, while Maggie threw herself upon the damp ground at her feet, her face lighted with eager curiosity and her lustrous eyes bright as stars with excitement. For a moment Hagar bent forward, and, folding her hands one above the other, laid them upon the head of the young girl as if to gather strength for what she was to say. But all in vain; for when she essayed to speak her tongue clave to the roof of her mouth, and her lips gave forth unmeaning sounds.

"It must be something terrible to affect her so," thought Maggie, and, taking the bony hands between her own, she said, "I would not tell it, Hagar; I do not wish to hear."

The voice aroused the half-fainting woman, and, withdrawing her hand from Maggie's grasp, she replied, "Turn away your face, Margaret Miller, so I cannot see the hatred settling over it, when I tell you what I must."

"Certainly; my back if you prefer it," answered Maggie, half playfully; and turning round she leaned her head against the feeble knees of Hagar.

"Maggie, Maggie," began the poor old woman, lingering long and lovingly over that dear name, "nineteen years ago, next December, I took upon my soul the secret sin which has worn my life away, but I did it for the love I had for you. Oh, Margaret, believe it, for the love I had for you, more than for my own ambition;" and the long fingers slid nervously over the bands of shining hair just within her reach.

At the touch of those fingers, Maggie shuddered involuntarily. There was a vague, undefined terror stealing over her, and, impatient to know the worst, she said, " Go on, tell me what you did."

" I can't—I can't—and yet I must! " cried Hagar. " You were a beautiful baby, Maggie, and the other one was sickly, pinched, and blue. I had you both in my room the night after Hester died ; and the devil— Maggie, do you know how the devil will creep into the heart, and whisper, whisper till the brain is all on fire ? This thing he did to me, Maggie, nineteen years ago, he whispered—whispered dreadful things, and his whisperings were of you! "

" Horrible, Hagar! " exclaimed Maggie. " Leave the devil, and tell me of yourself."

" That's it," answered Hagar. " If I had but left him then, this hour would never have come to me ; but I listened, and when he told me that a handsome, healthy child would be more acceptable to the Conways than a weakly, fretful one—when he said that Hagar Warren's grandchild had far better be a lady than a drudge—that no one would ever know it, for none had noticed either—I did it, Maggie Miller ; I took you from the pine-board cradle where you lay—I dressed you in the other baby's clothes—I laid you on her pillow—I wrapped her in your coarse white frock—I said that she was mine, and Margaret—oh, Heaven ! can't you see it ? Don't you know that I, the shrivcled, skinny hag who tells you this, am your own grandmother ! "

There was no need for Maggie Miller to answer that appeal. The words had burned into her soul— scorching her very life-blood, and maddening her brain. It was a fearful blow—crushing her at once.

She saw it all, understood it all, and knew there was no hope. The family pride at which she had often laughed was strong within her, and could not at once be rooted out. All the fond household memories, though desecrated and trampled down, were not so soon to be forgotten. She could not own that half-crazed woman for her grandmother! As Hagar talked Maggie had risen, and now, tall, and erect as the mountain ash which grew on her native hills, she stood before Hagar, every vestige of color faded from her face, her eyes dark as midnight and glowing like coals of living fire, while her hands, locked despairingly together, moved slowly towards Hagar, as if to thrust her aside.

"Oh, speak again!" she said, "but not the dreadful words you said to me just now. Tell me they are false—say that my father perished in the storm, that my mother was she who held me on her bosom when she died—that I—oh, Hagar, I am not—I will not be the creature you say I am! Speak to me," she continned; "tell me; is it true?" and in her voice there was not the olden sound.

Hoarse—hollow—full of reproachful anguish it seemed; and, bowing her head in very shame, old Hagar made her answer: "Would to Heaven 'twere not true—but it is—it is! Kill me, Maggie," she continned, "strike me dead, if you will, but take your eyes away! You must not look thus at me, a heart-broken wretch."

But not of Hagar Warren was Maggie thinking then. The past, the present, and the future were all embodied in her thoughts. She had been an intruder all her life; had ruled with a high hand people on whom she had no claim, and who, had they known her parentage, would have spurned her from them. Theo, whom she had held in her arms so oft, calling her sister and loving her as such, was hers no longer; nor yet the fond woman who had cherished her so tenderly —neither was hers; and in fancy she saw the look of scorn upon that woman's face when she should hear the tale, for it must be told—and she must tell it, too. She would not be an impostor; and then there flashed upon her the agonizing thought, before which all else seemed as naught—in the proud heart of Arthur Carrollton was there a place for Hagar Warren's grandchild? " No, no, no! " she moaned; and the next moment she lay at Hagar's feet, white, rigid, and insensible

" She's dead! " cried Hagar; and for one brief instant she hoped that it was so.

But not then and there was Margaret to die; and slowly she came back to life, shrinking from the touch of Hagar's hand when she felt it on her brow.

" There may be some mistake," she whispered; but Hagar answered, " There is none "; at the same time relating so minutely the particulars of the deception that Maggie was convinced, and, covering her face with her hands, sobbed aloud, while Hagar, sitting by in silence, was nerving herself to tell the rest.

The sun had set, and the twilight shadows were stealing down upon them, when, creeping abjectly upon her knees towards the wretched girl, she said, " There is more, Maggie, more—I have not told you all."

But Maggie had heard enough, and, exerting all her strength, she sprang to her feet, while Hagar clutched eagerly at her dress, which was wrested from her grasp, as Maggie fled away—away—she knew not, cared not, whither, so that she were beyond the reach of the trembling voice which called after her to return. Alone in the deep woods, with the darkness falling around her, she gave way to the mighty sorrow which had come so suddenly upon her. She could not doubt what she had heard. She knew that it was true, and as proof after proof crowded upon her, until the chain of evidence was complete, she laid her head upon the rain-wet grass, and shudderingly stopped her ears, to shut out, if possible, the memory of the dreadful words, "I, the shriveled, skinny hag who tells you this, am your own grandmother." For a long time she lay there thus, weeping till the fountain of her tears seemed dry; then, weary, faint, and sick, she started for her home. Opening cautiously the outer door, she was gliding up the stairs when Madam Conway, entering the hall with a lamp, discovered her, and uttered an exclamation of surprise at the strangeness of her appearance. Her dress, bedraggled and wet, was torn in several places by the briery bushes she had passed; her hair, loosened from its confinement, hung down her back, while her face was so white and ghastly that Madam Conway in much alarm followed her up the stairs, asking what had happened.

"Something dreadful came to me in the woods,' said Maggie; "but I can't tell you to-night. To-morrow I shall be better—or dead—oh, I wish I could b dead—before you hate me so, dear grand—— No, I didn't mean that—you aint; forgive me, do;'" and sinking to the floor she kissed the very hem of Madam Conway's dress.

Unable to understand what she meant, Madam Conway divested her of her damp clothing, and, placing her in bed, sat down beside her, saying gently, " Can you tell me now what frightened you? "

A faint cry was Maggie's only answer, and taking the lady's hand she laid it upon her forehead, where the drops of perspiration were standing thickly. All night long Madam Conway sat by her, going once to communicate with Arthur Carrollton, who, anxious and alarmed, came often to the door, asking if she slept. She did sleep at last—a fitful feverish sleep; but ever at the sound of Mr. Carrollton's voice a spasm of pain distorted her features, and a low moan came from her lips. Maggie had been terribly excited, and when next morning she awoke she was parched with burning fever, while her mind at intervals seemed wandering; and ere two days passed she was raving with delirium, brought on, the physician said, by some sudden shock, the nature of which no one could even guess.

For three weeks she hovered between life and death, whispering oft of the horrid shape which had met her in the woods, robbing her of happiness and life. Winding her feeble arms around Madam Conway's neck, she would beg of her most piteously not to cast her off—not to send her away from the only home she had ever known—" For I couldn't help it," she would say. " I didn't know it, and I've loved you all so much—so much! Say, grandma, may I call you grandma all the same? Will you love poor Maggie a little? " and Madam Conway, listening to words whose meaning she could not fathom, would answer by laying the aching head upon her bosom, and trying to soothe the *xcited girl. Theo, too, was summoned home, but at her Maggie at first refused to look, and, covering her eyes with her hand, she whispered scornfully, "Pinched, and blue, and pale; that's the very look. I couldn't see it when I called you sister."

Then her mood would change, and motioning Theo to her side she would say to her, "Kiss me once, Theo, just as you used to do when I was Maggie Miller."

Towards Arthur Carrollton she from the first manifested fear, shuddering whenever he approached her, and still exhibiting signs of uneasiness if he left her sight. "He hates me," she said, "hates me for what I could not help;" and when, as he often did, he came to her bedside, speaking words of love, she would answer mournfully: "Don't, Mr. Carrollton; your pride is stronger than your love. You will hate me when you know all."

Thus two weeks went by, and then with the first May day reason returned again, bringing life and strength to the invalid, and joy to those who had so anxiously watched over her. Almost her first rational question was for Hagar, asking if she had been there.

"She is confined to her bed with inflammatory rheumatism," answered Madam Conway; "but she inquires for you every day, they say; and once when told you could not live she started to crawl on her hands and knees to see you, but fainted near the gate, and was carried back."

"Poor old woman!" murmured Maggie, the tears rolling down her cheeks, as she thought how strong must be the love that half-crazed creature bore her, and how little it was returned, for every feeling of her nature revolted from claiming a near relationship with one whom she had hitherto regarded as a servant. The secret, too, seemed harder to divulge, and day by day she put it off, saying to them when they asked what had so much affected her that she could not tell them yet—she must wait till she was stronger.

So Theo went back to Worcester as mystified as ever, and Maggie was left much alone with Arthur Carrollton, who strove in various ways to win her from the melancholy into which she had fallen. All day long she would sit by the open window, seemingly immovable, her large eyes, now intensely black, fixed upon vacancy, and her white face giving no sign of the fierce struggle within, save when Madam Conway, coming to her side, would lay her hand caressingly on her in token of sympathy. Then, indeed, her lips would quiver, and turning her head away, she would say, " Don't touch me—don't ! "

To Arthur Carrollton she would listen with apparent composure, though often as he talked her long, tapering nails left their impress in her flesh, so hard she strove to seem indifferent. Once when they were left together alone he drew her to his side, and bending very low, so that his lips almost touched her marble cheek, he told her of his love, and how full of anguish had been his heart when he thought that she would die.

" But God kindly gave you back to me," he said; " and now, my precious Margaret, will you be my wife? Will you go with me to my English home, from which I have tarried now too long because I would not leave you? Will Maggie answer me? " and he folded her lovingly in his arms.

Oh, how could she tell him No, when every fiber of her heart thrilled with the answer Yes. She mistook him—mistook the character of Arthur Carrollton, for, though pride was strong within him, he loved the beautiful girl who lay trembling in his arms better than he loved his pride; and had she told him then who and what she was, he would not have deemed it a disgrace to love a child of Hagar Warren. But Margaret did not know him, and when he said again, "Will Maggie answer me?" there came from her lips a piteous, wailing cry, and turning her face away she answered mournfully: "No, Mr. Carrollton, no, I cannot be your wife. It breaks my heart to tell you so; but if you knew what I know, you would never have spoken to me words of love. You would have rather thrust me from you, for indeed I am unworthy."

"Don't you love me, Maggie?" Mr. Carrollton said, and in the tones of his voice there was so much tenderness that Maggie burst into tears, and, involuntarily resting her head upon his bosom, answered sadly: "I love you so much, Arthur Carrollton, that I would die a hundred deaths could that make me worthy of you, as not long ago I thought I was. But it cannot be. Something terrible has come between us."

"Tell me what it is. Let me share your sorrow," he said; but Maggie only answered: "Not yet, not yet! Let me live where you are a little longer. Then I will tell you all, and go away forever."

This was all the satisfaction he could obtain; but after a time she promised that if he would not mention the subject to her until the first of June, she would then tell him everything; and satisfied with a promise which he knew would be kept, Mr. Carrollton waited impatiently for the appointed time, while Maggie, too, counted each sun as it rose and set, bringing nearer and nearer a trial she so much dreaded.

CHAPTER XX.

THE RESULT.

Two days only remained ere the first of June, and in the solitude of her chamber Maggie was weeping bitterly. "How can I tell them who I am?" she thought. "How bear their pitying scorn, when they learn that she whom they call Maggie Miller has no right to that name?—that Hagar Warren's blood is flowing in her veins?—and Madam Conway thinks so much of that! Oh, why was Hagar left to do me this great wrong? why did she take me from the pine-board cradle where she says I lay, and make me what I was not born to be?" and, falling on her knees, the wretched girl prayed that it might prove a dream from which she would ere long awake.

Alas for thee, poor Maggie Miller! It is not a dream, but a stern reality; and you who oft have spurned at birth and family, why murmur now when both are taken from you? Are you not still the same, —beautiful,—accomplished, and refined,—and can you ask for more? Strange that theory and practice so seldom should accord. And yet it was not the degradation which Maggie felt so keenly, it was rather the loss of love she feared; without that the blood of royalty could not avail to make her happy.

Maggie was a warm-hearted girl, and she loved the stately lady she had been wont to call her grandmother with a filial, clinging love which could not be severed, and still this love was naught compared to what she felt for Arthur Carrollton, and the giving up of him was the hardest part of all. But it must be done, she thought; he had told her once that were she Hagar Warren's grandchild he should not be riding with her —how much less, then, would he make that child his wife! and rather than meet the look of proud disdain on his face when first she stood confessed before him, she resolved to go away where no one had ever heard of her or Hagar Warren. She would leave behind a letter telling why she went, and commending to Madam Conway's care poor Hagar, who had been sorely punished for her sin. " But whither shall I go, and what shall I do when I get there? " she cried, trembling at the thoughts of a world of which she knew so little. Then, as she remembered how many young girls of her age went out as teachers, she determined to go at all events. " It will be better than staying here where I have no claim," she thought; and, nerving herself for the task, she sat down to write the letter which, on the first of June, should tell to Madam Conway and Arthur Carrollton the story of her birth.

It was a harder task than she supposed, the writing that farewell, for it seemed like severing every hallowed tie. Three times she wrote " My dear grandma," then with a throb of anguish she dashed her pen across the revered name, and wrote simply " Madam Conway." It was a rambling, impassioned letter, full of tender love—of hope destroyed—of deep despair—and though it shadowed forth no expectation that Madam Conway or Mr. Carrollton would ever take her to their hearts again, it begged of them most touchingly to think sometimes of " Maggie " when she was gone forever. Hagar was then commended to Madam Conway's forgiveness and care. " She is old," wrote Maggie, " her life is nearly ended, and if you have in your heart one feeling of pity for her who used to call you grandma, bestow it, I pray you, on poor old Hagar Warren."

The letter was finished, and then suddenly remembering Hagar's words, that "all had not been told," and feeling it her duty to see once more the woman who had brought her so much sorrow, Maggie stole cautiously from the house, and was soon walking down the woodland road, slowly, sadly, for the world had changed to her since last she trod that path. Maggie, too, was changed, and when at last she stood before Hagar, who was now able to sit up, the latter could scarcely recognize in the pale, haggard woman the blooming, merry-hearted girl once known as Maggie Miller.

" Margaret! " she cried, " you have come again— come to forgive your poor old grand—— No, no," she added, as she saw the look of pain flash over Maggie's face, " I'll never insult you with that name. Only say that you forgive me, will you, Miss Margaret? " and the trembling voice was choked with sobs, while the aged form shook as with a palsied stroke.

Hagar had been ill. Exposure to the damp air on that memorable night had brought on a second severe attack of rheumatism, which had bent her nearly double. Anxiety for Margaret, too, had wasted her to a skeleton, and her thin, sharp face, now of a corpse-like pallor, contrasted strangely with her eyes, from which the wildness all was gone. Touched with pity,

Maggie drew a chair to her side, and thus replied: "I do forgive you, Hagar, for I know that what you did was done in love; but by telling me what you have you've ruined all my hopes of happiness. In the new scenes to which I go, and the new associations I shall form, I may become contented with my lot, but never can I forget that I once was Maggie Miller."

"Magaret," gasped Hagar, and in her dim eye there was something of its olden fire, "if by new associations you mean Henry Warner, it must not be. Alas, that I should tell this! but Henry is your brother —your father's only son. Oh, horror! horror!" and dreading what Margaret would say, she covered her face with her cramped, distorted hands.

But Margaret was not so much affected as Hagar had anticipated. She had suffered severely, and could not now be greatly moved. There was an involuntary shudder as she thought of her escape, and then her next feeling was one of satisfaction in knowing that she was not quite friendless and alone, for Henry would protect her, and Rose, indeed, would be to her a sister.

"Henry Warner my brother!" she exclaimed; "how came you by this knowledge?" And very briefly Hagar explained to her what she knew, saying that Hester had told her of two young children, but she had forgotten entirely of their existence, and now that she was reminded of it she could not help fancying that Hester said the stepchild was a boy. But the peddler knew, of course, and she must have forgotten.

"When the baby they thought was you died," said Hagar, "I wrote to the minister in Meriden, telling him of it, but I did not sign my name, and I thought

that was the last I should ever hear of it. Why don't
you curse me?" she continued. "Haven't I taken
from you your intended husband, as well as your
name?"

Maggie understood perfectly now why the secret
had been revealed, and involuntarily she exclaimed,
"Oh, had I told you first, this never need have been!"
and then hurriedly she explained to the repentant
Hagar how at the very moment when the dread confession was made she, Maggie Miller, was free from
Henry Warner.

From the window Maggie saw in the distance the
servant who had charge of Hagar, and, dreading the
presence of a third person, she arose to go. Offering
her hand to Hagar, she said: "Good-by. I may never
see you again, but if I do not, remember that I forgive
you freely."

"You are not going away, Maggie. Oh, are you
going away!" and the crippled arms were stretched
imploringly towards Maggie, who answered: "Yes,
Hagar, I must go. Honor requires me to tell Madam
Conway who I am, and after that you know that I cannot stay. I shall go to my brother."

Three times old Hagar essayed to speak, and at last,
between a whisper and a moan, she found strength to
say: "Will you kiss me once, Maggie darling? 'Twill
be something to remember, in the lonesome nights
when I am all alone. Just once, Maggie! Will you?"

Maggie could not refuse, and gliding to the bowed
woman's side she put back the soft hair from off the
wrinkled brow, and left there token of her forgiveness.

The last May sun had set, and ere the first June morning rose Maggie Miller would be nowhere found in the home her presence had made so bright. Alone, with no eye upon her save that of the Most High, she had visited the two graves, and, while her heart was bleeding at every pore, had wept her last adieu over the sleeping dust so long held sacred as her mother's. Then kneeling at the other grave, she murmured, "Forgive me, Hester Hamilton, if in this parting hour my heart clings most to her whose memory I was first taught to revere; and if in the better world you know and love each other—oh, will both bless and pity me, poor, wretched Maggie Miller!"

Softly the night air moved through the pine that overshadowed the humble grave, while the moonlight, flashing from the tall marble, which stood a sentinel over the other mound, bathed Maggie's upturned face as with a flood of glory, and her throbbing heart grew still as if indeed at that hushed moment the two mothers had come to bless their child. The parting with the dead was over, and Margaret sat again in her room, waiting until all was still about the old stone house. She did not add to her letter another line telling of her discovery, for she did not think of it; her mind was too intent upon escaping unobserved; and when sure the family had retired she moved cautiously down the stairs, noiselessly unlocked the door, and without once daring to look back, lest she should waver in her purpose, she went forth, heartbroken and alone, from what for eighteen happy years had been her home. Very rapidly she proceeded, coming at last to an open field through which the railroad ran, the depot being nearly a quarter of a mile away. Not until then had she reflected that her appearance at the station at that hour of the night would excite suspicion, and she was beginning to feel uneasy, when suddenly around a curve the cars appeared in view. Fearing lest she should be too late, she quickened her footsteps, when to her great surprise she saw that the train was stopping! But not for her they waited; in the bright moonlight the engineer had discovered a body lying across the track, and had stopped in time to save the life of a man, who, stupefied with drunkenness, had fallen asleep. The movement startled the passengers, many of whom alighted and gathered around the inebriate.

In the meantime Margaret had come near, and, knowing she could not now reach the depot in time, she mingled unobserved in the crowd, and entering the rear car, took her seat near the door. The train at last moved on, and as at the station no one save the agent was in waiting, it is not strange that the conductor passed unheeded the veiled figure which in the dark corner sat ready to pay her fare.

"He will come to me by and by," thought Maggie, but he did not, and when Worcester was reached the fare was still uncollected. Bewildered and uncertain what to do next, she stepped upon the platform, deciding finally to remain at the depot until morning, when a train would leave for Leominster, where she confidently expected to find her brother. Taking a seat in the ladies' room, she abandoned herself to her sorrow, wondering what Theo would say could she see her then. But Theo, though dreaming it may be of Maggie, dreamed not that she was near, and so the night wore on, Margaret sleeping towards daylight, and dreaming, too, of Arthur Carrollton, who she thought had followed her—nay, was bending over her now and whispering in her ear, " Wake, Maggie, wake."

Starting up, she glanced anxiously around, uttering a faint cry when she saw that it was not Arthur Carrollton, but a dark, rough-looking stranger, who rather rudely asked her where she wished to go.

" To Leominster," she answered, turning her face fully towards the man, who became instantly respectful, telling her when the train would leave, and saying that she must go to another depot, at the same time asking if she had not better wait at some hotel.

But Maggie preferred going at once to the Fitchburg depot, which she accordingly did, and drawing her veil over her face, lest some one of her few acquaintances in the city should recognize her, she sat there until the time appointed for the cars to leave. Then, weary and faint, she entered the train, her spirits in a measure rising as she felt that she was drawing near to those who would love her for what she was and not for what she had been. Rose would comfort her, and already her heart bounded with the thought of seeing one whom she believed to be her brother's wife, for Henry had written that ere his homeward voyage was made Rose would be his bride.

Ah, Maggie! there is for you a greater happiness in store—not a brother, but a sister—your father's child is there to greet your coming. And even at this early hour her snow-white fingers are arranging the fair June blossoms into bouquets, with which she adorns her home, saying to him who hovers at her side that somebody, she knows not whom, is surely coming to-day; and then, with a blush stealing over her cheek, she adds, "I wish it might be Margaret"; while Henry, with a peculiar twist of his comical mouth, winds his arm around her waist, and playfully responds, "Anyone save her."

CHAPTER XXI.

THE SISTERS.

ON a cool piazza overlooking a handsome flower garden the breakfast table was tastefully arranged. It was Rose's idea to have it there, and in her cambric wrapper, her golden curls combed smoothly back, and her blue eyes shining with the light of a new joy, she occupies her accustomed seat beside one who for several happy weeks has called her his, loving her more and more each day, and wondering how thoughts of any other could ever have filled his heart. There was much to be done about his home, so long deserted, and as Rose was determined upon a trip to the seaside he had made arrangements to be absent from his business for two months or more, and was now enjoying all the happiness of a quiet, domestic life, free from care of any kind. He had heard of Maggie's illness, but she was better now, he supposed, and when Theo hinted vaguely that a marriage between her and Arthur Carrollton was not at all improbable, he hoped it would be so, for the Englishman, he knew, was far better adapted to Margaret than he had ever been. Of Theo's hints he was speaking to Rose as they sat together at breakfast, and she had answered, " It will be a splendid match," when the doorbell rang, and the servant announced, " A lady in the parlor, who asks for Mr. Warner."

"I told you someone would come," said Rose. "Do, pray, see who it is. How does she look, Janet?"

"Tall, white as a ghost, with big black eyes," was Janet's answer; and, with his curiosity awakened, Henry Warner started for the parlor, Rose following on tiptoe, and listening through the half-closed door to what their visitor might say.

Margaret had experienced no difficulty in finding the house of Mrs. Warner, which seemed to her a second Paradise, so beautiful and cool it looked, nestled amid the tall, green forest trees. Everything around it betokened the fine taste of its occupants, and Maggie, as she reflected that she too was nearly connected with this family, felt her wounded pride in a measure soothed, for it was surely no disgrace to claim such people as her friends. With a beating heart she rang the bell, asking for Mr. Warner, and now, trembling in every limb, she awaited his coming. He was not prepared to meet her, and at first he did not know her, she was so changed; but when, throwing aside her bonnet, she turned her face so that the light from the window opposite shone fully upon her, he recognized her in a moment, and exclaimed, "Margaret— Margaret Miller! why are you here?"

The words reached Rose's ear, and darting forward she stood within the door, just as Margaret, staggering a step or two towards Henry, answered passionately, "I have come to tell you what I myself but recently have learned"; and wringing her hands despairingly, she continued, "I am not Maggie Miller, I am not anybody; I am Hagar Warren's grandchild, the child of her daughter and your own father! Oh, Henry, don't you see it? I am your sister. Take me as such, will you? Love me as such, or I shall surely die. I have nobody now in the wide world but you. They are all gone, all—Madam Conway, Theo too, and—and——" She could not speak that name. It died upon her lips, and tottering to a chair she would have fallen had not Henry caught her in his arms.

Leading her to the sofa, while Rose, perfectly confounded, still stood within the door, he said to the half-crazed girl: "Margaret, I do not understand you. I never had a sister, and my father died when I was six months old. There must be some mistake. Will you tell me what you mean?"

Bewildered and perplexed, Margaret began a hasty repetition of Hagar's story, but ere it was three-fourths told there came from the open door a wild cry of delight, and quick as lightning a fairy form flew across the floor, white arms were twined round Maggie's neck, kiss after kiss was pressed upon her lips, and Rose's voice was in her ear, never before half so sweet as now, when it murmured soft and low to the weary girl: "My sister Maggie—mine you are—the child of my own father, for I was Rose Hamilton, called Warner, first to please my aunt, and next to please my Henry. Oh, Maggie darling, I am so happy now!" and the little snowy hands smoothed caressingly the bands of hair, so unlike her own fair waving tresses.

It was, indeed, a time of almost perfect bliss to them all, and for a moment Margaret forgot her pain, which, had Hagar known the truth, need not have come to her. But she scarcely regretted it now, when she felt Rose Warner's heart throbbing against her own, and knew their father was the same.

"You are tired," Rose said, at length, when much had been said by both. "You must have rest, and then I will bring to you my aunt, our aunt, Maggie— our father's sister. She has been a mother to me. She will be one to you. But stay," she continued, "you have had no breakfast. I will bring you some," and she tripped lightly from the room.

Maggie followed her with swimming eyes, then turning to Henry she said, "You are very happy, I am sure."

"Yes, very," he answered, coming to her side. "Happy in my wife, happy in my newly found sister," and he laid his hand on hers with something of his former familiarity.

But the olden feeling was gone, and Maggie could now meet his glance without a blush, while he could talk with her as calmly as if she had never been aught to him save the sister of his wife. Thus often changeth the human heart's first love.

After a time Rose returned, bearing a silver tray heaped with the most tempting viands; but Maggie's heart was too full to eat, and after drinking a cup of the fragrant black tea, which Rose herself had made, she laid her head upon the pillow which Henry brought, and, with Rose sitting by, holding lovingly her hand, she fell into a quiet slumber. For several hours she slept, and when she awoke at last the sun was shining in at the western window, casting over the floor a glimmering light, and reminding her so forcibly of the dancing shadows on the grass which grew around the old stone house that her eyes filled with tears, and, thinking herself alone, she murmured, "Will it never be my home again?"

A sudden movement, the rustling of a dress, startled her, and lifting up her head she saw standing near a pleasant-looking, middle-aged woman, who, she rightly guessed, was Mrs. Warner, her own aunt.

"Maggie," the lady said, laying her hand on the fevered brow, "I have heard a strange tale to-day. Heretofore I had supposed Rose to be my only child, but though you take me by surprise you are not the less welcome. There is room in my heart for you, Maggie Miller, room for the youngest-born of my only brother. You are somewhat like him, too," she continned, "though more like your mother;" and with the mention of that name a flush stole over the lady's face, for she, too, was very proud, and her brother's marriage with a servant girl had never been quite forgiven.

Mrs. Warner had seen much of the world, and Maggie knew her to be a woman of refinement, a woman of whom even Madam Conway would not be ashamed; and, winding her arms around her neck, she said impulsively, "I am glad you are my aunt; and you will love me, I am sure, even if I am poor Hagar's grandchild."

Mrs. Warner knew nothing of Hagar save from Henry's amusing description, the entire truth of which she somewhat doubted; but she knew that whatever Hagar Warren might be, the beautiful girl before her was not answerable for it, and very kindly she tried to soothe her, telling her how happy they would be together. "Rose will leave me in the autumn," she said, "and without you I should be all alone." Of Hagar, too, she spoke kindly and considerately, and Maggie, listening to her, felt somewhat reconciled to the fate which had made her what she was. Still, there was much of pride to overcome ere she could calmly think of herself as other than Madam Conway's grandchild; and when that afternoon, as Henry and Rose were sitting with her, the latter spoke of her mother, saying she had a faint remembrance of a tall, handsome girl who sang her to sleep on the night when her own mother died, there came a visible shadow over Maggie's face, and instantly changing the conversation she asked why Henry had never told her anything definite concerning himself and family.

For a moment Henry seemed embarrassed. Both the Hamiltons and the Warners were very aristocratic in their feelings, and by mutual consent the name of Hester Warren was by them seldom spoken. Cousequently, if there existed a reason for Henry's silence with regard to his own and Rose's history, it was that he disliked bringing up a subject he had been taught to avoid, both by his aunt and the mother of Mr. Hamilton, who for several years after her son's death had lived with her daughter in Leominster, where she finally died. This, however, he could not say to Margaret, and after a little hesitancy he answered laughingly, " You never asked me for any particulars; and, then, you know, I was more agreeably occupied than I should have been had I spent my time in enlightening you with regard to our genealogy "; and the saucy mouth smiled archly, first on Rose, and then on Margaret, both of whom blushed slightly, the one suspecting he had not told her the whole truth, and the other knowing he had not.

Very considerate was Rose of Maggie's feelings, and not again that afternoon did she speak of Hester, though she talked much of their father; and Margaret, listening to his praises, felt herself insensibly drawn towards this new claimant for her filial love. " I wish I could have seen him," she said; and, starting to her feet, Rose answered: " Strange I did not think of it before. We have his portrait. Come this way," and she led the half-unwilling Maggie into an adjoining room, where from the wall a portly, good-humored-looking man gazed down upon the sisters, his eyes seeming to rest with mournful tenderness on the face of her whom in life they had not looked upon. He seemed older than Maggie had supposed, and the hair upon his head was white, reminding her of Hagar. But she did not for this turn away from him. There was something pleasing in the mild expression of his face, and she whispered faintly, " 'Tis my father."

On the right of this portrait was another, the picture of a woman, in whose curling lip and soft brown eyes Maggie recognized the mother of Henry. To the left was another still, and she gazed upon the angel face, with eyes of violet blue, and hair of golden brown, on which the fading sunlight now was falling, encircling it as it were with a halo of glory.

"You are much like her," she said to Rose, who made no answer, for she was thinking of another picture, which years before had been banished to the garret by her haughty grandmother, as unworthy a place beside him who had petted and caressed the young girl of plebeian birth and kindred.

" I can make amends for it, though," thought Rose, returning with Maggie to the parlor. Then, seeking out her husband, she held with him a whispered consultation, the result of which was that on the morrow

there was a rummaging in the garret, an absence from
home for an hour or two, and when about noon she
returned there was a pleased expression on her face, as
if she had accomplished her purpose, whatever it
might have been.

All that morning Maggie had been restless and uneasy, wandering listlessly from room to room, looking
anxiously down the street, starting nervously at the
sound of every footstep, while her cheeks alternately
flushed and then grew pale as the day passed on. Dinner being over she sat alone in the parlor, her eyes
fixed upon the carpet, and her thoughts away with
one who she vaguely hoped would have followed her
ere this. True, she had added no postscript to tell
him of her new discovery; but Hagar knew, and he
would go to her for a confirmation of the letter. She
would tell him where Maggie was gone, and he, if his
love could survive that shock, would follow her thither;
nay, would be there that very day, and Maggie's heart
grew wearier, fainter, as time wore on and he did not
come. "I might have known it," she whispered sadly.
"I knew that he would nevermore think of me," and
she wept silently over her ruined love.

"Maggie, sister," came to her ear, and Rose was at
her side. "I have a surprise for you, darling. Can
you bear it now?"

Oh, how eagerly poor Maggie Miller looked up in
Rose's face! The car whistle had sounded half an
hour before. Could it be that he had come? Was he
there? Did he love her still? No, Maggie, no; the
surprise awaiting you is of a far different nature, and
the tears flow afresh when Rose, in reply to the question "What is it, darling?" answers, "It is this," at

the same time placing in Maggie's hand an ambrotype which she bade her examine. With a feeling of keen disappointment Maggie opened the casing, involuntarily shutting her eyes as if to gather strength for what she was to see.

It was a young face—a handsome face—a face much like her own, while in the curve of the upper lip and the expression of the large black eyes there was a look like Hagar Warren. They had met together thus, the one a living reality, the other a semblance of the dead, and she who held that picture trembled violently. There was a fierce struggle within, the wildly beating heart throbbing for one moment with a newborn love, and then rebelling against taking that shadow, beautiful though it was, in place of her whose memory she had so long revered.

"Who is it, Maggie?" Rose asked, leaning over her shoulder.

Maggie knew full well whose face it was she looked upon, but not yet could she speak that name so interwoven with memories of another, and she answered mournfully, "It is Hester Hamilton."

"Yes, Margaret, your mother," said Rose. "I never called her by that name, but I respect her for your sake. She was my father's pet, so it has been said, for he was comparatively old, and she his young girl-wife."

"Where did you get this?" Maggie asked; and, coloring crimson, Rose replied, "We have always had her portrait, but grandmother, who was very old and foolishly proud about some things, was offended at our father's last marriage, and when after his death the portraits were brought here, she—— Forgive her,

Maggie—she did not know you, or she would not have done it——"

"I know," interrupted Maggie. "She despised this Hester Warren, and consigned her portrait to some spot from which you have brought it and had this taken from it."

"Not despised her!" cried Rose, in great distress, as she saw a dark expression stealing over the face of Maggie, in whose heart a chord of sympathy had been struck when she thought of her mother banished from her father's side. "Grandma could not despise her," continued Rose; "she was so good, so beautiful."

"Yes, she was beautiful," murmured Maggie, gazing earnestly upon the fair, round face, the soft, black eyes, and raven hair of her who for years had slept beneath the shadow of the Hillsdale woods. "Oh, I wish I were dead like her!" she exclaimed at last, closing the ambrotype and laying it upon the table. "I wish I was lying in that little grave in the place of her who should have borne my name, and been what I once was;" and bowing her face upon her hands she wept bitterly, while Rose tried in vain to comfort her. "I am not sorry you are my sister," sobbed Margaret through her tears. "That's the only comfort I have left me now; but, Rose, I love Arthur Carrollton so much—oh, so much, and how can I give him up!"

"If he is the noble, true-hearted man he looks to be, he will not give you up," answered Rose, and then for the first time since this meeting she questioned Margaret concerning Mr. Carrollton and the relations existing between them. "He will not cast you off," she said, when Margaret had told her all she had to tell. "He may be proud, but he will cling to you still. He will follow you, too—not to-day, perhaps, nor to-morrow, but ere long he will surely come;" and, listening to her sister's cheering words, Maggie herself grew hopeful, and that evening talked animatedly with Henry and Rose of a trip to the seaside that they were intending to make. "You will go, too, Maggie," said Rose, caressing her sister's pale cheek, and whispering in her ear, "Aunt Susan will be here to tell Mr. Carrollton where you are, if he does not come before we go, which I am sure he will."

Maggie tried to think so too, and her sleep that night was sweeter than it had been before for many weeks—but the next day came, and the next, and Maggie's eyes grew dim with watching and with tears, for up and down the road, as far as she could see, there came no trace of him for whom she waited.

"I might have known it; it was foolish of me to think otherwise," she sighed; and, turning sadly from the window where all the afternoon she had been sitting, she laid her head wearily upon the lap of Rose.

"Maggie," said Henry, "I am going to Worcester to-morrow, and perhaps George can tell me something of Mr. Carrollton."

For a moment Maggie's heart throbbed with delight at the thought of hearing from him, even though she heard that he would leave her. But anon her pride rose strong within her. She had told Hagar twice of her destination, Hagar had told him, and if he chose he would have followed her ere this; so somewhat bitterly she said: "Don't speak to George of me. Don't tell him I am here. Promise me, will you?"

The promise was given, and the next morning, which was Saturday, Henry started for Worcester on the early train. The day seemed long to Maggie, and when at nightfall he came to them again it was difficult to tell which was the more pleased at his return, Margaret or Rose.

"Did you see Theo?" asked the former; and Henry replied: "George told me she had gone to Hillsdale. Madam Conway is very sick."

"For me! for me! She's sick with mourning for me!" cried Maggie. "Darling grandma! she does love me still, and I will go home to her at once."

Then the painful thought rushed over her: "If she wished for me, she would send. It's the humiliation, not the love, that makes her sick. They have cast me off—grandma, Theo, all, all!" and, sinking upon the lounge, she wept aloud.

"Margaret," said Henry, coming to her side, "but for my promise I should have talked to George of you, for there was a troubled expression on his face when he asked me if I had heard from Hillsdale."

"What did you say?" asked Maggie, holding her breath to catch the answer, which was, "I told him you had not written to me since my return from Cuba, and then he looked as if he would say more, but a customer called him away, and our conversation was not resumed."

For a moment Maggie was silent. Then she said: "I am glad you did not intrude me upon him. If Theo has gone to Hillsdale, she knows that I am here, and does not care to follow me. It is the disgrace that troubles them, not the losing me!" and again burying her head in the cushions of the lounge, she wept bitterly. It was useless for Henry and Rose to try to comfort her, telling her it was possible that

Hagar had told nothing. "And if so," said Henry, "you well know that I am the last one to whom you would be expected to flee for protection." Margaret would not listen. She was resolved upon being unhappy, and during the long hours of that night she tossed wakefully upon her pillow, and when the morning came she was too weak to rise; so she kept her room, listening to the music of the Sabbath bells, which to her seemed sadly saying, "Home, home." "Alas! I have no home," she said, turning away to weep, for in the tolling of those bells there came to her no voice whispering of the darkness, the desolation, and the sorrow that were in the home for which she so much mourned.

Thus the day wore on, and ere another week was gone Rose insisted upon a speedy removal to the seashore, notwithstanding it was so early in the season, for by this means she hoped that Maggie's health would be improved. Accordingly, Henry went once more to Worcester, ostensibly for money, but really to see if George Douglas now would speak to him of Margaret. But George was in New York, they said; and, somewhat disappointed, Henry went back to Leominster, where everything was in readiness for their journey. Monday was fixed upon for their departure, and at an early hour Margaret looked back on what had been to her a second home, smiling faintly as Rose whispered to her cheerily, "I have a strong presentiment that somewhere in our travels we shall meet with Arthur Carrollton."

CHAPTER XXII.

THE HOUSE OF MOURNING.

COME now over the hills to the westward. Come to the Hillsdale woods, to the stone house by the mill, where all the day long there is heard but one name, the servants breathing it softly and low, as if she who had borne it were dead, the sister, dim-eyed now, and paler faced, whispering it oft to herself, while the lady, so haughty and proud, repeats it again and again, shuddering as naught but the echoing walls reply to the heartbroken cry of, " Margaret, Margaret, where are you now? "

Yes, there was mourning in that household—mourning for the lost one, the darling, the pet of them all.

Brightly had the sun arisen on that June morning which brought to them their sorrow, while the birds in the tall forest trees caroled as gayly as if no storm-cloud were hovering near. At an early hour Mr. Carrollton had arisen, thinking, as he looked forth from his window, " She will tell me all to-day," and smiling as he thought how easy and pleasant would be the task of winning her back to her olden gayety. Madam Conway, too, was unusually excited, and very anxiously she listened for the first sound of Maggie's footsteps on the stairs.

" She sleeps late," she thought, when breakfast was announced, and taking her accustomed seat she bade a servant see if Margaret were ill.

" She is not there," was the report the girl brought back.

" Not there!" cried Mr. Carrollton.

" Not there!" repeated Madam Conway, a shadowy foreboding of evil stealing over her. " She seldom walks at this early hour," she continued; and, rising, she went herself to Margaret's room.

Everything was in perfect order, the bed was undisturbed, the chamber empty; Margaret was gone, and on the dressing-table lay the fatal letter telling why she went. At first Madam Conway did not see it; but it soon caught her eye, and tremblingly she opened it, reading but the first line, " I am going away forever."

Then a loud shriek rang through the silent room, penetrating to Arthur Carrollton's listening ear, and bringing him at once to her side. With the letter still in her hand, and her face of a deathly hue, and her eyes flashing with fear, Madam Conway turned to him as he entered, saying, " Margaret has gone, left us forever—killed herself it may be! Read!" And she handed him the letter, herself bending eagerly forward to hear what he might say.

But she listened in vain. With lightning rapidity Arthur Carrollton read what Maggie had written— read that she, his idol, the chosen bride of his bosom, was the daughter of a servant, the grandchild of old Hagar! And for this she had fled from his presence, fled because she knew of the mighty pride which now, in the first bitter moment of his agony, did indeed rise up, a barrier between himself and the beautiful girl he loved so well. Had she lain dead before him, dead in all her youthful beauty, he could have folded her in his arms, and then buried her from his sight, with a feeling of perfect happiness compared to that which he now felt.

"Oh, Maggie, my lost one, can it be!" he whispered to himself, and pressing his hand upon his chest, which heaved with strong emotion, he staggered to a seat, while the perspiration stood in beaded drops upon his forehead and around his lips.

"What is it, Mr. Carrollton? 'Tis something dreadful, sure," said Mrs. Jeffrey, appearing in the door, but Madam Conway motioned her away, and, tottering to his side, said, "Read it to me—read."

The sound of her voice recalled his wandering mind, and covering his face with his hands he moaned in anguish; then, growing suddenly calm, he snatched up the letter, which had fallen to the floor, and read it aloud; while Madam Conway, stupefied with horror, sank at his feet, and clasping her hands above her head, rocked to and fro, but made no word of comment. Far down the long ago her thoughts were straying, and gathering up many bygone scenes which told her that what she heard was true.

"Yes, 'tis true," she groaned; and then, powerless to speak another word, she laid her head upon a chair, while Mr. Carrollton, preferring to be alone, sought the solitude of his own room, where unobserved he could wrestle with his sorrow and conquer his inborn pride, which whispered to him that a Carrollton must not wed a bride so far beneath him.

Only a moment, though, and then the love he bore for Maggie Miller rolled back upon him with an overwhelming power, while his better judgment, with that love, came hand in hand, pleading for the fair young girl, who, now that he had lost her, seemed a thousandfold dearer than before. But he had not lost her; he would find her. She was Maggie Miller still to him, and though old Hagar's blood were in her veins he would not give her up. This resolution once made, it could not be shaken, and when half an hour or more was passed he walked with firm, unfaltering footsteps back to the apartment where Madam Conway still sat upon the floor, her head resting upon the chair, and her frame convulsed with grief.

Her struggle had been a terrible one, and it was not over yet, for with her it was more than a matter of pride and love. Her daughter's rights had been set at naught; a wrong had been done to the dead; the child who slept beneath the pine had been neglected; nay, in life, had been, perhaps, despised for an intruder, for one who had no right to call her grandmother; and shudderingly she cried, "Why was it suffered thus to be?" Then as she thought of white-haired Hagar Warren, she raised her hand to curse her, but the words died on her lips, for Hagar's deed had brought to her much joy; and now, as she remembered the bounding step, the merry laugh, the sunny face, and loving words which had made her later years so happy, she involuntarily stretched out her arms in empty air, moaning sadly: "I want her here. I want her now, just as she used to be." Then, over the grave of her buried daughter, over the grave of the sickly child, whose thin, blue face came up before her just as it lay in its humble coffin, over the deception of eighteen years, her heart bounded with one wild, yearning throb, for every bleeding fiber clung with a deathlike grasp to her who had been so suddenly taken from her.

" I love her still! " she cried; " but can I take her
back?" And then commenced the fiercest struggle of
all, the battling of love and pride, the one rebelling
against the child of Hagar Warren, and the other
clamoring loudly that without that child the world to
her was nothing. It was the hour of Madam Conway's humiliation, and in bitterness of spirit she
groaned: " That I should come to this! Theo first,
and Margaret, my bright, my beautiful Margaret,
next! Oh, how can I give her up when I loved her
best of all—best of all!"

This was true, for all the deeper, stronger love of
Madam Conway's nature had gone forth to the merry,
gleeful girl whose graceful, independent bearing she
had so often likened to herself and the haughty race
with which she claimed relationship. How was this
illusion dispelled! Margaret was not a Conway, nor
yet a Davenport. A servant-girl had been her mother,
and of her father there was nothing known. Madam
Conway was one who seldom wept for grief. She
had stood calmly at the bedside of her dying husband, had buried her only daughter from her sight,
had met with many reverses, and shed for all no tears,
but now they fell like rain upon her face, burning,
blistering as they fell, but bringing no relief.

" I shall miss her in the morning," she cried, " miss
her at noon, miss her in the lonesome nights, miss her
everywhere—oh, Margaret, Margaret, 'tis more than
I can bear! Come back to me now, just as you are.
I want you here—here where the pain is hardest,"
and she clasped her arms tightly over her heaving
bosom. Then her pride returned again, and with it
came thoughts of Arthur Carrollton. He would scoff

at her as weak and sentimental; he would never take beyond the sea a bride of " Hagarish " birth; and duty demanded that she too should be firm, and sanction his decision. " But when he's gone," she whispered, " when he has left America behind, I'll find her, if my life is spared. I'll find poor Margaret, and see that she does not want, though I must not take her back."

This resolution, however, did not bring her comfort, and the hands pressed so convulsively upon her side could not ease her pain. Surely never before had so dark an hour infolded that haughty woman, and a prayer that she might die was trembling on her lips when a footfall echoed along the hall, and Arthur Carrollton stood before her. His face was very pale, bearing marks of the storm he had passed through; but he was calm, and his voice was natural as he said: " Possibly what we have heard is false. It may be a vagary of Hagar's half-crazed brain."

For an instant Madam Conway had hoped so too; but when she reflected, she knew that it was true. Old Hagar had been very minute in her explanations to Margaret, who in turn had written exactly what she had heard, and Madam Conway, when she recalled the past, could have no doubt that it was true. She remembered everything, but more distinctly the change of dress at the time of the baptism. There could be no mistake. Margaret was not hers, and so she said to Arthur Carrollton, turning her head away as if she too were in some way answerable for the disgrace.

" It matters not," he replied, " whose she has been. She is mine now, and if you feel able we will consult together as to the surest method of finding her."

A sudden faintness came over Madam Conway, and, while the expression of her face changed to one of joyful surprise, she stammered out: "Can it be I hear aright? Do I understand you? Are you willing to take poor Maggie back?"

"I certainly have no other intention," he answered. "There was a moment, the memory of which makes me ashamed, when my pride rebelled; but it is over now, and though Maggie cannot in reality be again your child, she can be my wife, and I must find her."

"You make me so happy—oh, so happy!" said Madam Conway. "I feared you would cast her off, and in that case it would have been my duty to do so too, though I never loved a human being as at this moment I love her."

Mr. Carrollton looked as if he did not fully comprehend the woman who, loving Margaret as she said she did, could yet be so dependent upon his decision; but he made no comment, and when next he spoke he announced his intention of calling upon Hagar, who possibly could tell him where Margaret had gone. "At all events," said he, "I may ascertain why the secret, so long kept, was at this late day divulged. It may be well," he continued, "to say nothing to the servants as yet, save that Maggie has gone. Mrs. Jeffrey, however, had better be let into the secret at once. We can trust her, I think."

Madam Conway bowed, and Mr. Carrollton left the room, starting immediately for the cottage by the mine. As he approached the house he saw the servant who for several weeks had been staying there, and who now came out to meet him, telling him that since the night before Hagar had been raving crazy, talking continually of Maggie, who, she said, had gone where none would ever find her.

In some anxiety Mr. Carrollton pressed on, until the cottage door was reached, where for a moment he stood gazing silently upon the poor woman before him. Upon the bed, her white hair falling over her round, bent shoulders, and her large eyes shining with delirious light, old Hagar sat, waving back and forth, and talking of Margaret, of Hester, and "the little foolish child," who, with a sneer upon her lip, she said, "was a fair specimen of the Conway race."

"Hagar," said Mr. Carrollton; and at the sound of that voice Hagar turned toward him her flashing eyes, then with a scream buried her head in the bed-clothes, saying: "Go away, Arthur Carrollton! Why are you here? Don't you know who I am? Don't you know what Margaret is, and don't you know how proud you are?"

"Hagar," he said again, subduing, by a strong effort, the repugnance he felt at questioning her, "I know all, except where Margaret has gone, and if on this point you can give me any information, I shall receive it most thankfully."

"Gone!" shrieked Hagar, starting up in bed; "then she has gone. The play is played out, the performance is ended—and I have sinned for nothing!"

"Hagar, will you tell me where Maggie is? I wish to follow her," said Mr. Carrollton; and Hagar answered: "Maggie, Maggie—he said that lovingly enough, but there's a catch somewhere. He does not wish to follow her for any good—and though I know where she has gone I'll surely never tell. I kept one secret nineteen years. I can keep another as long ";

and, folding her arms upon her chest, she commenced
singing, " I know full well, but I'll never tell."

Biting his lips with vexation, Mr. Carrollton tried
first by persuasion, then by flattery, and lastly by
threats, to obtain from her the desired information,
but in vain. Her only answer was, " I know full well,
but I'll never tell," save once, when tossing towards
him her long white hair, she shrieked: " Don't you
see a resemblance—only hers is black—and so was
mine nineteen years ago—and so was Hester's too—
glossy and black as the raven's wing. The child is
like the mother—the mother was like the grandmother,
and the grandmother is like—me, Hagar Warren. Do
you understand? "

Mr. Carrollton made no answer, and with a feeling
of disappointment walked away, shuddering as he
thought, " And she is Margaret's grandmother."

He found Madam Conway in hysterics on Margaret's bed, for she had refused to leave the room,
saying she would die there, or nowhere. Gradually
the reality of her loss had burst upon her, and now,
gasping, choking, and wringing her hands, she lay
upon the pillows, while Mrs. Jeffrey, worked up to a
pitch of great nervous excitement, fidgeted hither and
thither, doing always the wrong thing, fanning the
lady when she did not wish to be fanned, and ceasing
to fan her just when she was " dying for want of air."

As yet Mrs. Jeffrey knew nothing definite, except
that something dreadful had happened to Margaret;
but very candidly Mr. Carrollton told her all, bidding
her keep silent on the subject; then, turning to Madam
Conway, he repeated to her the result of his call on old
Hagar.

" The wretch!" gasped Madam Conway, while Mrs. Jeffrey, running in her fright from the window to the door, and from the door back to the window again, exclaimed: " Margaret not a Conway, nor yet a Davenport, after all! It is just what I expected. I always knew she came honestly by those low-bred ways!"

" Jeffrey," and the voice of the hysterical woman on the bed was loud and distinct, as she grasped the arm of the terrified little governess, who chanced to be within her reach. " Jeffrey, either leave my house at once, or speak more deferentially of Miss Miller. You will call her by that name, too. It matters not to Mr. Carrollton and myself whose child she has been. She is ours now, and must be treated with respect. Do you understand me?"

" Yes, ma'am," meekly answered Jeffrey, rubbing her dumpy arm, which bore the mark of a thumb and finger, and as her services were not just then required she glided from the room to drown, if possible, her grievance in the leather-bound London edition of Baxter!

Meanwhile Madam Conway was consulting with Mr. Carrollton as to the best mode of finding Margaret. " She took the cars, of course," said Mr. Carrollton, adding that he should go at once to the depot and ascertain which way she went. " If I do not return to-night you need not be alarmed," he said, as he was leaving the room, whereupon Madam Conway called him back, bidding him telegraph for Theo at once, as she must have someone with her besides that vexatious Jeffrey.

Mr. Carrollton promised compliance with her request, and then went immediately to the depot, where he learned that no one had entered the cars from that place on the previous night, and that Maggie, if she took the train at all, must have done so at some other station. This was not unlikely, and before the day was passed Mr. Carrollton had visited several different stations, and had talked with the conductors of the several trains, but all to no purpose; and, very much disheartened, he returned at nightfall to the old stone house, where to his surprise he found both Theo and her husband. The telegram had done its mission, and feeling anxious to know the worst George had come up with Theo to spend the night. It was the first time that Madam Conway had seen him since her memorable encounter with his mother, for though Theo had more than once been home, he had never before accompanied her, and now when Madam Conway heard his voice in the hall below she groaned afresh. The sight of his good-humored face, however, and his kind offer to do whatever he could to find the fugitive, restored her composure in a measure, and she partially forgot that he was in any way connected with the blue umbrella, or the blue umbrella connected with him! Never in her life had Theo felt very deeply upon any subject, and now, though she seemed bewildered at what she heard, she manifested no particular emotion, until her grandmother, wringing her hands, exclaimed, "You have no sister now, my child, and I no Margaret!" Then, indeed, her tears flowed, and when her husband whispered to her, "We will love poor Maggie all the same," she cried aloud, but not quite as demonstratively as Madam Conway wished; and, in a very unamiable frame of mind, the old lady accused her of being selfish and hard-hearted.

At this stage of proceedings Mr. Carrollton returned, bringing no tidings of Maggie, whereupon another fit of hysterics ensued, and as Theo behaved
much worse than Mrs. Jeffrey had done, the latter was
finally summoned again to the sickroom, and at last
succeeded in quieting the excited woman. The next
morning George Douglas visited old Hagar, but he
too was unsuccessful, and that afternoon he returned
to Worcester, leaving Theo with her grandmother,
who, though finding fault with whatever she did. refused to let her go until Margaret was found.

During the remainder of the week Mr. Carrollton
rode through the country, making the most minute inquiries, and receiving always the same discouraging
answer. Once he thought to advertise, but from making the affair thus public he instinctively shrank, and,
resolving to spare neither his time, his money, nor his
health, he pursued his weary way alone. Once, too,
Madam Conway spoke of Henry Warner, saying it
was possible Maggie might have gone to him, as she
had thought so much of Rose; but Mr. Carrollton
" knew better." A discarded lover, he said, was the
last person in the world to whom a young girl like
Margaret would go, particularly as Theo had said that
Henry was now the husband of another.

Still the suggestion haunted him, and on the Monday following Henry Warner's first visit to Worcester,
he, too, went down to talk with Mr. Douglas, asking
him if it were possible that Maggie was in Leominster.

" I know she is not," said George, repeating the particulars of his interview with Henry, who, he said, was
at the store on Saturday. " Once I thought of telling
him all," said he, " and then, considering the rela-

tion which formerly existed between them, I concluded to keep silent, especially as he manifested no
desire to speak of her, but appeared, I fancied, quite
uneasy when I casually mentioned Hillsdale."

Thus was that matter decided, and while not many
miles away Maggie was watching hopelessly for the
coming of Arthur Carrollton, he, with George Douglas, was devising the best means for finding her,
George generously offering to assist in the search, and
suggesting finally that he should himself go to New
York City, while Mr. Carrollton explored Boston and
its vicinity. It seemed quite probable that Margaret
would seek some of the large cities, as in her letter
she had said she could earn her livelihood by teaching
music; and quite hopeful of success, the young men
parted, Mr. Carrollton going immediately to Boston,
while Mr. Douglas, after a day or two, started for
New York, whither, as the reader will remember, he
had gone at the time of Henry's last visit to
Worcester.

Here for a time we leave them, Hagar raving mad,
Madam Conway in strong hysterics, Theo wishing
herself anywhere but at Hillsdale, Mrs. Jeffrey ditto,
George Douglas threading the crowded streets of the
noisy city, and Mr. Carrollton in Boston, growing
paler and sadder as day after day passed by, bringing
him no trace of the lost one. Here, I say, we leave
them, while in another chapter we follow the footsteps
of her for whom this search was made.

CHAPTER XXIII.

NIAGARA.

FROM the seaside to the mountains, from the mountains to Saratoga, from Saratoga to Montreal, from Montreal to the Thousand Isles, and thence they scarce knew where, the travelers wended their way, stopping not long at any place, for Margaret was ever seeking change. Greatly had she been admired, her pale, beautiful face attracting attention at once; but from all flattery she turned away, saying to Henry and Rose, "Let us go on."

So onward still they went, pausing longest at Montreal, for it was there Arthur Carrollton had been, there a part of his possessions lay, and there Margaret willingly lingered, even after her companions wished to be gone.

"He may be here again," she said; and so she waited and watched, scanning eagerly the passers-by, and noticing each new face as it appeared at the table of the hotel where they were staying. But the one she waited for never came. "And even if he does," she thought, "he will not come for me."

So she signified her willingness to depart, and early one bright July morning she left, while the singing birds from the treetops, the summer air from the Canada hills, and, more than all, a warning voice within her, bade her "Tarry yet a little, stay till the sun was set," for far out in the country, and many miles away, a train was thundering on. It would reach the city at nightfall, and among its jaded passengers was a worn and weary man. Hopeless, almost aimless now, he would come, and why he came he scarcely knew. "She would not be there, so far from home," he felt sure, but he was coming for the sake of what he hoped and feared when last he trod those streets. Listlessly he entered the same hotel from whose windows, for five long days, a fair young face had looked for him. Listlessly he registered his name, then carelessly turned the leaves backward—backward—backward still, till only one remained between his hand and the page bearing date five days before. He paused and was about to move away, when a sudden breeze from the open window turned the remaining leaf, and his eye caught the name, not of Maggie Miller, but of " Henry Warner, lady, and sister."

Thus it stood, and thus he repeated it to himself, dwelling upon the last word "sister," as if to him it had another meaning. He had heard from Madam Conway that neither Henry Warner nor Rose had a sister, but she might be mistaken; probably she was; and dismissing the subject from his mind, he walked away. Still the names haunted him, and thinking at last that if Mr. Warner were now in Montreal he would like to see him, he returned to the office, asking the clerk if the occupants of Nos. — were there still.

"Left this morning for the Falls," was the laconic answer; and, without knowing why he should particularly wish to do so, Mr. Carrollton resolved to follow them.

He would as soon be at the Falls as in Montreal, he thought. Accordingly he left the next morning for

Niagara, taking the shortest route by river and lake, and arriving there on the evening of the second day after his departure from the city. But nowhere could a trace be found of Henry Warner, and determining now to wait until he came Mr. Carrollton took rooms at the International, where after a day or two, worn out with travel, excitement, and hope deferred, he became severely indisposed, and took his bed, forgetting entirely both Henry Warner and the sister, whose name he had seen upon the hotel register. Thoughts of Maggie Miller, however, were constantly in his mind, and whether waking or asleep he saw always her face, sometimes radiant with healthful beauty, as when he first beheld her, and again, pale, troubled, and sad, as when he saw her last.

"Oh, shall I ever find her?" he would sometimes say, as in the dim twilight he lay listening to the noisy hum which came up from the public room below.

And once, as he lay there thus, he dreamed, and in his dreams there came through the open window a clear, silvery voice, breathing the loved name of Maggie. Again he heard it on the stairs, then little tripping feet went past his door, followed by a slow, languid tread, and with a nervous start the sick man awoke. The day had been cloudy and dark, but the rain was over now, and the room was full of sunshine —sunshine dancing on the walls, sunshine glimmering on the floor, sunshine everywhere. Insensibly, too, there stole over Mr. Carrollton's senses a feeling of quiet, of rest, and he slept ere long again, dreaming this time that Margaret was there.

Yes, Margaret was there—there, beneath the same roof which sheltered him, and the same sunshine which filled his room with light had bathed her white brow, as, leaning from her window, she listened to the roar of the falling water. They had lingered on their way, stopping at the Thousand Isles, for Margaret would have it so; but they had come at last, and the tripping footsteps in the hall, the silvery voice upon the stairs, was that of the golden-haired Rose, who watched over Margaret with all a sister's love and a mother's care. The frequent jokes of the fun-loving Henry, too, were not without their good effect, and Margaret was better now than she had been for many weeks.

"I can rest here," she said, and a faint color came to her cheeks, making her look more like herself than at any time since that terrible night of sorrow in the woods.

And so three days went by, and Mr. Carrollton, on his weary bed, dreamed not that the slender form which sometimes, through his half-closed door, cast a shadow in his room, was that of her for whom he sought. The tripping footsteps, too, went often by, and a merry, childish voice, which reminded him of Maggie, rang through the spacious halls, until at last the sick man came to listen for that party as they passed. They were a merry party, he thought, a very merry party; and he pictured to himself her of the ringing voice; she was dark-eyed, he said, with braids of shining hair, and when, as they were passing once, he asked of his attendant if it were not as he had fancied, he felt a pang of disappointment at the answer, which was, "The girl the young gentleman hears so much has yellow curls and dark blue eyes."

"She is not like Maggie, then," he sighed, and when again he heard that voice a part of its music was gone.

Still, it cheered his solitude, and he listened for it again, just as he had done before.

Once, when he knew they were going out, he went to the window to see them, but the large straw hats and close carriage revealed no secret, and disappointed he turned away.

" It is useless to stay here longer," he said; " I must be about my work. I am able to leave, and I will go to-morrow. But first I will visit the Falls once more. I may never see them again."

Accordingly, next morning, after Margaret and Rose had left the house, he came down the stairs, sprang into an open carriage, and was driven to Goat Island, which, until his illness, had been his favorite resort.

.   .   .   .   .

Beneath the tall forest trees which grow upon the island there is a rustic seat. Just on the brink of the river it stands, and the carriage road winds by. It is a comparatively retired spot, looking out upon the foaming water rushing so madly on. Here the weary often rest; here lovers sometimes come to be alone; and here Maggie Miller sat on that summer morning, living over again the past, which to her had been so bright, and musing sadly on the future, which would bring her she knew not what.

She had struggled to overcome her pride, nor deemed it now a disgrace that she was not a Conway. Of Hagar, too, she often thought, pitying the poor old half-crazed woman who for her sake had borne so much. But not of her was she thinking now. Hagar was shriveled and bent and old, while the image present in Margaret's mind was handsome, erect, and young, like the gentleman riding by—the man whose

carriage wheels, grinding into the gravelly road, at.
tracted no attention. Too intent was she upon a
shadow to heed aught else around, and she leaned
against a tree, nor turned her head aside, as Arthur
Carrollton went by!

A little further on, and out of Maggie's sight, a
fairy figure was seated upon the grass; the hat was
thrown aside, and her curls fell back from her upturned face as she spoke to Henry Warner. But the
sentence was unfinished, for the carriage appeared in
view, and with woman's quick perception Rose ex-
claims, " 'Tis surely Arthur Carrollton!"

Starting to her feet, she sprang involuntarily forward to meet him, casting a rapid glance around for
Margaret. He observed the movement, and knew that
somewhere in the world he had seen that face before
—those golden curls—those deep blue eyes—that child,
ish form—they were not wholly unfamiliar. Who
was she, and why did she advance towards him?

"Rose," said Henry, who would call her back,
"Rose!" and looking towards the speaker Mr. Carrollton knew at once that Henry Warner and his bride
were standing there before him.

In a moment he had joined them, and though he
knew that Henry Warner had once loved Maggie
Miller he spoke of her without reserve, saying to Rose,
when she asked if he were there for pleasure: "I am
looking for Maggie Miller. A strange discovery has
been made of late, and Margaret has left us."

"She is here—here with us!" cried Rose; and in the
exuberance of her joy she was darting away, when
Henry held her back until further explanations were
made.

This did not occupy them long, for sitting down again upon the bank Rose briefly told him all she knew; and when with eager joy he asked "Where is she now?" she pointed towards the spot, and then with Henry walked away, for she knew that it was not for her to witness that glad meeting.

The river rolls on with its heaving swell, and the white foam is tossed towards the shore, while the soft summer air still bears on its wing the sound of the cataract's roar. But Margaret sees it not, hears it not. There is a spell upon her now—a halo of joy; and she only knows that a strong arm is around her, and a voice is in her ear, whispering that the bosom on which her weary head is pillowed shall be her resting-place forever.

It had come to her suddenly, sitting there thus—the footfall upon the sand had not been heard—the shadow upon the grass had not been seen, and his presence had not been felt, till, bending low, Mr. Carrollton said aloud, "My Maggie!"

Then indeed she started up, and turned to see who it was that thus so much like him had called her name. She saw who it was, and looking in his face she knew she was not hated, and with a moaning cry went forward to the arm extended to receive her.

.   .   .   .   . .

Four guests, instead of one, went forth that afternoon from the International—four guests homeward bound, and eager to be there. No more journeying now for happiness; no more searching for the lost; for both are found; both are there—happiness and Maggie Miller.

CHAPTER XXIV.

HOME.

IMPATIENT, restless, and cross, Madam Conway lay in Margaret's room, scolding Theo and chiding Mrs. Jeffrey, both of whom, though trying their utmost to suit her, managed unfortunately to do always just what she wished them not to do. Mrs. Jeffrey's hands were usually too cold, and Theo's were too hot. Mrs. Jeffrey made the head of the bed too high, Theo altogether too low. In short, neither of them ever did what Margaret would have done had she been there, and so day after day the lady complained, growing more and more unamiable, until at last Theo began to talk seriously of following Margaret's example, and running away herself, at least as far as Worcester; but the distressed Mrs. Jeffrey, terrified at the thought of being left there alone, begged of her to stay a little longer, offering the comforting assurance that " it cannot be so bad always, for Madam Conway will either get better—or something."

So Theo stayed, enduring with a martyr's patience the caprices of her grandmother, who kept the whole household in a constant state of excitement, and who at last began to blame George Douglas entirely as being the only one in fault. " He didn't half look," she said, " and she doubted whether he knew enough to keep from losing himself in New York. It was the most foolish thing Arthur Carrollton had ever done, hiring George Douglas to search!"

"Hiring him, grandma!" cried Theo; "George offered his services for nothing," and the tears came to her eyes at the injustice done her husband.

But Madam Conway persisted in being unreasonable, and matters grew gradually worse until the day when Margaret was found at the Falls. On that morning Madam Conway determined upon riding. "Fresh air will do me good," she said, "and you have kept me in a hot chamber long enough."

Accordingly, the carriage was brought out, and Madam Conway carefully lifted in; but ere fifty rods were passed the coachman was ordered to drive back, as she could not endure the jolt. "I told you I couldn't, all the time;" and her eyes turned reprovingly upon poor Theo, sitting silently in the opposite corner.

"The Lord help me, if she isn't coming back so soon!" sighed Mrs. Jeffrey, as she saw the carriage returning, and went to meet the invalid, who had "taken her death of cold," just as she knew she should when they insisted upon her going out.

That day was far worse than any which had preceded it. It was probably her last, Madam Conway said, and numerous were the charges she gave to Theo concerning Margaret, should she ever be found. The house, the farm, the furniture and plate were all to be hers, while to Theo was given the lady's wardrobe, saving such articles as Margaret might choose for herself, and if she never were found the house and farm were to be Mr. Carrollton's. This was too much for Theo, who resolved to

go home on the morrow, at all hazards, and she
had commenced making preparations for leaving,
when to her great joy her husband came, and in re-
counting to him her trials she forgot in a measure
how unhappy she had been. George Douglas was
vastly amused at what he heard, and resolved to experiment a little with the lady, who was so weak as
to notice him only with a slight nod when he first entered the room. He saw at a glance that nothing in
particular was the matter, and when towards night she
lay panting for breath, with her eyes half closed, he
approached her and said, " Madam, in case you
die——"

" In case I die ! " she whispered indignantly. " It
doesn't admit of a doubt. My feet are as cold as
icicles now."

" Certainly," said he. " I beg your pardon; of
course you'll die."

The lady turned away rather defiantly for a dying
woman, and George continued, " What I mean to say
is this—if Margaret is never found, you wish the house
to be Mr. Carrollton's? "

" Yes, everything, my wardrobe and all," came from
beneath the bedclothes ; and George proceeded : " Mr.
Carrollton cannot of course take the house to England, and, as he will need a trusty tenant, would you
object greatly if my father and mother should come
here to live? They'd like it, I——"

The sentence was unfinished—the bunches in the
throat which for hours had prevented the sick woman
from speaking aloud, and were eventually to choke
her to death, disappeared; Madam Conway found her
voice, and, starting up, screamed out, " That abomi-

nable woman and heathenish girl in this house, in my house; I'll live forever, first!" and her angry eyes flashed forth their indignation.

"I thought the mention of mother would revive her," said George, aside, to Theo, who, convulsed with laughter, had hidden herself behind the window curtain.

Mr. Douglas was right, for not again that afternoon did Madam Conway speak of dying, though she kept her bed until nightfall, when an incident occurred which brought her at once to her feet, making her forget that she had ever been otherwise than well.

In her cottage by the mine old Hagar had raved and sung and wept, talking much of Margaret, but never telling whither she had gone. Latterly, however, she had grown more calm, talking far less than heretofore, and sleeping a great portion of the day, so that the servant who attended her became neglectful, leaving her many hours alone, while she, at the stone house, passed her time more agreeably than at the lonesome hut. On the afternoon of which we write she was as usual at the house, and though the sun went down she did not hasten back, for her patient, she said, was sure to sleep, and even if she woke she did not need much care.

Meantime old Hagar slumbered on. It was a deep, refreshing sleep, and when at last she did awake, her reason was in a measure restored, and she remembered everything distinctly up to the time of Margaret's last visit, when she said she was going away. And Margaret had gone away, she was sure of that, for she remembered Arthur Carrollton stood once within that room, and besought of her to tell if she knew aught of Maggie's destination. She did know, but she had not told, and perhaps they had not found her yet. Raising herself in bed, she called aloud to the servant, but there came no answer; and for an hour or more she waited impatiently, growing each moment more and more excited. If Margaret were found she wished to know it, and if she were not found it was surely her duty to go at once and tell them where she was. But could she walk? She stepped upon the floor and tried. Her limbs trembled beneath her weight, and, sinking into a chair, she cried, "I can't! I can't!"

Half an hour later she heard the sound of wheels. A neighboring farmer was returning home from Richland, and had taken the cross road as his shortest route. "Perhaps he will let me ride," she thought, and, hobbling to the door, she called after him, making known her request. Wondering what "new freak" had entered her mind, the man consented, and just as it was growing dark he set her down at Madam Conway's gate, where, half fearfully, the bewildered woman gazed around. The windows of Margaret's room were open, a figure moved before them; Margaret might be there; and entering the hall door unobserved, she began to ascend the stairs, crawling upon her hands and knees, and pausing several times to rest.

It was nearly dark in the sickroom, and as Mrs. Jeffrey had just gone out, and Theo, in the parlor below, was enjoying a quiet talk with her husband, Madam Conway was quite alone. For a time she lay thinking of Margaret; then her thoughts turned upon George and his "amazing proposition." "Such un-

heard of insolence!" she exclaimed, and she was pro-
ceeding farther with her soliloquy, when a peculiar
noise upon the stairs caught her ear, and raising. herself upon her elbow she listened intently to the sound,
which came nearer and nearer, and seemed like someone creeping slowly, painfully, for she could hear at
intervals a long-drawn breath or groan, and with a
vague feeling of uneasiness she awaited anxiously the
apearance of her visitor; nor waited long, for the
half-closed door swung slowly back, and through the
gathering darkness the shape came crawling on, over
the threshold, into the room, towards the corner, its
limbs distorted and bent, its white hair sweeping the
floor. With a smothered cry Madam Conway hid beneath the bedclothes, looking cautiously out at the
singular object which came creeping on until the bed
was reached. It touched the counterpane, it was
struggling to regain its feet, and with a scream of hor-
rcr the terrified woman cried out, " Fiend, why are you
here?" while a faint voice replied, " I am looking for
Margaret. I thought she was in bed"; and, rising up
from her crouching posture, Hagar Warren stood face
to face with the woman she had so long deceived.

"Wretch!" exclaimed the latter, her pride returning as she recognized old Hagar and thought of her
as Maggie's grandmother. " Wretch, how dare you
come into my presence? Leave this room at once,"
and a shrill cry of " Theo! Theo!" rang through the
house, bringing Theo at once to the chamber, where
she started involuntarily at the sight which met her
view.

"Who is it? who is it?" she exclaimed.

"It's Hagar Warren. Take her away!" screamed

Madam Conway; while Hagar, raising her withered hand deprecatingly, said: "Hear me first. Do you know where Margaret is? Has she been found?"

"No, no," answered Theo, bounding to her side, while Madam Conway forgot to scream, and bent eagerly forward to listen, her symptoms of dissolution disappearing one by one as the strange narrative proceeded, and ere its close she was nearly dressed, standing erect as ever, her face glowing, and her eyes lighted up with joy.

"Gone to Leominster! Henry Warner's half-sister!" she exclaimed. "Why didn't she add a postscript to that letter, and tell us so? though the poor child couldn't think of everything;" and then, unmindful of George Douglas, who at that moment entered the room, she continued: "I should suppose Douglas might have found it out ere this. But the moment I put my eyes upon *that woman* I knew no child of hers would ever know enough to find Margaret. The Warners are a tolerably good family, I presume. I'll go after her at once. Theo, bring my broché shawl, and wouldn't you wear my satin hood? 'Twill be warmer than my leghorn."

"Grandma," said Theo, in utter astonishment, "What do you mean? You surely are not going to Leominster to-night, as sick as you are?"

"Yes, I am going to Leominster to-night," answered the decided woman; "and this gentleman," waving her hand majestically towards George, "will oblige me much by seeing that the carriage is brought out."

Theo was about to remonstrate, when George whispered: "Let her go; Henry and Rose are probably no at home, but Margaret may be there. At all events, a little airing will do the old lady good;" and, rather pleased than otherwise with the expedition, he went after John, who pronounced his mistress "crazier than Hagar."

But it wasn't for him to dictate, and, grumbling at the prospect before him, he harnessed his horses and drove them to the door, where Madam Conway was already in waiting.

"See that everything is in order for our return," she said to Theo, who promised compliance, and then, herself bewildered, listened to the carriage as it rolled away; it seemed so like a dream that the woman who three hours before could scarcely speak aloud had now started for a ride of many miles in the damp night air! But love can accomplish miracles, and it made the eccentric lady strong, buoying up her spirits, and prompting her to cheer on the coachman, until just as the day grew rosy in the east Leominster appeared in view. The house was found, the carriage steps let down, and then with a slight trembling in her limbs Madam Conway alighted and walked up the graveled path, casting eager, searching glances around and commenting as follows:

"Everything is in good taste; they must be somebody, these Warners. I'm glad it is no worse." And with each new indication of refinement in Margaret's relatives the disgrace seemed less and less in the mind of the proud Englishwoman.

The ringing of the bell brought down Janet, who, with an inquisitive look at the satin hood and bundle of shawls, ushered the stranger into the parlor, and then went for her mistress. Taking the card her serv-

ant brought, Mrs. Warner read with some little trepi-
dation the name " Madam Conway, Hillsdale." From
what she had heard, she was not prepossessed in the
lady's favor; but, curious to know why she was there
at this early hour, she hastened the making of her
toilet, and went down to the parlor, where Madam
Conway sat, coiled in one corner of the sofa, which
she had satisfied herself was covered with real broca-
tel, as were also the chairs within the room. The
tables of rosewood and marble, and the expensive
curtains had none of them escaped her notice, and in a
mood which more common furniture would never have
produced Madam Conway arose to meet Mrs. Warner,
who received her politely, and then waited to hear her
errand.

It was told in a few words. She had come for
Margaret—Margaret, whom she had loved for eighteen years, and could not now cast off, even though she
were not of the Conway and Davenport extraction.

" I can easily understand how painful must have
been the knowledge that Maggie was not your own,"
returned Mrs. Warner, " for she is a girl of whom anyone might be proud; but you are laboring under a mistake—Henry is not her brother;" and then very
briefly she explained the matter to Madam Conway,
who, having heard so much, was now surprised at
nothing, and who felt, it may be, a little gratified in
knowing that Henry was, after all, nothing to Margaret, save the husband of her sister. But a terrible
disappointment awaited her. Margaret was not
there; and so loud were her lamentations that some
time elapsed ere Mrs. Warner could make her listen
while she explained that Mr. Carrollton had found

Maggie the day previous at the Falls, that they were probably in Albany now, and would reach Hillsdale that very day; such at least was the import of the telegram which Mrs. Warner had received the evening before. " They wish to surprise you, undoubtedly," she said, " and consequently have not telegraphed to you."

This seemed probable, and forgetting her weariness Madam Conway resolved upon leaving John to drive home at his leisure, while she took the Leominster cars, which reached Worcester in time for the upward train. This matter adjusted, she tried to be quiet; but her excitement increased each moment, and when at last breakfast was served she did but little justice to the tempting viands which her hostess set before her. Margaret's chamber was visited next, and very lovingly she patted and smoothed the downy pillows, for the sake of the bright head which had rested there, while to herself she whispered abstractedly, " Yes, yes," though to what she was giving her assent she could not tell. She only knew that she was very happy, and very impatient to be gone, and when at last she did go it seemed to her an age ere Worcester was reached.

Resolutely turning her head away, lest she should see the scene of her disaster when last in that city, she walked up and down the ladies' room, her satin hood and heavy broché shawl, on that warm July morning, attracting much attention. But little did she care. Margaret was the burden of her thoughts, and the appearance of Mrs. Douglas herself would scarcely have disturbed her. Much less, then, did the presence of a queerly dressed young girl, who, entering the car with her, occupied from necessity the same seat, feeling herself a little annoyed at being thus obliged to sit so near one whom she mentally pronounced "mighty unsociable," for not once did Madam Conway turn her face that way, so intent was she upon watching their apparent speed, and counting the number of miles they had come.

When Charlton was reached, however, she did observe the women in a shaker, who, with a pail of huckleberries on her arm, was evidently waiting for someone.

An audible groan from the depths of the satin hood, as Betsy Jane passed out and the cars passed on, showed plainly that the mother and sister of George Douglas were recognized, particularly as the former wore the red and yellow calico, which, having been used as a "dress up" the summer before, now did its owner service as a garment of everyday wear. But not long did Madam Conway suffer her mind to dwell upon matters so trivial. Hillsdale was not far away, and she came each moment nearer. Two more stations were reached—the haunted swamp was passed—Chicopee River was in sight—the bridge appeared in view—the whistle sounded, and she was there.

Half an hour later, and Theo, looking from her window, started in surprise as she saw the village omnibus drive up to their door.

"'Tis grandmother!" she cried, and running to meet her she asked why she had returned so soon.

"They are coming at noon," answered the excited woman—then, hurrying into the house and throwing off her hood, she continued: "He's found her at the Falls; they are between here and Albany now; tell

everybody to hurry as fast as they can; tell Hannah
to make a chicken pie—Maggie was fond of that; and
turkey—tell her to kill a turkey—it's Maggie's favorite dish—and ice cream, too! I wish I had some
this minute," and she wiped the perspiration from her
burning face.

No more hysterics now; no more lonesome nights;
no more thoughts of death—for Margaret was coming home—the best loved of them all. Joyfully the
servants told to each other the glad news, disbelieving
entirely the report fast gaining circulation that the
queenly Maggie was lowly born—a grandchild of old
Hagar. Up and down the stairs Madam Conway ran,
flitting from room to room, and tarrying longest in
that of Margaret, where the sunlight came in softly
through the half-closed blinds and the fair summer
blossoms smiled a welcome for the expected one.

Suddenly the noontide stillness was broken by a
sound, deafening and shrill on ordinary occasions, but
falling now like music on Madam Conway's ear, for
by that sound she knew that Margaret was near.
Wearily went the half-hour by, and then, from the
head of the tower stairs, Theo cried out, " She is coming!" while the grandmother buried her face in the
pillows of the lounge, and asked to be alone when she
took back to her bosom the child which was not hers.

Earnestly, as if to read the inmost soul, each looked
into the other's eyes—Margaret and Theo—and while
the voice of the latter was choked with tears she wound
her arms around the graceful neck, which bent to the
caress, and whispered low, " You are my sister still."

Against the vine-wreathed balustrade a fairy form
was leaning, holding back her breath lest she should

break the deep silence of that meeting. In her bosom there was no pang of fear lest Theo should be loved the best; and, even had there been, it could not surely have remained, for stretching out her arm Margaret drew Rose to her side, and placing her hand in that of Theo said, "You are both my sisters now," while Arthur Carrollton, bending down, kissed the lips of the three, saying as he did so, "Thus do I acknowledge your relationship to me."

"Why don't she come?" the waiting Madam Conway sighed, just as Theo, pointing to the open door, bade Margaret go in.

There was a blur before the lady's eyes—a buzzing in her ears—and the footfall she had listened for so long was now unheard as it came slowly to her side. But the light touch upon her arm—the well-remembered voice within her ear, calling her " Madam Conway," sent through her an electric thrill, and starting up she caught the wanderer in her arms, crying imploringly, " Not that name, Maggie darling; call me grandma, as you used to do—call me grandma still," and smoothing back the long black tresses, she looked to see if grief had left its impress upon her fair young face. It was paler now, and thinner too, than it was wont to be, and while her tears fell fast upon it, Madam Conway whispered: "You have suffered much, my child, and so have I. Why did you go away? Say, Margaret, why did you leave me all alone?"

"To learn how much you loved me," answered Margaret, to whom this moment brought happiness second only to that which she had felt when on the river bank she sat with Arthur Carrollton, and heard him tell how much she had been mourned—how lonesome was the house without her—and how sad were all their hearts.

But that was over now—no more sadness, no more tears; the lost one had returned; Margaret was home again—home in the hearts of all, and nothing could dislodge her—not even the story of her birth, which Arthur Carrollton, spurning at further deception, told to the listening servants, who, having always respected old Hagar for her position in the household as well as for her education, so superior to their own, set up a deafening shout, first for "Hagar's grandchild," and next for "Miss Margaret forever!"

CHAPTER XXV.

HAGAR.

By Theo's request old Hagar had been taken home the day before, yielding submissively, for her frenzied mood was over—her strength was gone—her life was nearly spent—and Hagar did not wish to live. That for which she had sinned had been accomplished, and, though it had cost her days and nights of anguish, she was satisfied at last. Margaret was coming home again—would be a lady still—the bride of Arthur Carrollton, for George Douglas had told her so, and she was willing now to die, but not until she had seen her once again—had looked into the beautiful face of which she had been so proud.

Not to-day, however, does she expect her; and just as the sun was setting, the sun which shines on Margaret at home, she falls away to sleep. It was at this hour that Margaret was wont to visit her, and now, as the treetops grew red in the day's departing glory, a graceful form came down the woodland path, where for many weeks the grass has not been crushed beneath her feet. They saw her as she left the house,—Madam Conway, Theo, all,—but none asked whither she was going. They knew, and one who loved her best of all followed slowly after, waiting in the woods until that interview should end.

Hagar lay calmly sleeping. The servant was as

usual away, and there was no eye watching Margaret as with burning cheeks and beating heart she crossed the threshold of the door, pausing not, faltering not, until the bed was reached—the bed where Hagar lay, her crippled hands folded meekly upon her breast, her white hair shading a whiter face, and a look about her half-shut mouth as if the thin, pale lips had been much used of late to breathe the word " Forgive." Maggie had never seen her thus before, and the worn-out, aged face had something touching in its sad expression, and something startling too, bidding her hasten, if to that woman she would speak.

" Hagar," she essayed to say, but the word died on her lips, for standing there alone, with the daylight fading from the earth, and the lifelight fading from the form before her, it seemed not meet that she should thus address the sleeper. There was a name, however, by which she called another—a name of love, and it would make the withered heart of Hagar Warren bound and beat and throb with untold joy. And Margaret said that name at last, whispering it first softly to herself; then, bending down so that her breath stirred the snow-white hair, she repeated it aloud, starting involuntarily as the rude walls echoed back the name " Grandmother ! "

" Grandmother ! " Through the senses locked in sleep it penetrated, and the dim eyes, once so fiery and black, grew large and bright again as Hagar Warren woke.

Was it a delusion, that beauteous form which met her view, that soft hand on her brow, or was it Maggie Miller?

" Grandmother," the low voice said again, " I am

Maggie—Hester's child. Can you see me? Do you know that I am here?"

Yes, through the films of age, through the films of coming death, and through the gathering darkness, old Hagar saw and knew, and with a scream of joy her shrunken arms wound themselves convulsively around the maiden's neck, drawing her nearer, and nearer still, until the shriveled lips touched the cheek of her who did not turn away, but returned that kiss of love.

"Say it again, say that word once more," and the arms closed tighter round the form of Margaret, who breathed it yet again, while the childish woman sobbed aloud, "It is sweeter than the angels' song to hear you call me so."

She did not ask her when she came—she did not ask her where she had been; but Maggie told her all, sitting by her side with the poor hands clasped in her own; then, as the twilight shadows deepened in the room, she struck a light, and coming nearer to Hagar, said, "Am I much like my mother?"

"Yes, yes, only more winsome," was the answer, and the half-blind eyes looked proudly at the beautiful girl bending over the humble pillow.

"Do you know that?" Maggie asked, holding to view the ambrotype of Hester Hamilton.

For an instant Hagar wavered, then hugging the picture to her bosom, she laughed and cried together, whispering as she did so, "My little girl, my Hester, my baby that I used to sing to sleep in our home away over the sea."

Hagar's mind was wandering amid the scenes of bygone years, but it soon came back again to the present time, and she asked of Margaret whence that picture came. In a few words Maggie told her, and then for a time there was silence, which was broken at last by Hagar's voice, weaker now than when she spoke before.

"Maggie," she said, "what of this Arthur Carrollton? Will he make you his bride?"

"He has so promised," answered Maggie; and Hagar continued: "He will take you to England, and you will be a lady, sure. Margaret, listen to me. 'Tis the last time we shall ever talk together, you and I, and I am glad that it is so. I have greatly sinned, but I have been forgiven, and I am willing now to die. Everything I wished for has come to pass, even the hearing you call me by that blessed name; but, Maggie, when to-morrow they say that I am dead— when you come down to look upon me lying here asleep, you needn't call me 'Grandmother,' you may say 'poor Hagar!' with the rest; and, Maggie, is it too much to ask that your own hands will arrange my hair, fix my cap, and straighten my poor old crooked limbs for the coffin? And if I should look decent, will you, when nobody sees you do it—Madam Conway, Arthur Carrollton, nobody who is proud—will you, Maggie, kiss me once for the sake of what I've suffered that you might be what you are?"

"Yes, yes, I will," was Maggie's answer, her tears falling fast, and a fear creeping into her heart, as by the dim candlelight she saw a nameless shadow settling down on Hagar's face.

The servant entered at this moment, and, glancing at old Hagar, sunk into a chair, for she knew that shadow was death.

"Maggie," and the voice was now a whisper, "I wish I could once more see this Mr. Carrollton. 'Tis the nature of his kin to be sometimes overbearing, and though I am only old Hagar Warren he might heed my dying words, and be more thoughtful of your happiness. Do you think that he would come?"

Ere Maggie had time to answer there was a step upon the floor, and Arthur Carrollton stood at her side. He had waited for her long, and growing at last impatient had stolen to the open door, and when the dying woman asked for him he had trampled down his pride and entered the humble room. Winding his arm round Margaret, who trembled violently, he said: "Hagar, I am here. Have you aught to say to me?"

Quickly the glazed eyes turned towards him, and the clammy hand was timidly extended. He took it unhesitatingly, while the pale lips murmured faintly, "Maggie's too." Then, holding both between her own, old Hagar said solemnly, "Young man, as you hope for heaven, deal kindly with my child," and Arthur Carrollton answered her aloud, "As I hope for heaven, I will," while Margaret fell upon her knees and wept. Raising herself in bed, Hagar laid her hands upon the head of the kneeling girl, breathing over her a whispered blessing; then the hands pressed heavily, the fingers clung with a loving grasp, as it were, to the bands of shining hair—the thin lips ceased to move—the head fell back upon the pillow, motionless and still, and Arthur Carrollton, leading Margaret away, gently told her that Hagar was dead.

.   .   .   .   .

Carefully, tenderly, as if she had been a wounded dove, did the whole household demean themselves to-

wards Margaret, seeing that everything needful was
done, but mentioning never in her presence the name of
the dead. And Margaret's position was a trying one,
for though Hagar had been her grandmother she had
never regarded her as such, and she could not now
affect a grief she did not feel. Still, from her earliest
childhood she had loved the strange old woman, and
she mourned for her now, as friend mourneth for
friend, when there is no tie of blood between them.

Her promise, too, was kept, and with her own hands
she smoothed the snow-white hair, tied on the muslin
cap, folded the stiffened arms, and then, unmindful
who was looking on, kissed twice the placid face,
which seemed to smile on her in death.

.   .   .   .   .

By the side of Hester Hamilton they made another
grave, and, with Arthur Carrollton and Rose standing
at either side, Margaret looked on while the weary and
worn was laid to rest; then slowly retraced her steps,
walking now with Madam Conway, for Arthur Carrollton and Rose had lingered at the grave, talking
together of a plan which had presented itself to the
minds of both as they stood by the humble stone which
told where Margaret's mother slept. To Margaret,
however, they said not a word, nor yet to Madam Conway, though they both united in urging the two ladies
to accompany Theo to Worcester for a few days.

"Mrs. Warner will help me keep house," Mr. Carrollton said, advancing the while so many good reasons why Margaret at least should go, that she finally
consented, and went down to Worcester, together with
Madam Conway, George Douglas, Theo, and Henry,
the latter of whom seemed quite as forlorn as did she

herself, for Rose was left behind, and without her he was nothing.

Madam Conway had been very gracious to him; his family were good, and when as they passed the Charlton depot thoughts of the leghorn bonnet and blue umbrella intruded themselves upon her, she half wished that Henry had broken his leg in Theo's behalf, and so saved her from bearing the name of Douglas.

The week went by, passing rapidly as all weeks will, and Margaret was again at home. Rose was there still, and just as the sun was setting she took her sister's hand, and led her out into the open air toward the resting-place of the dead, where a change had been wrought; and Margaret, leaning over the iron gate, comprehended at once the feeling which had prompted Mr. Carrollton and Rose to desire her absence for a time. The humble stone was gone, and in its place there stood a handsome monument, less imposing and less expensive than that of Mrs. Miller, it is true, but still chaste and elegant, bearing upon it simply the names of " Hester Hamilton, and her mother Hagar Warren," with the years of their death. The little grave, too, where for many years Maggie herself had been supposed to sleep, was not beneath the pine tree now; that mound was leveled down, and another had been made, just where the grass was growing rank and green beneath the shadow of the taller stone, and there side by side they lay at last together, the mother and her infant child.

" It was kind in you to do this," Margaret said, and then, with her arm round Rose's waist, she spoke of the coming time when the sun of another hemisphere would be shining down upon her, saying she should think often of that hour, that spot, and that sister, who answered: " Every year when the spring rains fall I shall come to see that the grave has been well kept, for you know that she was my mother, too," and she pointed to the name of " Hester," deep cut in the polished marble.

" Not yours, Rose, but mine," said Maggie. " My mother she was, and as such I will cherish her memory." Then, with her arm still around her sister's waist, she walked slowly back to the house.

A little later, and while Arthur Carrollton, with Maggie at his side, was talking to her of something which made the blushes burn on her still pale cheeks, Madam Conway herself walked out to witness the improvements, lingering longest at the little grave, and saying to herself, " It was very thoughtful in Arthur, very, to do what I should have done myself ere this had I not been afraid of Margaret's feelings."

Then, turning to the new monument, she admired its chaste beauty, but hardly knew whether she was pleased to have it there or not.

" It's very handsome," she said, leaving the yard, and walking backward to observe the effect. " And it adds much to the looks of the place. There is no question about that. It is perfectly proper, too, or Mr. Carrollton would never have put it here, for he knows what is right, of course," and the still doubtful lady turned away, saying as she did so, "On the whole, I think I am glad that Hester has a handsome monument, and I know I am glad that Mrs. Miller's is a little the taller of the two!"

CHAPTER XXVI.

AUGUST EIGHTEENTH, 1858.

YEARS hence, if the cable resting far down in the mermaids' home shall prove a bond of perfect peace between the mother and her child, thousands will recall the bright summer morning when through the caverns of the mighty deep the first electric message came, thrilling the nation's heart, quickening the nation's pulse, and, with the music of the deep-toned bell and noise of the cannon's roar, proclaiming to the listening multitude that the isle beyond the sea, and the lands which to the westward lie, were bound together, shore to shore, by a strange, mysterious tie. And two there are who, in their happy home, will oft look back upon that day, that 18th day of August, which gave to one of Britain's sons as fair and beautiful a bride as e'er went forth from the New England hills to dwell beneath a foreign sky.

They had not intended to be married so soon, for Margaret would wait a little longer; but an unexpected and urgent summons home made it necessary for Mr. Carrollton to go, and so by chance the bridal day was fixed for the 18th. None save the family were present, and Madam Conway's tears fell fast as the words were spoken which made them one, for by those words she knew that she and Margaret must part. But not forever; for when the next year's autumn leaves shall fall the old house by the mill will again be without a mistress, while in a handsome country-seat beyond the sea Madam Conway will demean herself right proudly, as becometh the grandmother of Mrs. Arthur Carrollton. Theo, too, and Rose will both be there, for their husbands have so promised, and when the Christmas fires are kindled on the hearth and the ancient pictures on the wall take a richer tinge from the ruddy light, there will be a happy group assembled within the Carrollton halls; and Margaret, the happiest of them all, will then almost forget that ever in the Hillsdale woods, sitting at Hagar's feet, she listened with a breaking heart to the story of her birth.

But not the thoughts of a joyous future could dissipate entirely the sadness of that bridal, for Margaret was well beloved, and the billows which would roll ere long between her and her childhood's home stretched many, many miles away. Still they tried to be cheerful, and Henry Warner's merry jokes had called forth more than one gay laugh, when the peal of bells and the roll of drums arrested their attention; while the servants, who had learned the cause of the rejoicing, struck up " God Save the Queen," and from an adjoining field a rival choir sent back the stirring note of " Hail, Columbia, Happy Land." Mrs. Jeffrey, too, was busy. In secret she had labored at the rent made by her foot in the flag of bygone days, and now, perspiring at every pore, she dragged it up the tower stairs, planting it herself upon the house-top, where side by side with the royal banner it waved in the summer breeze. And this she did, not because she cared aught for the cable, in which she " didn't believe " and declared " would never work," but because. she would celebrate Margaret's wedding-day, and so make some amends for her interference when

once before the " Stars and Stripes " had floated above
the old stone house.

And thus it was, amid smiles and tears, amid bells
and drums, and waving flags and merry song, amid
noisy shout and booming guns, that double bridal day
was kept; and when the sun went down it left a glory
on the western clouds, as if they, too, had donned their
best attire in honor of the union.

.   .   .   .   .

It is moonlight on the land—glorious, beautiful
moonlight.   On Hagar's peaceful grave it falls, and
glancing from the polished stone shines across the
fields upon the old stone house, where all is cheerless
now, and still.   No life—no sound—no bounding step
—no gleeful song.   All is silent, all is sad.   The light
of the household has departed; it went with the hour
when first to each other the lonesome servants said,
" Margaret is gone."

Yes, she is gone, and all through the darkened rooms
there is found no trace of her, but away to the east-
ward the moonlight falls upon the sea, where a noble
vessel rides.   With sails unfurled to the evening
breeze, it speeds away—away from the loved hearts
on the shore which after that bark, and its precious
freight, have sent many a throb of love.   Upon the
deck of that gallant ship there stands a beautiful bride,
looking across the water with straining eye, and smiling through her tears on him who wipes those tears
away, and whispers in her ear, " I will be more to you,
my wife, than they have ever been."

So, with the love-light shining on her heart, and the
moonlight shining on the wave, we bid adieu to one
who bears no more the name of Maggie Miller.

EDNA'S SACRIFICE

BY FRANCES HENSHAW BADEN

EDNA'S SACRIFICE

IT WAS a cold night in September. For three days the rain had fallen almost unceasingly. It had been impossible for us to get out; and no visitors had been in. Everything looked dreary enough, and we felt so, truly. Of course the stoves were not prepared for use; and this night we (that is, Nell, Floy, Aunt Edna, and myself) were huddled in the corners of the sofa and arm-chairs, wrapped in our shawls. We were at our wits' end for something to while the hours away. We had read everything that was readable; played until we fancied the piano sent forth a wail of complaint, and begged for rest; were at the backgammon board until our arms ached; and I had given imitations of celebrated actresses, until I was hoarse, and Nell declared I was in danger of being sued for scandal. What more could we do? To dispel the drowsiness that was stealing over me, I got up, walked up and down the floor, and then drew up the blind, and gazed out into the deserted street. Not a footfall to be heard, neither man's nor beast's; nothing but patter, patter, patter. At length, after standing fully fifteen minutes — oh, joyful sound! — a coming footstep, firm and quick. My first thought was that those steps would stop at our door. But, directly after, I felt that very improbable for who was there that *would* come such a night? Papa was up north with mamma; Nell and Floy were visiting Aunt Edna

3

and me, the only ones home, save the servants.
Neither of us had as yet a lover so devoted or so de-
mented as to come out, if he had anywhere to *stay in*.

On and past went the steps. Turning away, I
drew down the blind, and said: "Some one must be
ill, and that was the doctor, surely: for no one else
would go out, only those from direst necessity sent."

A deep sigh escaped Aunt Edna's lips, and although
partially shaded by her hand, I could see the shadow
on the beautiful face had deepened.

Why my aunt had never married was a mystery to
me, for she was lovable in every way, and must have
been very beautiful in her youth. Thirty-six she
would be next May-day, she had told me. Thirty-six
seemed to me, just sixteen, a very great many years
to have lived. But aunt always was young to us;
and the hint of her being an old maid was always re-
sented, very decidedly, by all her nieces.

"Aunt Edna," I said, "tell us a story — a love-
story, please."

"Oh, little one, you have read *so* many! And what
can I tell you more?" she answered, gently.

"Oh, aunty, I want a *true* story! Do, darling
aunty, tell us your own. Tell us why you are blessing
our home with your presence, instead of that of some
noble man, for noble he must have been to have won
your heart, and — hush-sh! Yes, yes; I know something about somebody, and I must know all. Do,
please!"

I plead on. I always could do more with Aunt
Edna than any one else. I was named for her, and
many called me like her — "only not nearly so pretty" was always added.

At last she consented, saying:

"Dear girls, to only one before have I given my entire confidence, and that was my mother. I scarce know why I have yielded to your persuasions, little Edna, save that this night, with its gloom and rain, carries me back long years, and my heart seems to join its pleading with yours, yearning to cast forth some of its fulness, and perchance find relief by pouring into your loving heart its own sorrows. But, darling, I would not cast my shadow over your fair brow, even for a brief time."

With her hand still shading her face, Aunt Edna began:

"Just such a night as this, eighteen years ago, dear child, my fate was decided. The daughter of my mother's dearest friend had been with us about a year. Dearly we all loved the gentle child, for scarcely more than child she was — only sixteen. My mother had taken her from the cold, lifeless form of her mother into her own warm, loving heart, and she became to me as a sister. So fair and frail she was! We all watched her with the tenderest care, guarding her from all that could chill her sensitive nature or wound the already saddened heart. Lilly was her name. Oh, what a delicate while lily she was when we first brought her to our home; but after a while she was won from her sorrow, and grew into a maiden of great beauty. Still, with child-like, winning ways.

"Great wells of love were in her blue eyes — violet hue *he* called them. Often I wondered if any one's gaze would linger on my dark eyes when hers were near? Her pale golden hair was pushed off her broad forehead and fell in heavy waves far down below her graceful shoulders and over her black dress. Small delicately formed features, a complexion so fair and clear that it seemed transparent. In her blue eyes there was always such a sad, wistful look; this, and the gentle smile that ever hovered about her lips, gave an expression of mingled sweetness and sorrow that was very touching. You may imagine now how beautiful she was.

"Her mother had passed from earth during the absence of Lilly's father. Across the ocean the sorrowful tidings were borne to him. He was a naval officer. Lilly was counting the days ere she should see him. The good news had come that soon he would be with her. At last the day arrived, but oh! what a terrible sorrow it brought! When her heart was almost bursting with joy, expecting every moment to be clasped in those dear arms — a telegraphic dispatch was handed in. Eagerly she caught it, tore it open, read — and fell lifeless to the floor.

"Oh! the fearful, crushing words. We read, not of his coming to Lilly, but of his going to her, his wife, in heaven. Yes, truly an orphan the poor girl was then.

"In vain proved all efforts to restore her to consciousness. Several times, when she had before fainted, mother was the only physician needed. But that night she shook her head and said:

" 'We must have a doctor, and quickly.'

"It was a terrible night. Our doctor was very remote. Your father suggested another, near by.

"Dr. ——, well, never mind his name. Your father said he had lately known him, and liked him much.

"Through the storm he came, and by his skilful

treatment Lilly was soon restored to consciousness, but not to health. A low nervous fever set in, and many days we watched with fearful hearts. Ah! during those days I learned to look too eagerly for the doctor's coming. Indeed, he made his way into the hearts of all in our home. After the dreaded crisis had passed, and we knew that Lilly would be spared to us, the doctor told mother he should have to prescribe for me. I had grown pale, from confinement in the sickroom, and he must take me for a drive, that the fresh air should bring the roses back to my cheeks. Willingly mother consented. After that I often went. When Lilly was able to come down-stairs, this greatest pleasure of my life then was divided with her. One afternoon I stood on the porch with her, waiting while the doctor arranged something about the harness.

" 'Oh! *how* I wish it was my time to go!' she whispered.

" 'Well, darling, it shall be your time. I can go tomorrow. Run, get your hat and wrap,' I said, really glad to give any additional pleasure to this child of many sorrows.

" 'No, no, that would not be fair. And, Edna, don't you know that *tomorrow* I would be so sorry if I went today? I do not mean to be selfish, but, oh, indeed, I cannot help it! I am wishing *every time* to go. Not that I care for a ride—' She hesitated, flushed, and whispered: 'I like to be with my doctor. Don't you, Edna? Oh! I wish he was my father, or brother, or cousin—just to be with us all the time, you know.'

"Just then the doctor came for me, and I had to

leave her.   As we drove off I looked back and kissed
my hand to her, saying:

" 'Dear little thing!   I wish she was going with us.'

" 'I do not,' the doctor surprised me by saying.

"I raised my eyes inquiringly to his.   In those
beautiful, earnest eyes I saw something that made me
profoundly happy.   I could not speak.   After a moment he added:

" 'She is a beautiful, winning child, and I enjoy her
company.   But when with her, I feel as if it was my
duty to devote myself entirely to her — in a word, to
take care of her, or, I should say, to care for *her* only.
And this afternoon, of all others, I do not feel like
having Lilly with us.'

"That afternoon was one of the happiest of my
life.   Although not a word of love passed his lips, I
knew it filled his heart, and was for me.   He told me
of his home, his relatives, his past life.   Of his
mother he said:

" 'When you know her, you will love her dearly.'

"He seemed to be sure that I should know her.
And then — ah, well, I thought so too, then.

"Lilly was waiting for us when we returned.   He
chided her for being out so late.   It was quite dark.
Tears filled her eyes as she raised them to his and said:

" 'Don't be angry.   I could not help watching.
Oh, why did you stay *so* long?   I thought you would
never come back.   I was afraid something had happened — that the horse had run away, or—'

" 'Angry I could not be with you, little one.   But
I don't want you to get sick again.   Come, now, smile
away your tears and fears!   Your friend is safe and
with you again,' the doctor answered.

Taking her hand, he led her into the parlor.

"He had not understood the cause of her tears. Only for him she watched and wept.

" '*Do* stay,' she plead, when her doctor was going.

"He told her he could not, then; there was another call he must make, but would return after a while.

"She counted the minutes, until she should see him again. Never concealing from any of us how dearly she loved him. She was truly as guileless as a child of six years.

"From the first of her acquaintance with him, she had declared 'her doctor' was like her father. Mother too, admitted, the resemblance was very decided.

"This it was, I think, that first made him so dear to her.

"Several times, after the doctor returned that evening, I saw he sought opportunity to speak to me, unheard by others. But Lilly was always near.

"Ah! it was better so. Better that from his *own* lips I heard not those words he would have spoken. Doubly hard would have been the trial. Oh, that night when he said, 'good-bye!' He slipped in my hand a little roll of paper. As Lilly still stood at the window, watching as long as she could see him, I stole away to open the paper. Then, for a while, I forgot Lilly, aye, forgot everything, in my great happiness. He loved me! On my finger sparkled the beautiful diamond — my engagement ring — to be worn on the morrow, 'if I could return his love,' he said.

"Quickly I hid my treasures away, his note, and the ring — Lilly was coming.

"She was not yet strong, and soon tired. I helped her to get off her clothes, and as she kissed me good-night, she said:

" 'I wish we had a picture of him — don't you?'

" 'Who, dear?' I asked.

" 'My doctor! Who else? You tease. You *knew* well enough,' she answered, as she nestled her pretty head closer to mine.

"Soon she was sleeping and dreaming of him. Sweet dreams at first I knew they were; for soft smiles flitted over her face.

"I could not sleep. A great fear stole in upon my happiness. Did not Lilly love him too? How would she receive the news which soon must reach her? Was her love such as mine? Such as is given to but one alone? Or only as a brother did she love him? I must *know* how it was. Heaven grant that joy for one would not bring sorrow to the other, I prayed. I had not long to wait. Her dreams became troubled. Her lips quivered and trembled, and then with a cry of agony she started up.

" 'Gone, gone, gone!' she sobbed.

"It was many minutes ere I succeeded in calming and making her understand 'twas but a dream.

" 'Oh, but *so* real, so *dreadfully* real. I thought he did not care for me. That he had gone and left me, and they told me he was married!'

"Telling this, she began to sob again.

" 'Lilly, dear, tell me truly — tell your sister, your very best friend — how it is you love your doctor?' I asked.

" 'How?' she returned. 'Oh, Edna, more than all the world! He is all that I have lost and more;

and if he should die, or I should lose him, I would not wish to live. I *could* not live. He loves me a little, does he not, Edna?'

"I could not reply. Just then there was a terrible struggle going on in my heart. *That* must be ended, the victory won ere I could speak. She waited for my answer and then said, eagerly:

" 'Oh, speak, *do!* What *are* you thinking about?'

"Pressing back the sigh — back and far down into the poor heart — I gave her the sweet, and kept the bitter part, when I could answer.

" 'Yes, dear, I *do* think he loves you a little now, and will, by-and-by, love you dearly. God grant he may!'

" 'Oh, you darling Edna! You have made me so happy!' she cried, kissing me, and still caressing me she fell asleep.

"Next morning I enclosed the ring, with only these words:

" 'Forgive if I cause you sorrow, and believe me your true friend. I return the ring that I am not *free* to accept.'

"I intended that my reply should mislead him, when I wrote that I was not free, and thus to crush any hope that might linger in his heart. While at breakfast that morning, we received a telegram that grandma was extremely ill, and wanted me. Thus, fate seemed to forward my plans. I had thought to go away for a while. I told mother all. How her dear heart ached for me! Yet she dared not say aught against my decision. She took charge of the note for the doctor, and by noon I was on my journey. Two years passed ere I returned home. Mother wrote me but little news of either Lilly or her doctor. After the first letter, telling that my note was a severe shock and great disappointment. Three or four months elapsed before grandma was strong enough for me to leave her. An opportunity at that time presented for my going to Europe. I wanted such an entire change, and gladly accepted. Frequently came letters from Lilly. For many months they were filled with doubts and anxiety; but after a while came happier and shorter ones. Ah, she had only time to be with him, and to think in his absence of his coming again.

"When I was beginning to tire of all the wonders and grandeur of the old world, and nothing would still the longing for home, the tidings came they were married, Lilly and her doctor, and gone to his western home to take charge of the patients of his uncle, who had retired from practice. Then I hastened back, and ever since, dear girls, I have been contented, finding much happiness in trying to contribute to that of those so dear. Now, little Edna, you have my only love-story, its beginning and ending."

"But, aunty, do tell me his name," I said. "Indeed, it is not merely idle curiosity. I just feel as if I must know it — that it is for something very important. Now you need not smile. I'm very earnest, and I shall not sleep until I know. I really felt a presentiment that if I knew his name it might in some way affect the conclusion of the story."

"Well, my child, I may as well tell you. Dr. Graham it was — Percy Graham," Aunt Edna answered, low.

"Ah! did I not tell you? It was not curiosity.
Listen, aunty mine. While you were away last winter, papa received a paper from St. Louis; he handed
it to me, pointing to an announcement. But I will
run get it. He told me to show it to you, and I forgot. I did not dream of all this."

From my scrap-book I brought the slip, and Aunt
Edna read:

"DIED.—Suddenly, of heart disease, on the morning
of the 15th, Lilly, wife of Doctor Percy Graham, in
the 34th year of her age."

Aunt Edna remained holding the paper, without
speaking, for some minutes; then, handing it back to
me, she said, softly, as if talking to her friend:

"*Dear* Lilly! Thank heaven, I gave to *you* the
best I had to give, and caused you naught but happiness. God is merciful! Had *he* been taken, and you
left, how *could* we have comforted you?" And then,
turning to me, she said: "Nearly a year it is since
Lilly went to heaven. 'Tis strange I have not heard
of this."

" 'Tis strange from him you have not heard," I
thought; "and stranger still 'twill be if he comes not
when the year is over. For surely he *must* know that
you are free—" But I kept my thoughts, and soon
after kissed aunty goodnight.

One month passed, and the year was out. And
somebody was in our parlor, making arrangements to
carry away Aunt Edna. I knew it was he, when he
met me at the hall door, and said:

"Edna — Miss Linden! *can* it be?"

"Yes and no, sir — both — Edna Linden; but, Doctor Graham, not *your* Edna. You will find her in the

parlor," I answered, saucily, glad and sorry, both, at his coming.

Ah, she welcomed him with profound joy, I know. He knew all; papa had told him. And if he loved the beautiful girl, he then worshipped that noble woman.

"Thank God! Mine at last!" I heard him say, with fervent joy, as I passed the door, an hour after.

How beautiful she was, when, a few weeks after, she became his very own. I stood beside her and drew off her glove. How happy he looked as he placed the heavy gold circlet on her finger! How proudly he bore her down the crowded church aisle!

Ah, little Lilly was no doubt his dear and cherished wife. But *this* one, 'twas plain to see, was the one love of his life.

THE END.

ADELPHI LIBRARY

OF POPULAR WORKS OF FICTION

A unique, thoroughly up-to-date series of books by the most popular authors. *Undoubtedly the most startling, attractive series of 12mos. ever made to sell at a popular price.* Bound in green English vellum cloth, stamped with a beautiful cover design, having large artistic green side and back title letterings, making altogether a highly artistic decorative cover, bound flat back, printed from large clear type on a good quality of laid paper, each book in wrapper.

135 Titles. Price 50 cents.

59	Macaria	98	Staunch of Heart
60	Magdalen's Vow	99	Stella's Fortune
61	Marble Faun, The	100	St Cuthbert's Tower
62	Marquis, The	101	Stepping Heavenward
63	Martyred Love, A	102	Story of a Wedding Ring
64	Mary St. John	103	Study in Scarlet
65	Micah Clarke	104	Sunshine and Roses
66	Not Like Other Girls	105	Tale of Two Cities
67	Nurse Revel's Mistake	106	Ten Nights in a Bar Room
68	Old Mam'sell's Secret	107	Terrible Temptation
69	Old Myddleton's Money	108	Thaddeus of Warsaw
70	Oliver Twist	109	Thelma
71	Olivia	110	Thorns and Orange
72	Only a Girl's Love		Blossoms
73	Only the Governess	111	Three Guardsmen, The
74	Only One Love	112	Throne of David
75	Our Mutual Friend	113	Those Westerton Girls
76	Owl's Nest, The	114	Treasure Island
77	Pastor's Daughter	115	Twin Lieutenants, The
78	Prince of the House of	116	Two Orphans
	David	117	Uncle Tom's Cabin
79	Princess of the Moor	118	Under Two Flags
80	Put Yourself in His Place	119	Unseen Bridegroom
81	Queen of the Isle, The	120	Usurper The
82	Quo Vadis	121	Vendetta
83	Queenie's Whim	122	Very Hard Cash
84	Robinson Crusoe	123	Vicar of Wakefield
85	Romance of Two Worlds	124	Wasted Love, A
86	Russian Gypsy, The	125	We Two
87	Samantha at Saratoga	126	Wee Wifie
88	Scarlet Letter, The	127	White Company, The
89	Scottish Chiefs	128	Wife of Monte Cristo
90	Second Wife, The	129	Who Wins
91	She Loved Him	130	Woman Against Woman
92	Sign of the Four, The	131	Woman's Soul, A
93	Silas Marner	132	Won by Waiting
94	Sketch Book	133	Wormwood
95	So Fair, So False	134	Wounded Heart, A
96	So Nearly Lost	135	Wooed and Married
97	Son of Monte Cristo		

THE
Sweet Clover Stories
FOR GIRLS

BY MRS. CARRIE L. MAY

INCLUDING

Brownie Sanford

Nellie Milton's Housekeeping

Sylvia's Burden

Ruth Lovell

M. A. DONOHUE & COMPANY
415 Dearborn St. - Chicago

CPSIA information can be obtained
at www.ICGtesting.com
Printed in the USA
BVHW04*1233140918
527538BV00007B/308/P